GALLIMORE

GALLIMORE

Michelle Griep

Black Lyon Publishing, LLC

Our books may be ordered through your local bookstore or by visiting the publisher:

www.BlackLyonPublishing.com

Black Lyon Publishing, LLC
PO Box 567
Baker City, OR 97814

This is a work of fiction. All of the characters, names, events, organizations and conversations in this novel are either the products of the author's vivid imagination or are used in a fictitious way for the purposes of this story.

ISBN-10:   1-934912-11-5
ISBN-13:   978-1-934912-11-9
Library of Congress Control Number: 2008939187

Written, published and printed in
the United States of America.

Black Lyon Historical Romance

*To my own Captain of the Guard
who will soon come for me.
Rev. 22:20*

I would also like to acknowledge:
Mark Griep, Kelly Klepfer, Shannon McNear,
Gina Holmes, Jessica Dotta, Ane Mulligan,
Lisa Ludwig, Donita K. Paul, Penwrights, y and e,
Terri Thompson, Grant and Cheryl Higgins,
Linda Ahlmann, Jeff Gerke, Brenda Henry,
and Marsha Wilder.

Prologue

Two Years Past

Is this what it feels like to die?

Daniel Neale grasped onto the floating question as a child would clasp his fingers around a balloon string. It bobbed about, somewhere overhead. First near, then far. Elusive.

Red light. No, white. Bright. One eyeball then the other, forced open to the terrible, blinding beam.

"... coming around. Hey. Hey, buddy. Stay with us."

Buddy? Buddy's what he called his little boy. His own boy. His Jack.

"Come on, pal. Wake up."

Dan opened his eyes, this time of his own accord, and then— pain.

Pain of unimaginable height and depth. Stabbing, slicing, biting... shocking. His body pulsated with raw agony.

And his wail blended with the sirens.

"That's it. Easy now. We're going to straighten out this leg before we get you in the ambulance. It's going to hurt. Hang on."

It sounded like a chicken drumstick ripped from a carcass, a slipping kind of popping crack, then—nothing.

Quiet.

The balloon floated back to him, and this time he held the string loosely. He couldn't decide if he wanted to own the scarlet question, or if it wanted to own him.

Is this what it feels like to die?

No. He'd let it drift away. Drift away on the cold wind shivering against his skin.

"... convulsing. Stat!"

The voices returned, but Dan struggled to shut them out. Too loud and urgent. Too frightening.

"Come on. Come on."

Prodding. Poking. Pain again ... sharp.

His eyes blinked open. Faces he didn't know breathed life all around him.

"Hang on. Stay with us. Do you know who you are?"

"Dan." Even his voice hurt. "Daniel Neale."

"Good. Good. We're taking you to the hospital, Dan. You were in an accident. Do you understand?"

Accident? Understand? Oh, God. Oh, Jess.

"My ... my wife. I need ... I need my—"

His stomach cramped, and a thick liquid, salty and foul smelling, cut off his words. The vomit changed to blood, and Dan was helpless against the flowing river.

Is this what it feels like to die?

The balloon popped.

Chapter 1

"Would you mind terribly?"

The obtrusive words broke into Jessica Neale's thoughts, making no sense. Turning away from a clouded pane of double-thick glass, she glanced up into a pair of startling green eyes. "What?"

"I said, I see you've room beneath the seat in front of you, and being that the overheads are near to full, would you mind terribly if that's where I stored my bag?"

Other passengers continued to file in, bumping and jostling in an odd sort of dance. She'd hoped the empty seat next to her would remain vacant. No such luck.

"Sure." She resigned herself to accept his leather briefcase.

"It's very kind of you. Thank you."

For a fleeting moment, Jess studied the man as he stuffed a second bag into the small space at his feet. The width of his broad shoulders as he worked and wiggled to wedge his baggage into place all but blocked her view of his face. The accent struck her as decidedly British, and his manners seemed polished. Satisfied he wasn't an axe-murderer, the little interest she held in her seatmate evaporated.

She returned her attention to the outside world where baggage handlers scurried like ants around a dropped piece of candy. A fiery sunset dazzled the dusky horizon off the farthest wing tip, but the orange beauty failed to impress her.

What am I doing here? No clear answer came. Only echoes of her sister and mother nagging her to leave her ten-year-old son with Gramma and get away. "Take a vacation," they said. "You need some time to regroup and refresh."

It sounded easy enough, but she doubted she'd return home being the Jessica Neale they once knew.

"Welcome all passengers aboard flight 1409 bound for London Gatwick. This is Captain Morris speaking. We're fourth in line for takeoff, expecting a flight duration of around eight hours. That should put us at a touchdown of 8:35 AM local time. With fair winds, we're looking forward to a relatively smooth ride. Our flight attendants will provide you with a few safety precautions, and as always, thank you for flying Northwest."

A precise voice went on to discuss oxygen masks and the like, but Jess paid little heed. If the plane went down, so be it.

Jet engines roared as the attendants finished their tutorial, and blue runway lights changed from individual beacons into a neon streak. A vague sense of guilt attempted to invade her conscience as the force of the lift set in and the plane became airborne. She should probably be excited or anxious with anticipation. She should be ... something. Anything. In truth, the void of endless black sky outside her window mirrored her spirit.

Running her fingers through her short curls, she willed away such philosophical thoughts, then bent to move her carry-on in front of her seatmate's briefcase at her feet. She retrieved one of several travel guides and paged past the historical tourist traps. All the glitzy medieval hype spread throughout rolling English hills just seemed wrong.

"On holiday?"

Great, she'd once again caught only the tail-end of one of Mr. Green Eyes' questions. "What?"

"I said, I see you've a book on sightseeing. Are you on holiday?"

She looked up, meeting his gaze. How wise would it be to give out personal information to a stranger?

He must've noted her hesitation, for he continued with a smile. "I'm sorry. No need to answer to my curiosity. It's a long flight home for me, and I'm a bit antsy to have the time pass quickly."

He seemed genuine enough, like a puppy looking for someone to play ball. She forced a pleasantness to her voice. "Have you been away for long?"

"Quite. A year-long residency as part of a teaching exchange."

"Where?"

"A small, Midwestern college—Wheaton. Have you heard of it?"

"No, I'm not really that well versed on Midwestern colleges."

His easy smile flashed again. "Not to worry. As I've said, it's relatively small. I enjoyed the change of pace."

"Sounds like you're used to a more hectic schedule."

"Yes, life at Cambridge can be, well ... a bit hairy I should say."

A red flag of skepticism unfurled in her head. "So, you're a professor at Cambridge?"

"Yes."

"And what do you profess?"

His grin widened. "You don't believe me, do you?"

"No, not a bit. Sounds like you're trying to impress me."

He laughed outright at that. "I didn't realize I could use my exciting position of British historian to attract women. I'll have to try it sometime."

She would've blushed, if she could remember how. Instinct told her he spoke truth, that he'd intended nothing more than conversation. He did look the scholarly type. His dark hair, finger-combed and ragged at his collar's edge announced that his profession held priority over outward impressions.

"Sorry, Professor. I'm a cynic at heart. I suppose I should let you prove yourself before jumping to conclusions."

"No need to apologize. No offense taken."

Laugh lines gathered in crinkles from his cheekbones to temples, a testimony to a lifetime of laughter, though she doubted he was much more than thirty.

"So, what exactly does a professor of history do all day? Read dusty books? Lecture on facts and dates and such?"

She listened as he related his position, but put her mind on autopilot when he continued to explain his recently published collection of medieval essays. Was this guy for real? Pleasing to the eye, amiable, intelligent, his manner gentle yet he commanded attention. His soft-spoken, self-assured presence reminded her of someone. Someone she'd been trying to forget.

Oh, Dan.

No. She'd not let that surface now.

Holding out her travel book, she derailed her train of thought and interrupted his discourse. "What do you recommend?"

"I beg your pardon?"

"I'm on vacation and would like to see a bit of history. Being that's basically your life, what do you recommend?"

"Oh, well." He took the book and paged through glossy advertisements. "I suppose it depends on your intent."

"Intent?"

"Yes. You see—" He paused. "How shall I put this? There are sights to see, of legitimate historical value mind you, that have been renovated to the point of distraction. You'll find well-maintained artifacts in glass display cases, and gift shops selling replicated trinkets. If you'd like to see history all laced-up and trimmed 'round the edges, then any place mentioned in this book ought to suit you."

Though she bore no inherent love for the past, a strange urge to rise to his challenge came out in a rush of words. "What if that were not my intent? What if I wanted to not only see history in its polished state, but to live and breathe it?"

His searching gaze seemed to weigh the integrity of her response as if, perhaps, she mocked him. Did she? Whatever had gotten into her to spout such questions?

"What part of the country?" he replied at length.

"I'd like to keep London as my base, so I suppose nothing that would take more than a day."

Retrieving a pen from the pack at his feet, he indicated her travel guide. "Shall I?"

At her approval, he turned to the blank pages at the back and wrote for quite some time. Her interest waned when the snack cart came down the aisle, but his focus was such that he didn't look up at the tinkle of ice cubes or the whiff of ham salad.

Her eyelids weighed heavy by the time he handed back the book. She flipped through the pages, the detail overwhelming her, but one entry in particular commanded more than its fair share of space.

"I'm guessing that Gallimore Castle is the one site I really shouldn't miss."

"Yes, well." A sheepish grin lit his face. "I suppose I did get a bit carried away."

"Why?"

"It's quite a long story actually."

"Well, let's see," she looked at her watch, exaggerating his ludicrous answer, and let a playful edge soften her tone. "I've got about six hours worth of listening time. Think that's enough to squeeze in your long story?"

"Certainly, if you'd like the shortened version."

Cole Hawksworth, as she discovered the professor's true identity, no doubt held the foremost position in his field, for he excelled in bringing the past to life. His tale began in the early 1300s with someone named Tagerwynn the Noble, fifth Earl of Gallimore. Before long, knights battled and ladies swooned in Jess's mind.

"That's pretty amazing." And it was, or more like he was. *What?* She swallowed back that renegade thought and ignored the aftertaste. "Do you know this much history about all the castles in England?"

"If I did, I dare say they ought to increase my salary. Gallimore's rather a pet project of mine that's taken years of research. I've only uncovered information back to the fifth earl, but I'd love to discover what happened to the four before him. Someday I hope to compile it all into a book, perhaps in novel form."

"Hmm." She raised one brow, a trait she'd perfected in front of a mirror during third grade. "I'd say, professor, that you're hiding a romantic streak behind that lofty career of yours."

"Perhaps, though I've never really thought of myself—"

The plane dropped, not a smooth descent, but a severe vertical plummet. Shrieks of panic masked whatever Cole had intended to say.

Jess's stomach lurched and she grasped the armrest where Cole's hand lay. Is this it? Is this where I'll die? Will Dan's face be the first I see?

Cabin lights blinked from on to off, then on again. The crazy downward motion changed into an insane rollercoaster ride. Up and down, down and up, the plane skidded on air currents.

"This is the Captain. Do not panic. We've hit some rough turbulence. Though the situation is disturbing, everything's under control. Please remain seated with seatbelts fastened until further notice."

The captain's calm voice soothed most passengers. Jess let out her own slow exhale, suddenly aware she'd been holding her breath—but that wasn't the only thing she held.

With a jerk, she pulled her hand free of the professor's. "Sorry, didn't mean to freak out and grab you like that. I don't usually scare so easily."

"On the contrary, I thought you were very brave. You didn't scream once. You must have a firm faith."

Right, about as firm as Jell-O. Years ago she would've described her faith as firm, but not lately.

"Well, Professor, I didn't see you squirm either. Your own faith must be pretty solid."

He chuckled. "Well, it would hardly do to leave God behind with our families, would it?"

His words stabbed, ripping a hole in the fabric of her apathy. That's exactly what she'd done—left God behind—and a twinge of guilt nicked her soul. This conversation was beginning to feel like the plane ride ... sickening. She flailed mentally for a new topic. "You, uh, you left your family behind for an entire year?"

"Oh, sorry, didn't mean to imply a family of my own. My sister and I have always been very close, and I must say, I've missed my nephew and two nieces terribly. Would you like to see a photo?"

Why in the world would he show her a picture of his relatives? This was one eccentric character, but her apathetic reserve was hardly a match against his boyish earnestness. "Sure."

Shifting in his seat, he produced a worn wallet with a creased photograph inside, and she gazed at a snapshot of the perfect family.

"That's my sister, Jenny, and her husband, Martin. Margie and Olivia are the two angels on the left, and Ben is the tiger-eyed rascal in the middle."

Jess smiled. "They're beautiful. You've a very nice family to go home to, Professor."

"And you?"

"Me?"

"Have you a picture of your family?"

Jess bit her lip and paused. How to explain without going into detail why the family snapshot she carried consisted of only one person?

"I shouldn't have asked you that." He crinkled his laugh lines at her again. "Please don't feel obligated to share something so personal."

This was ridiculous. He'd only asked to see a picture, not tell him her whole life story. "No, I don't feel obligated at all."

After coercing the belt buckle out of the way, she opened the Velcro flap on the front pocket of her waistpack and retrieved a laminated wallet-sized photo. "This is my son, Jack. He's ten-years-old now, but this was taken a year ago."

Cole studied the picture. "He looks a lot like you."

"Not really. Most people say he doesn't take after me a bit."

"No." Cole shook his head. "I'm sure of it. Even though it's a photo, I can tell he's got your strength of spirit. I think he'll grow to be a very fine man one day."

His fingertips brushed hers as he handed back the photo, and a shot of warmth traveled up her arm. She pulled back and tucked away the picture, taking longer than necessary. Weird. It'd been a long time since she'd given anyone a second thought, least of all a man. She might almost be sorry they neared the end of the flight.

Once again, the captain's voice reminded everyone to remain seated, but gave permission for the flight attendants to prepare for landing. Sighs chorused around her, and she guessed many would be exceedingly glad to put this wild ride behind them.

"I hope your holiday goes well." The professor's tone carried a warm sincerity.

"Thanks. And thanks for the tourist information."

"Not a problem. You know, I was thinking, I hope you won't think me too forward if ..."

Fabulous, here it came. She should've known he'd hit on her sooner or later. Lonely professor meets single woman showing mild interest in his lengthy tales. She never should've put her hand on his. "No, I just don't think it would work out."

A puzzled look crossed his face. "What an odd name."

He hadn't been asking her out—he'd been asking her name. A battering-ram of shame tried to breach her well-structured wall of isolation, and she cleared her throat. "I guess I misunderstood. My name is Jess. Jessica Neale. I can't believe I've been so rude that for this entire flight I never introduced myself."

"No need to apologize. I could've asked sooner. It's been a pleasure, Ms. Neale." He offered his hand in belated greeting.

Jess cringed inside at being called Ms. A prickly peeve, it poked her like a pin each time someone gave her that label. Since Dan's death, she wandered like a vagabond between Miss and Mrs. It fit her, though, and that annoyed her most. "You can call me Jess.

Most people do."

"Very well, Jess. You've been a delightful audience and I'm glad to have met you. I hope you have the kind of historical experience that will tie your future to the past."

The candid glimmer in his eyes tempered the strange comment. Whatever did he mean?

"Uh, I was thinking again, and—" His words were lost as he bent over to rummage through his backpack once more. After a few moments, he handed her a ripped-off piece of notebook paper on which he'd scrawled a woman's name and phone number.

"What's this for?"

"Jenny Clayborn is my sister, and that's where I can be reached if you find my directions aren't clear enough, or you end up getting lost. I'll warn you, though, the sites I listed are quite off the beaten path and can be a challenge to find even when you know where you're going."

"Oh, uh, well." She stopped, unsure if she should be insulted or grateful. "Thanks."

"I hope you won't mind if I dash off. As I've said, I am awfully anxious."

"Hey, don't worry about it." She wrenched his briefcase free from behind her bag on the floor.

The wheels barely came to a stop on the tarmac before Cole loosed his seatbelt and bounded down the aisle. Scores of people followed in his wake, and Jess let them all shuffle past.

Being one of the last off the plane, she assumed the activity of customs would be lessened. Wrong. Lines of travelers clogged the passport check. Clusters of people boarded the train. Even a great swarm of humanity queued up to ride the tube.

After braving a confusing maze of streets, she arrived at a brownstone guesthouse in a quiet section of town. Three flights of narrow stairs led her to a small room. It appeared tidy, if not cramped, and had a faint aroma of mothballs. Not the Hilton, but it would do.

She released her suitcase and dropped her shoulder bag next to it, then glanced at her watch through travel-weary eyes. It'd been more than twenty-four hours since she'd last slept. Though the early afternoon sun shone and her stomach growled in loud complaint, the lumpy little bed magnetized her. She plopped on top of the chenille bedspread and gave in to a fitful sleep.

He came to her then, as he always did. Dan lived only in her dreams, for she chose to shut out his memory in her daily life. It held too much pain.

Of course she had prayed. Prayed for the grief to be removed. Prayed to endure the loneliness that shrouded her every waking minute. Prayed even for her own life to end. She knew better than to have asked, but at the time, it'd been the honest state of her heart. Through it all, God remained silent. She knew He hadn't turned from her, but neither did she truthfully turn to Him. Fear blocked that path—fear that if she did lay all her emotions and her heart at His altar, He might call her to pick it back up and love again, and she couldn't do that.

She wouldn't do that. Ever.

Strange, though, how the longer she lay there trying to remember Dan's face, all she could see was the professor's.

Chapter 2

Jess woke to a dragged suitcase banging an annoying cadence in the stairwell outside the thin door to her hotel room. The picture frame cast a diagonal shadow on the worn papered wall. Was it dusk already? How long had she slept?

Groggy, she rose, ignoring the receding thumpity-thump. She stepped over her shoes she'd left strewn on the floor and peered out the only window gracing the room. A patchwork of roofs and crumbling chimneys—pigeon heaven. No wonder this room had been such a bargain.

Pulling herself away from the less than scenic view, she glanced at the fake-gold sunburst clock. It looked more like early American garage sale than uppity-British décor, but the needle-nosed hands told her what she needed to know. Pubs from Picadilly to Mayfair would be serving up fish and chips for dinner right about now, and her pinched stomach cried out for a meal.

Her feet complained as she tugged on her leather loafers. She snatched up her purse, and as an afterthought, grabbed the sweater heaped across her duffle bag.

Suitcase Thumper must've found his home because the staircase was empty as Jess trotted down. No one manned the chipped-veneer podium masquerading as a front-desk either. Patting her pocket to make sure she had a key, she slipped out the front door unconcerned. She'd seen several restaurants when passing the area earlier. It shouldn't be a problem to find one now.

The first breath of cool evening air revived her flagging senses. A brisk walk to a neighboring café would be the ideal way to begin a vacation.

The refreshing breeze soon turned chill, and she pulled on her sweater. Wanting to remain in daylight as long as possible, she headed west. A leftover newspaper skittered across her path and landed in the gutter, but tap-dancing litter was all she encountered. Why weren't any of the eateries open? The three she'd passed displayed closed signs in their lifeless windows.

Her stomach grumped again. She might have to give up the quintessential fish and chips dinner and take the tube to a station with fast-food outlets. Picking up her pace, she looked for an underground entry, but mostly succeeded in working her way into an industrial area.

As her footsteps reverberated off the building walls, she shivered. Creepy black alleys punctuated the long city blocks and the night air carried a stink of wet cardboard and marinated dumpster trash. Her nerves prickled when she realized someone followed a short distance back. Great. What was she doing here?

She scooted around the next corner, the footsteps behind her increasing in tempo as well. Fear tasted sour in her mouth, driving away the hunger that'd been gnawing at her. Jess sprinted, uncaring of how foolish she might look. She'd not become a statistic.

Down the length of street, sporadic sets of headlights whizzed past. She slipped in an oily puddle camouflaged by black shadows, catching herself before losing balance, and raced toward the lights.

Her tension eased as she reached a main thoroughfare with a red BT booth. Closing herself up in the glass cocoon, she wrenched the phone off the cradle, ready to call for help. Only then did she allow herself to look back for a solid description of her pursuer.

But the street was empty.

Whoa, girl, you are losing it. After a few cleansing breaths, she willed her racing heartbeat to slow. Chagrined at her own foolishness, she scanned the rest of the world through the view of the phone booth. Nothing looked familiar, of course. Other than lost, she had no idea where she was.

She unzipped her waistpack and fished around, her fingers searching for the card with the phone number of the inn. All she found was a scrap of ripped notebook paper with a name and numbers written in blue ink. Jenny Clayborn. Jenny Clayborn?

Jenny Clayborn is my sister, and that's where I can be reached if you find my directions aren't clear enough, or you end up getting lost. The professor's words replayed like a prophecy of doom. He had offered to help her, though this probably wasn't the situation he had in mind. She could give it a try. Why not? Worst case scenario, he'd hang up on her, and she'd call a cab.

She inserted her credit card and punched in the numbers for the Jenny Clayborn residence.

A somewhat familiar voice answered. "Clayborns."

"Uh." Should she really go through with this? "Cole?"

"Yes?"

The uncertainty in his tone spoke louder than if he'd demanded to know who in the world she was. "This is Jess. Jessica Neale. Remember me? The one on the plane? You said I could call you if I happened to get lost, and—"

"Have you tried to find a castle already?"

"No. No, it's not that. I was, well, this will probably sound ridiculous, but I left my hotel to try to find a restaurant, and I—"

"In London?"

Oh, why did I call him? "Yes, in London." He probably couldn't help her unless she was lost back in the Middle Ages, and she sighed.

"I didn't mean to offend you. I just wasn't sure."

"Look, I'm sorry to have bothered you."

"No bother. Can you tell me where you are?"

She squinted into the darkness outside the glare of the bright phone booth. "I'm at the intersection of Wincott Street and Gilbert Road."

"And where are you trying to go?"

"I was trying to get something to eat, but now I'd be just as happy to get back to my hotel, the St. James on Tonbridge and Welsh."

"All right. Hold on."

The silence on the receiver continued for so long, she wondered if he might've gotten into a car himself to come rescue her.

"Are you still there?" she heard him at last.

"Yes."

"Can you write this down? It's lengthy. You must've been walking for quite some time."

Tell me about it.

"The directions are from my sister, and she says though it's roundabout, at least you'll avoid the warehouse district. It's not very safe, you know."

Jess bit her lip. Of course she knew that. Firsthand.

"She also said it might take you past a convenience store for a bite to eat, which is about the best you'll find at this time of night in that part of town."

Her pen took on a life of its own as her fingers flew to keep up with his narration. Writer's cramp threatened to set in by the time he finished. How had she possibly gotten so far off course? "Okay. Got it. Thanks a lot."

"Why don't you ring me when you get back to your hotel so I'll know you made it safely?"

Why would he care? "I'm sure I'll be fine. Tell your sister thanks. Bye."

Reading her scribbled directions, she understood why she'd gotten lost. There were at least five different streets named Tonbridge with subtle variations. Tonbridge Road crossed Tonbridge Street, but then turned into Tonbridge Place, where Tonbridge Lane veered off to just plain Tonbridge.

By the time she returned to her room, the clock neared midnight. She released her feet from loafer prison and fell on the bed, not caring to brush her teeth or wash her face. As she began to surrender to a deep sleep, the shrill ring of the telephone startled her awake.

"Hello?" She forced her voice to cooperate.

"Jess?"

"That's me." She stifled a yawn.

"This is Cole. Just wanted to make sure you got back safely to your room."

"Yeah, uh, okay." She rubbed her eyes with her free hand. "I made it back just fine, though I never found anything to eat. I'll try again in the morning. So for now, I think we can all go to sleep."

"All right then. Good night."

She fumbled the receiver back to the night stand. Dead-tired, beyond hungry, and more than a little annoyed, she flopped back onto the bed. What more would this vacation have to offer?

•

Though she slept till noon, Jess wandered in a haze for the rest of the next day. After checking in with her mom and son via telephone, she ventured out for a few hours, but didn't know where to go or what to do. The Tower of London sounded depressing, Picadilly Circus too garish, the guards at Buckingham Palace much too implacable—nothing even remotely interested her. She spent the evening with a carton of Chinese take-out and dozed off to *The History of the Monarchy* on the BBC.

Slants of sunrise tickled her eyelids and she woke, running her tongue across teeth wearing sweaters of plaque. The jangling telephone broke the early morning silence, and she snapped her head toward it, immediately grabbing the back of her neck. Wincing from the sharp pain, she cursed hard European pillows and reached with her free hand for the receiver.

"Hello?"

"Hello, Jess?"

The voice was way too deep to be her son, and she didn't remember her sister or mother sounding that bass even when they had a cold. "Yes."

"Hello there. This is Cole Hawksworth. How's your holiday going so far?"

"You called me this early to ask how my vacation is?" Was he nuts?

"Hope I didn't wake you. I didn't realize the hour what with the chatter and patter of busy feet around here. I'm taking the little ones, my sister's children I should say, out to Gallimore today. Being we discussed it in such measure on the plane, I wondered if you might like to tag along."

She reached up to knead the knot in her neck that still smarted from the nerve pinch. "Are you serious?"

"Of course. Why not?"

Why not? He was nuts. She sealed her lips to keep from blurting her thoughts. How wise could it be to spend an entire day with a man she'd recently met? She'd probably get stuck babysitting those kids while he took professor-type notes or something. Still, the alternative of repeating the day before didn't hold any appeal either.

"We could come over and pick you up in an hour or so."

"No, I'll— " She stopped. She'd what? Ride the tube all day and top it off with fried rice and a Brit comedy blaring from a thirteen-inch screen? "I'll rent a car and meet you."

"All right, then. How about Tetbury? It's a small hamlet near

Gallimore. We could meet, oh, say noon or thereabouts. Have you a map? I wouldn't want you getting lost again."

"No, but I'm sure I can pick one up at the car rental place."

"Very good. Noon in Tetbury at the petrol station. Can't miss it. And watch out for those roundabouts."

She'd heard of roundabouts—circular junctions with offshoots for various intersecting streets. However, until she experienced one behind the wheel, on the opposite side of the road, whizzing along at 90K, she couldn't fully comprehend his warning. It took several rotations before she got the hang of it and shot off on the chute toward Tetbury.

Even with her roundabout trials, she managed to arrive five minutes ahead of schedule. A few small houses and one rag-tag store, a sort of mercantile-pub-petrol station, made up the entire village.

Cole shouldn't have been hard to spot, especially with children in tow, but her mini-Cooper was the only car around. She'd have to wait.

She did. She waited, and waited, giving him plenty of time. Then she waited some more.

At one o'clock, she tried calling, but no one answered. It struck her as odd that he'd stand her up like this, but maybe he held more traits of an absent-minded professor than she gave him credit for.

By two o'clock, she had to make a decision. She'd not turn tail and head back to London, wasting another day of her vacation in the process. She'd go it alone, find that castle, snap a picture or two to prove it, and when her head hit the uncomfortable pillow that night, she'd feel like she'd accomplished something.

According to the professor's directions, she drove to a gravel turn-off, which eventually narrowed into a wide dirt path. She veered left and kept going until the hedgerow ended abruptly by a forked oak, then parked the car near the brush at the side of the road.

Stepping out, she pocketed the keys and shut the door. Determined to find Gallimore, she tramped into the wilds of rural England. Her feet slipped trying to find a solid foothold amidst tangled roots. Would this silly castle be worth all the effort?

Beads of sweat trickled down her back as the exceptionally warm weather closed in around her. She wished now she'd gotten more than her feet wet when crossing that winding river a ways back. Through rutted ravines and a steady uphill climb, she persevered. At least she could say she'd seen the English countryside in its natural state.

Near the crest of the hill, she slowed in front of a wire fence. After a glance around for any 'no trespassing' signs, she scampered over without a second thought. A thick edging of trees slowed her, but she broke through—and came face-to-face with a large ram bearing an impressive pair of sharpened curled horns.

She locked eyes with the goat-monster and swallowed, preparing to take a flying leap back downhill.

But the ram obviously had better things to do. He ambled away toward a bleating flock grazing off to her left. They didn't seem threatened by her presence. Goats. Didn't they make rugs out of those things?

Perspiration dotted her brow and she swiped at it with the back of her hand, then shaded her eyes against the sun to scan a rocky meadow. She must be getting close. Trudging over to the nearest rock, she sank down.

The field presented a picturesque scene, walled off by thick oaks and flanked farther on with cedar. Grass grew in clumps where it hadn't been nibbled, and right at her feet, by the base of a square boulder, a dainty yellow wildflower flashed its brazen petals. Digging through her waistpack, she retrieved her small set of pencils and nature journal, but in the process her son's photo fluttered to the ground. She snatched it up and brushed away any minute bits of dirt. His chipped-tooth smile endured her caress the same as if he'd stood there in person. Sweet boy. Sweet boy who needed a father. *Oh, Dan.*

With pressed lips, she tucked the picture into the rear zipper of her waistpack and slid from the rock to the ground, focusing on the tiny flower instead of the emotion nipping inside like a hound from hell. She lost herself in trying to capture its delicate essence against the canvas of rough gray stone. Her artistic skills never quite lived up to her expectations, but after a while, her persistence paid off with a rendering she could live with.

The sun tucked itself behind a blanket of clouds, lending a cooling effect. She rose to perch on the rock again, then re-packed the drawing tools and pulled out her travel guide to re-read Cole's directions.

She'd followed every detail. She should be standing right at the gates of Gallimore itself. Wait a minute ... standing? What about sitting? She looked with a whole new perspective. Sure enough, those rocks in the field lay in a pattern too strategic to be formed by nature. This must be the ruins of Gallimore Castle.

She walked the perimeter and mentally conjured an image of the structure as it might have been. Centuries before, this exact piece of land had supported a hub of people and power—hard to reconcile with a lazy goat pasture.

Swapping travel guide for sketchbook, she once more cozied into a niche on the ground. Pencil in hand, she drew her own version of the glory days of Gallimore Castle. Undaunted by the cooling temperature, she continued her fantasy and ignored the wind tugging at the edges of her paper. It took the first drops of rain splattering against her shaded battlements to catch her attention.

She snapped shut her book, then tucked it away and stood up to be slapped in the face by a chill wind and needles of rain. Alarmed by the green-gray sky, she decided she'd seen enough of Gallimore. She jogged through the field, noting that the calm bleating of goats had been replaced by the bass drone of approaching thunder.

Rain poured in earnest as she reached the overhang of trees. Crossing the fence required more effort with wet clothes clinging to her, and descending the face of the hill posed an especially treacherous challenge. By the time she reached the ravines, night fell in earnest blackness. The underbrush tangled her steps, causing her to fall more than once. Lightning lit her path, sending macabre shadows dancing around. The placid little creek she'd practically skipped across in the afternoon swirled in a frenzy, straining against its banks.

What am I doing here? That frantic thought stabbed her as an unwelcome reminder of her own ignorance. She should've gone back to London sooner.

It took several lifetimes to reach the small rental car. Her shivering fingers fought with the keys for an intolerable amount of time before she succeeded in opening the door. Once she shut out the incessant wind and driving rain, she slumped exhausted against the seat.

The respite didn't last long. She couldn't help but think the narrow dirt road must've morphed into mud by now. The urgency of the situation put an end to her inaction. A turn of the key brought the engine to life, and she coaxed the little car to the middle of the road.

Tree branches skittered across the path as her windshield wipers did double-time in vain effort. The bizarre scene outside looked like something out of a Hollywood movie set.

A chest-rattling crack of thunder lifted her several inches off the seat. Another blinding flash of lightning followed. In the split second of intense light, something moved off to the side of the road ahead of her. What?

She hunched over the steering wheel, squinting through the windshield. Did her eyes play tricks on her? Hard to tell with the tempest highlighting the landscape in an irregular strobe of electric white.

There it was again. Something more than the glare of her headlights reflected off the tree-lined road as a flash of silver crossed her path.

It looked like ... Couldn't be ... The shape of a man. Someone tried to cross directly in front of her. She swerved, and the tires slid.

Thunder cracked.

And so did her head.

A spray of shattered glass mingled with the pouring rain, creating a diamond kaleidoscope—before everything faded to black.

Chapter 3

A determined ray of morning light pierced through Jess's lids, calling her from the depths of hazy unconsciousness. Birdsong gave chorus to a light, shushing breeze, but she paid that scant attention. Reality throbbed in her head and ached in her neck.

She pushed herself upright, and her vision swam in a wave of dizziness. With a force of will, she concentrated on deep breathing. Her fuzzy focus sharpened by increments until at last she could fully take in her surroundings.

Immense trees. Tangled brush. A forest. The memory of her hazardous trek through the storm of the night before barreled back to mind with striking clarity. The last thing she remembered was a burst of white light as her head took the brunt of impact. She must've been thrown free from the car. Glancing around, she didn't see it. Strange. She couldn't have been thrown that far.

She stood in slow motion to stave off light-headedness and scanned the immediate area. No car. No road. No road? Ridiculous. No way could she have been cast such a distance and live to tell about it. On a whim, she reached to feel for a pulse. *No doubt about it ol' girl. You're alive.*

Upon further examination, she traced a trail of dried blood along the side of her face to the origin at the top of her forehead. No wonder her head pounded. From what she could tell, however, this gash and some mighty sore muscles were the extent of her injuries.

With a slow stretch, she worked out the kinks. As she moved, a strange glint caught at the periphery of her sight, and she turned to investigate the shimmer of silver.

Behind gnarled roots of a massive oak, a shiny piece of metal lay forgotten on the ground. Drawing closer, she discovered two matching discs curved and formed into rather ornate knee pads, on legs wearing a mesh of small chain links. Thighs the size of tree trunks were covered in part by finely woven blue material edged with golden embroidery. The remainder of the fabric rested over a torso that would've been the envy of any linebacker. A sleeveless tunic revealed arms with powerful biceps enclosed in more polished chain mail. The flash of silver she'd seen last night? The man who'd insanely crossed the road in front of her? What kind of idiot would prance around in the woods dressed as a knight?

She gnawed her lip. Since hit and run wasn't exactly on her agenda, she'd have to at least see if he were breathing. Stupid man. Crouching beside the still form, she grasped the visor of his helmet. It lifted easily enough. Shadow hid much of the man's face, but from what she could see, he had good color. Being so near, she inhaled the scent of him. He smelled of wood smoke and the balminess that lingers in the air after an autumn rain.

As she tentatively reached out, his light breath brushed against her knuckles. Relieved, she drew back. He was fine. In fact, probably better than her, considering the splitting headache that nagged her.

Without warning, his dark lashes opened and she found herself staring into eyes so green, they were almost crystalline. Those eyes looked familiar. Mesmerized by their brilliance, she didn't know what to say, nor even where her voice had gone.

He rose to a sitting position, and the next moment, his gloved hand tightened around her throat.

•

Battle instincts heightened, Colwyn studied his quarry. Cropped hair and curious garments suggested that perhaps he'd landed an older boy. The telltale curves of womanhood gave him cause to consider otherwise. A woman? Out here?

What kind of sorcery was this? But the real enigma wasn't the foreign woman who clawed and wriggled against his firm grip. How had he gotten to the King's own wood? Even now he should be leagues from here, leading a charge of men to battle with the King. Where were his men? Where was his horse?

The girl's wide eyes and pale face warned him he'd pinched her air supply long enough. Releasing her, he stood, allowing time for her to gasp and cough, and for him to tug off his helm and padded arming cap.

He let forth a sharp, short whistle and looked for movement in the thick growth of trees. Nothing. Not a snap of twig, nor rustle of brush. Pushing air past his teeth once more, he still received no whickering response.

His horse, and his men, had vanished. Impossible.

He returned his attention to the girl, who yet spluttered for breath on the ground. "Namesake," he commanded.

She gave no answer, save for a piercing look of scorn. If this woman held a weapon, no doubt she'd see his blood spilled here and now. Such a look could not be entertained.

He whumped her face down in the dirt and ground his foot into the small of her back. "Thy name!"

At the lack of response, he dug in his heel, increasing the pressure. Woman or not, he would be obeyed. "Speak thee thy name forsooth."

A grunt of pain served as her only reply. This one was either brave or ignorant. He couldn't afford to waste time on a mute peasant, but neither could he let a mercenary spy slip through his fingers. In either case, hard to make an assessment as she lay prostrate on the forest floor.

"Forthwith I release you, yet free you are not. Rise and hail answer to me."

Removing his boot from her back, he watched warily as she rose. She wavered unsteady on her feet as she brushed herself off. Defiant eyes glared into his, speaking not of serfdom. Dried blood encrusted her face from forehead to temple, but that only added to his host of unanswered questions. "Speak thee thy name."

Spitting out bits of dirt that had lodged in her mouth, she finally answered. "Jess. Jessica Neale."

The name sounded as foreign as her accent. "Shire?"

Her silence communicated indignation, not fear. How interesting. "From what shire have you journeyed, and wherein lies your allegiance?"

"Look mister, I don't know what you're talking about. Maybe if you dropped the corny old English accent. Was it you that crossed in front of me like an idiot last night in that storm?"

Her dialect perplexed him, but he understood the tone—one that he'd not suffer from this snip of a girl. He unsheathed the dagger at his side and snatched her to him, pressing the blade's edge against her throat. "You owe me your life, for thus far have I spared it. Do not tread upon my patience for you will find it scarce. How come you to be here and for what purpose?"

"I thought …" She tensed and swallowed, her breaths shallow and fast. "I thought you were hurt, that I might've hit you with my car. Let me go!"

Her bold speech held too much authority for a peasant, and serfs cowered at the sight of him. This one not only lacked a proper amount of fright but made demands on him as well. Letting her go was out of the question.

No doubt his brother, the Earl, would be sorely displeased at this outcome. 'Twas by Tarne's decree that Colwyn should've been several days' ride from Gallimore Castle, not merely a swift hike's distance. Tarne's rage would be certain, and Colwyn shuddered to face it. Nay, he wouldn't. Far better that this girl in strange garments should bear the brunt of his brother's wrath.

"I spare you for the present. So be it if you will answer not to me. There are others to whom you shall. Walk at my command or I'll cast you over my shoulder. What say you?"

"I'll walk," came her cold response.

He released her, tensing for the inevitable escape attempt. She didn't move. This one was unpredictable, making her all the more dangerous. "Turn and set face toward Warnborough."

She merely looked at him, almost as if he were the one who should be told where to go.

"Go!"

"Why should I? How do I know you won't stab me in the back as soon as I turn around?"

"Front or back makes no difference to my blade." He glowered and took a menacing step toward her.

"All right! All right. If you want me to head toward Warnborough, you'll have to tell me where in the world it is."

"Fie! Follow me then and keep pace. Think not to stray either. My temper is such that I'll slay you in an instant to rid me of your uncommon tongue."

Retrieving his helm and cap from the ground, he set off with a stride that a lesser man would tremble to match. All the while, he minded her trailing behind, surprised she didn't lapse far at all. No doubt she'd be exhausted within minutes and he'd be heaving her over his shoulder. Not that it mattered. He cared not a fig whether the terrain or his speed suited her, and he pressed on.

After nearly an hour, slick sweat dripped from his skin beneath the weight of the metal fabric, soaking his linen undergarments clear through to the padded gambeson. Amazing that as of yet, he'd not had to add to his burden by carrying the girl. She followed without falter. She even followed without complaint. His own men would not have been so compliant.

At last Warnborough came within view. He'd soon be home.

•

Heart pounding and head reeling, Jess tagged behind the medieval maniac. Though his speech pattern confused her with a unique blend of Shakespeare and Yoda, she knew the meaning of 'slay you.' Hopefully if she pacified him, he wouldn't freak out, and she'd have a better chance of negotiating freedom. Besides which, they might come across people, a road, or some other remote kind of salvation. Instead, she saw no one and nothing other than the long legs of the man in front of her.

Above the continual rustle of batted branches and crushed twigs, a new sound hovered. Jess cocked her head. Something nearby bubbled like a Zen fountain.

The man picked up speed, and soon an unspoken race began. After a near-tumble and a skidding stop at the bottom of a steep bank, they both went to their knees. The man cupped water to his mouth fast enough to splash quite a spray. So, the physical strain of the wild hike hadn't belonged to her alone. Satisfaction tasted as good as the quenching drink.

He sat back but she lingered, washing off itchy, dried bits of blood caked on her cheek. The hateful man watched her every movement. Running away would be a challenge.

"We rest here, woman."

Turning from the rushing water, she eyed him. "I thought you said we were going to Warnborough?"

"Be ye daft? Herein lies Warnborough."

She looked around. Trees, weeds, rocks—pretty much the same scene she'd seen all morning with no sign of inhabitants anywhere. She thought for sure they'd been headed for one of the small English townships she'd driven through yesterday. "All that's here is this stream."

"Aye. Warnborough. The felon stream."

"Felon stream?"

An impatient frown pulled down his lips. "Where criminals are drowned. Look well upon it for perhaps 'tis where you'll meet your end."

"My end?" She narrowed her eyes. "Listen here buddy, it seems to me you'd be the one taking the criminal action prize today."

On his feet in an instant, he towered over her with dagger drawn. "Forsooth, wench, guard your tongue."

Violent and sexist? Bad combo. Obviously political correctness wasn't a big deal to him. "Wench?"

"Aye, and no doubt a harlot or heretic as well."

Where did this guy get off? Pounding heart or not, she pulled herself up and leveled her own challenging gaze. "I've had it with you. I'm out of here, and if you want to stop me with your fancy pocketknife, go ahead. I hope you get life in prison."

She spun away, but when her worn sneaker tread met a mossy rock, her foot shot out. Flailing her arms didn't help regain her balance, and she landed flat in the rushing water. It might've served to cool her off if not for the belly laugh behind her.

Picking her way to the other bank, she stood dripping, and glared back at him. But beyond, the backdrop of trees ... Weird, almost déjà vu. She whirled, and ravines gaped in front of her—ravines that would lead to a hill? If so, a goat pasture ought to follow, and surely someone nearby must tend those goats. Someone who could help her. She sprinted ahead, ignoring the splash of metal-encased feet.

All the hours she'd spent at the health club paid off, giving her the needed edge to keep ahead, but not by much. Leaving the cover of thick woods, she scrambled up a steep embankment. Not an oak to dodge nor a fence to hurdle like she remembered. Had she been mistaken? No time now to stop and reconsider. Laboring on, she reached the crest.

Then stopped.

No pasture. No goats. Only a rock wall loomed in front of her. A wall that spanned an imposing fortress where the ruins of Gallimore should've been. No, couldn't be. It made no sense. She must've made a wrong turn somewhere or been disoriented from the beginning.

Rough hands clamped her tight and twisted her around, then hoisted her up and flung her like a sack of potatoes. She found herself heaped over a tin shoulder looking down the backside of the man. Kicking and pounding dented her resolve but not his armor.

"Put me down!" No answer. Just the continual plodding of his heavy feet leaving tracks in the dirt.

She arched her neck and saw they followed the perimeter of the wall. Could this maybe be a castle open to the public? The thought became a life raft in the middle of an ocean of desperation. Hope swelled as she heard distinct sounds of movement other than the clanking and clinking of the knight's armor. The timbre of his steps changed when he left the dirt of the ground for an incline of slatted board. Light disappeared into shadows as cool stone walls surrounded them. It didn't last long. Once they went through the thick gate, they emerged into open air.

Manure, sweat and leather blended together on a puff of a breeze. A hammer beating against metal played a rhythmic tempo, competing with deep-toned conversations. Voices? Lifting her head, she thrilled to see two costumed guards standing at attention not five yards from where she'd passed.

"Hey! Stop this guy. He's holding me against my will."

At last this nightmare would be over. Some vacation this had turned out to be. A warm bath and the lumpy little bed would do much to restore her shredded nerves. She'd seen enough of England.

But something wasn't right. How could they not have seen or heard her? "Help me!"

The guards didn't move, and the man carrying her kept on eating up the ground with great strides. Another darkened corridor followed by a break into open grounds. Another set of historical guides dressed as uniformed guards with yet another chance to get her point across.

"Stop this man!"

No one paid any attention. Some even turned away at her cries. She caught a wider vision of the courtyard as she rose higher with each step the man mounted. This was taking historical accuracy too far. "Help me! Help—"

The slamming of a massive door cut off her words and the daylight. His metallic footsteps clanked up a grand stone stairway. The murky feel of the place eased somewhat when the staircase leveled off into a slit-windowed foyer. It didn't last long. After an abrupt right, he hoisted her up another flight of steps. This one, however, sent her empty stomach into nauseous circles. Round and round, spiraling ever upward.

Just when she thought the close walls and dark shadows would consume them both, he veered off through a side door and into a corridor. Now she had a view of an intricately patterned rug. At least it served to quiet the incessant stamp of his feet—but it didn't lessen the hammering of his fist against a solid door.

They barely stepped from the corridor into the room when, without warning, he sent her sprawling to the floor. He not only dropped her, he put a little muscle into it, and her backside smarted.

"Incompetent fool!"

Words not her own, but she couldn't have agreed more. As she rose, an angry retort rushed to her lips. She opened her mouth to speak, but the remark evaporated under the glare of a short and wiry man not two paces from where she stood. His hand raised to strike, and she cringed.

The blow landed full across the jaw of the knight. She stared wide-eyed, expecting more violence. The man didn't so much as flinch but remained a granite slab. Even more surprising, the hawk-nosed little man stepped toe-to-toe with him and shouted into the unmoving knight's face.

"Deserter. Traitor! How dare you return? We shall stand in violation of the King's decree because of you."

Jess's spirits plummeted. This man would be of no help to her. He lived in the same fairy tale as her tin-can abductor. Maybe she'd hit her head harder than she thought. This must be some kind of twisted hallucination.

"Sit ye down, Tarne. Your passion is wasted on a knave such as Colwyn. Save it for one more worthy." A woman's voice this time, edged with a raspiness brought about by age or hard living. From the looks of her, likely both. She sat at a table loaded with wine bottles, mostly empty, and scrutinized Jess. Her physical presence wasn't so intimidating, yet she wore a certain aura of power. The power to let her leave? Worth a try.

"Excuse me, ma'am, but I think there's been a mistake made here. You're all doing a super job. I mean, you've got the whole language thing going for you, and the costumes are great. I'm sure this is a first-rate tourist attraction, but I'm not part of this. You must've confused me with someone else on your staff. So, I'll just be leaving and—"

"Silence!"

The bristled reply brought an end to her appeal and a smirk to the face of the man named Tarne. His rage at the knight had been such that he'd paid no attention to Jess. An involuntary shiver ran through her as she realized this was about to change.

Tarne moved squarely in front of her, calculating and cold. The knight she'd been with suddenly seemed less frightening.

"Your account?" His words came on a gust of foul breath, and Jess recoiled. There was something disturbing about this man. Hidden. Deeper. Something not righteous, almost … evil.

Before she could answer, the man behind her spoke.

"We neared on Breckonshire, when of a sudden, a great tempest arose. Night had fallen, but all became day in the fingers of light reaching from the sky. Men scattered and horses reared bewitched. Trees felled left and right. A force struck me from my mount and all turned black. I know not how, nor by what means. I awoke in the King's own wood here at Gallimore by the hand of this woman. I give you Lady Jessica of Neale."

"I asked for the woman's account, brother, not your own." Though he spoke to the knight, Tarne's gaze didn't waver from her.

"Lady Neale?" The old woman across the room let the words dangle like a piece of meat from a hook. "Odd garments for a lady."

"You know, I've really had enough of this—" The woman broke in again, but this time Jess would not be put off, and she increased her own volume.

"Listen, wouldn't you be embarrassed if your king, or your boss, or the paying public showed up with me not in costume? So, guess I'll just leave, and you can continue with your, well, whatever it is that you're doing." She whipped around, but a side-step of the knight blocked her escape.

"The king? What know you of the king?" The woman's voice carried her suspicions across the room.

Jess turned back and couldn't stop the impatient sigh that rushed out of her. "I don't know anything. I don't even know who you people think is king. I just want to go home."

"No sovereign reigns but Edward!"

Frustration bubbled in her empty stomach. How to turn this situation around? Think. Think. Nothing came to mind.

This might be a good time to pray, if she could remember how. Instead, she opened her mouth and hoped for the best. "Oh all right, if I play your little game, then can I go? Let's see, I'm no history buff, but I'll guess Edward the first. The Braveheart guy. You've all seen the movie, right? Actually, you look like you were in the movie. Anyway, he was the one who trashed Scotland. I think Edward the second is the one Scotland paid back by chasing him out, but don't quote me on that. Or the third? There were three, right? The Hundred Years War or the plague or whatever."

Wide eyes gaped at her, the accompanying silence leaving her unnerved.

"A witch!" The accusation came from behind with the sound of armor indicating the man likely crossed himself.

"No." Tarne narrowed his eyes. "She is not a witch."

Takes one to know one. Jess swallowed the off-the-cuff remark she wanted to make. Knights, witches, kings. None of this made sense.

"Lady Neale," Tarne said, and she tried hard not to shrink at his nearness. The wild pounding of her heart moved from her chest to her throat.

"It would be remiss on our part should you not partake of our hospitality. I beg you to remain. My brother will oversee you to suitable quarters where you may prepare yourself for my table this eve."

"Uh, really, don't trouble yourself."

"I insist." He dismissed her with a flick of his hand and crossed the room to confer in hushed tones with the older woman.

Jess seized the opportunity and dashed to the door. This time the surly knight let her pass, but kept pace with her out to the corridor.

"Follow me." He set off without so much as a look over his

shoulder to see if she'd obey.

As if. She'd had quite enough of trailing after him. It couldn't be too hard to retrace her way back to the outside world. She headed the opposite direction and nearly gained the staircase when the weight of the knight's hand clamped on her shoulder.

"I told you to follow."

"I know what you told me." She shrugged off his grasp and faced him. "But I'm leaving, understand?"

"'Tis here you shall stay, prepare for my brother's table, and—"

"And what? Be served all trussed up with an apple in my mouth? No thanks. If you want to play games with those two freaks, you go right ahead. I won't, and I'm leaving."

Her head hit the wall at the same time the rough stone bit into her back. The bruises where he'd shoved her would surely be an ugly purple the following day.

"You will not speak such words against my family."

The sheer strength of that one small shove almost caused her to recant. Courage, what little she had left, was the only weapon she owned. Perhaps his apparent pride would prove to be his weakest link.

"Well, why don't I wait here then, while you run back to check with little brother? I mean, I understood him to offer a simple invitation, not issue an ultimatum. But, if that didn't make sense to you, go ahead and find out what he thinks you should do."

Close enough for her to practically read his mind, she still couldn't tell what he thought. His face revealed nothing. Not a hint. His strong cut jaw didn't so much as twitch. Jess held her breath.

A rumble from deep within his chest produced more of a growl than a word. "Go."

She didn't need any more encouragement than the lessening of his grasp. Set free, she descended like a twister from the sky down the sharp curve of stairs, his final words floating on the air behind her.

"Know that I'll find you should the need arise."

Chapter 4

Good riddance. Relief nudged Colwyn with as much power as the growl of his stomach. A good piece of meat and a bed to fall on took precedence over that snippety girl. Wending his way through cool corridors, he eventually confronted the contrasting environs of the kitchen. The smoky smell of fowl on a spit increased his appetite as he ignored the head nods of obedient servants.

"Sir Colwyn, I beg pardon, but 'tis not yet finished."

His hungry-eyed glare hushed the cook. At this point, roasted or raw mattered not. A reach of his armored forearm for a wooden trencher sent a basket of apples spinning in dizzying circles upon the floor. No one said a word even as a fleshy red fruit crushed to juicy bits beneath his boot.

The heat from the hearth baked his left side, but he ignored it as he transferred the sizzling bird to the trencher. He downed half a drumstick in one bite, leaving nothing but a bone as he crossed back to the door.

He crooked a finger and beckoned to a shaggy-headed page. "Come with me, boy." This time, no doubt his command would be obeyed without hesitation. It satisfied him almost as much as the greasy meat that filled his belly. By the time he reached his quarters, only stringy bits of ligament and unchewable knobs of cartilage remained on the fowl's carcass.

Colwyn surveyed the sparse room, relieved to see that nothing here had changed. He stood, arms outstretched, waiting for the boy to remove his armor. Piece by piece peeled from him, lifting weight from his tired muscles.

"The battle, Sir?"

"Nay. None was had." Colwyn sat and held out a foot.

With a grimace, the boy tugged until the boot slid off. "But the wild men of the North, surely they—"

"I said there was no battle." His tone forbade further speculation. He didn't know if a battle had or hadn't taken place, but he would not admit that to the boy.

"Will the men be returning tonight?"

He remained silent, letting the boy guess at an answer.

"Sir?"

He eyed the page. Lanky and ragged, the lad worshipped him with a look of adoration. A morsel of a story, any story, would be all the fodder he'd need to turn his master into the champion.

Colwyn exhaled, fighting a losing skirmish with the boy's wide eyes and raised brows. Besides which, it couldn't hurt to try to piece together what had happened one more time. "Two full-days journey from Gallimore we rode, nearing on Breckonshire to meet the King's men. 'Twas a gray day with a bubbling cauldron of a sky. A storm arose of such a sudden, we were caught unaware. I called for Faulk to gather the men, but I could not be heard. The tempest wind, the crashing of trees, horses cries, all was a mighty roar. A blinding flash sent me to the ground. And then—"

He rubbed his eyes with the back of his hand, trying to remember. Nothing. Not one memory. What happened to him out there? And what of his men? His horse? Revisiting the event revealed nothing new, no satisfactory explanation.

"And then?"

He almost allowed a smile at the boy's expectant persistence. Almost, but not quite. "I awoke in the King's wood here at Gallimore. I know not how nor why. Let us hope the men continued on to fight the battle of the King's bidding, or it will be the worse for us. Now, hie yourself to Warnborough to fetch my helm and gloves, and see to it that I remain undisturbed."

"Aye, Sir." The boy's face lit with a crooked-toothed smile, and he gathered the armor with animation. No doubt his travel-worn hauberk would gleam as never before by next morning.

The ache of weariness traveled along each muscle as Colwyn stretched out onto the softness of his bed. His body relaxed, but not the buzz of swarming thoughts that stung him. One last, unsolved mystery nagged at him as he sought the solace of sleep.

The girl. The wench who'd roused him. Hair cropped as a boy and dressed as such. From whence had she come? Her impertinence irked him and her gentility left much to be desired. Anger tarried from her boldness of speech. Neither maid nor lady, other than his own mother, dared to address him in such manner. As he gave in to a disturbed sleep, lingering images of the taunting girl defied and mocked him.

•

Jess followed a narrow, rutted road, little more than a path, weaving its way at will through the trees. An arched ceiling of oak leaves cooled the air, and though she took comfort in it, she was still tired and crabby. Her feet complained at each step.

How far had she gone? It'd been a long time since she'd passed a small village located at the base of the castle's rise. The tiny town had proved to be part of the same tourist attraction complete with costumed peasants. When she'd begged for help, they'd looked at her as if she'd recently landed a spaceship in their midst. Giving up, she'd set out at a clipped pace on the only road leading from town. For quite some time, the sun dripped its molten rays while she passed rocky fields with one crop or another. Born and bred a city girl, she couldn't tell wheat from oats or rye. It all looked like tall, wavy grass.

Eventually, the fields gave way to pastured hills and came to a halt at a line of trees. The cool shade had been a welcome relief at the time, but as light faded, the thought of a night alone in the woods spurred her pace.

Tales of Nottingham and Sherwood Forest flitted around the outskirts of her mind. She could use a band of merry men to direct her home right about now. As shadows increased, her thoughts darkened, and Ichabod Crane replaced Robin Hood. Her ears strained at the slightest sound for the approach of a headless horseman.

This was crazy. She reached up to massage the tension from her neck and took a few deep breaths. What a strange day. Knights and castles and a spooky forest. It had to be a dream. And if she were awake enough to realize this was a dream, maybe she could manipulate it into something better. *Think white sands and azure waters. Think palm fronds silhouetted against a ruby orange sunset. Think Hawaii.*

But the fat, dark oaks didn't change into slim coconut trees. The thick growth of ferns didn't flatten out into silky white beaches.

And that was definitely not a seagull she saw up ahead.

A plump, shiny bird sat in the middle of the road, the largest raven she'd ever seen. It stood in the dirt on ribbed talons, like an aberrant statue unafraid of her presence, without so much as a twitch the nearer she drew. Maybe it was wounded.

She stopped within arm's reach of the bird. Its bayonet beak looked sharp, and with a cocked head, one obsidian eye glistened at her with a hungry leer. Her nerves tingled as if fire ants crawled over her skin. *Pull yourself together, girl. It's only a stupid bird.*

"Caw!"

The piercing call cut the air, and she flinched. She'd never believed in superstitions but couldn't forget that those who did often heralded the raven as a harbinger of death.

Giving the bird a wide berth, she sidled around it. An eerie scratching of claws atop soil joined the darkness tagging at her heels. The creepy atmosphere closed in, and she broke into a run. She didn't slow until the trees thinned, and the hard-packed road led her out to the rosy glow of a lowered sun.

As if mirroring the sky, a red stippling brightened the green bushes rimming the woodland's edge. Berries! Without a pause, she waded into the thick growth not far from the road and feasted on the sweet harvest. The treat brought back memories of her grandmother's backyard. How many years had it been since she'd eaten herself sick on raspberries?

"You there! What are you doing?"

•

Icy water hit Colwyn full in the face. Gasping, he bounded to his feet, ready to murder whoever dared such a deed. And after he'd dealt with the intruder, he'd find that worthless page and wring his neck for the disturbance.

Tarne stood at the foot of his bed, water bucket in hand, and all fight drained from Colwyn, leaving behind an emotionless mask.

"What a sight, lazy sluggard. Dinner begins, yet here you lie."

"Since when has my presence, or lack thereof, caused you concern?" The words came out before Colwyn thought.

A genuine sneer of dislike crossed Tarne's face. "Since I required you to bring the wench to my table. Where is she?"

Dread settled over him like a fine, cold mist. He shouldn't have let her go. What a mistake. One he'd have to face. "Gone."

"Gone?" Displeasure hung thick and heavy on the air, closing in as the creeping dark of early evening. "Gone where?"

"I know not. She desired to leave, and she was nothing but trouble. I thought—"

A stinging slap twisted his face aside, ending his explanation.

"You thought? Your function is not to think, but to obey. I told you to escort her to quarters and return her to my table. Nothing remained to think about."

Colwyn contained but could not deny his contempt. He fought to maintain an unfeeling façade and clamped his lips together.

"I'll wager she's not gone far. Find her. Bring her back." Tarne took a moment to pick at his ear. "Lest you try to think again, be forewarned. I will not be so lenient with you in the future. Do not insult me with your presence until the girl is in your possession, and do not force me to have to come track you down. When I hunt, I hunt to kill."

The weight of Tarne's words bore down with sinister pressure, forcing the air from Colwyn's lungs.

He knew exactly the kind of evil his brother could inflict. To cross Tarne with the slightest infraction meant pain—pain brought about in unusual and unspeakable ways, and he wore the scars to prove it.

Tarne planted his fists on his hips. "Why do you stand there looking at me like a sheep to be slaughtered? Go. Find the girl."

He didn't wait for further dismissal. Striding past his brother, he picked up what little he needed on his way out of the antechamber without slowing a step. A thousand retorts bubbled like a vat of lye deep in his soul. Retorts he'd love to spit in Tarne's face. He hated the way his brother belittled him. He hated being told what to do and when to do it. Most of all, he hated because he didn't know what else to do with the past three decades of hurt that had buried his spirit in a crypt.

The sound of Tarne's wheedling voice still rang in his ears. Go find the girl. He'd find her all right. He'd find this wench who goaded him like a burning branding-iron. And when he did, he'd return her to Tarne posthaste. They deserved one another.

•

"Eat not that fruit!"

The command, though serious in intent, came from a voice that cracked on the last word. Jess peeked over her shoulder and saw a shaggy young man with a sheep in tow. He couldn't be more than a teen. His rough tunic tied with a length of rope hinted at his part in the same play-acting troupe from which she'd been running. This boy would be no help, not any more than the villagers she'd begged at earlier.

She ignored him and turned back to her dinner, making sure to avoid the nettles on the branches.

"That fruit belongs to Lord Gallimore. Ye'll be put in the stocks, or worse."

Had Dorothy in Oz felt as pestered by the Munchkins?

"Take heed, miss. If M'lord's men were to find ye—"

"Thanks for the warning. I'll take my chances. Goodbye."

"But, M'lady—"

"I said—" She turned back, skewering him with a determined look. "Goodbye."

With a shake of his head, the boy sauntered away, and she returned to her snack.

Though her stomach was filled now, she'd be hungry again soon enough. If she took care, she could put a handful of raspberries in the top of her waistpack and have some for later. She removed her son's photo, as well as her passport and driver's license, and slipped them into her back pocket. Then she began the challenge of picking berries ripe enough to eat, but not too soft to get mashed in her pack.

Job finished, she turned, but then paused. Rhythmic pounding grew louder the longer she listened. On the road, not twenty yards from where she stood, several horses galloped by, tearing up dirt into flying clods. Horses? Strange, though not any more weird than the rest of her day had been.

But the pounding hooves did not fade away and disappear. The big horses returned, pawing the earth at the bit of clearing where she'd entered.

She froze, hoping she'd blend into the greenery around her, all the while eyeing the horse-beasts with men atop. Though not clad in armor, the four of them weren't any less frightening than the knight of earlier in the day.

No words passed between them, but with a nod from the apparent leader, one of the men dismounted, walking her way.

What to do? She was no match for four hearty men. She wasn't a match for even one. Perhaps if she made a break for the forest, she could lose them in the thick growth. Flight won out over fight.

"She's taken to the trees. After her!"

The threat didn't slow her, but the bushy branches did. Her short-lived escape ended with a tug from behind, forcing her back to stand before the men still mounted.

"Bind her. Bring her to the bailiff."

"Come on, you can't do this. I'm a U.S. citizen. Aren't you people afraid of lawsuits? Ever hear of litigation?" Her words held no effect as one of them threw a length of rope to the man still holding her. Did he actually think she'd let him tie her up? Unbelievable. A quick stamp to his instep might change his mind.

In an instant, she found herself on the flat of her back, gasping for breath. Her hands bound in front of her, a pull on the rope set her back on her feet, tethered to the rear of a horse.

"Charges?" asked her captor, heaving himself up into the saddle.

"Thievery."

"I've not stolen anything!"

Ignoring her outburst, three of the men wheeled their horses and thundered off into the woods.

A click of the tongue sent the remaining horse into motion with her on a leash. The resulting jerk almost sent her face-first into the dirt. There was nothing to do but match pace or be dragged. She threatened for a while, accomplishing nothing but a coughing spell from the kicked-up dust.

By the time they reached a village square, flickering lights shone from thatched roof hovels. Not much of a village though, judging from its size. The one at the base of the castle had been much larger.

The horse finally halted, and she took the opportunity to sit on the ground, wrists raw and head throbbing.

"Bailiff," the man astride the horse hollered toward one of the huts.

"Aye, aye. Of what cause such a muckling ruckus?" A fat man emerged from a doorway. His pug-nosed face looked like a bulldog that'd scrapped in one too many fights. The closer he came, the stronger the stink of sauerkraut and sweat.

"This wench 'ere is charged with thievery. See to her justice."

"Thievery, eh? Put her in the stocks then, and we'll have a right fine time of it come the morn."

"That's your concern."

A quick slash of a sharp blade freed her from the horse, and she was left alone with the bailiff. Without a word, he picked up the rope lying in the dirt. Choosing not to wait for the inevitable tug, she scrambled to her feet and followed.

Buildings surrounded a kind of large chopping block, a well, and what she recognized to be stocks.

"Look, Sir, I—"

"Oh, 'tis Sir now, eh? Mighty noble of you to address the likes o' me."

"Okay, well, I didn't actually catch your name, but I'm an American. You can't ... What are you doing?"

He slit the rope dangerously close to her skin and grabbed her with firm hands from behind.

"In the stocks I'll settle ye. Then, on the morrow, 'tis your right hand I'll be taking for thievery." He nodded toward the stump she'd already identified as a chopping block. "You ought not to take things that don't belong to ye."

A grunt and a heave later, a wooden beam thudded shut over her neck and wrists, securing her between stout posts. Was she part of a show, or was this for real? The pain in her bent lower back screamed reality as did the crunch of the bailiff's retreating footsteps. She strained, tugged, pulled, twisted—nothing would wriggle her free from the grasp of the weathered wood. The insanity of the day sucked any remaining life from her.

Dropping her head, she closed her eyes. The longing to wake up and find herself safe in her own bed grew unbearable. This all had to be a dream, or rather, a nightmare. But how could everything look and feel so real? Even her eyes watered from the stench of fresh horse dung. Would a mere dream cause such a physical reaction? She'd heard that if you dreamt of falling off a cliff, and actually hit bottom, you'd die. What if she didn't wake up before the knife brandishing bailiff returned?

Maybe by some miracle she might open her eyes and this crazy, medieval ordeal would be gone. That would imply, however, that she'd have to ask for such a miracle. She'd tried asking for a miracle once.

She'd never ask again.

Utter exhaustion finally won out, shutting down her wearied mind. She gave into a fitful sleep, keeping at bay the speculation of what the morning might bring.

·

In the blackness of night, Colwyn needed all his senses to distinguish the woods from open road. A sky obscured by thick blankets of cloud hid any hint of starlight, and he knew rain was near. The smell of it certain. The taste of its approach brought apprehension. Last time he'd been caught in a storm, it almost killed him.

Old Black, the mighty warhorse he straddled, snorted a cloud of mist into the cool air. Nothing good had come of this day, except for that he still possessed his prized destrier. He could be thankful now that he'd opted to mount a younger horse that day he'd set off to do the king's bidding. Aye, it'd been a fine horse he'd lost in that storm, but the thought of losing Black brought a scowl to his face.

Against the ebony horizon, thatched roofs designating a small hamlet blended into near obscurity, but Colwyn knew they were there. Without urging, Black carried him to the center of the square. The night didn't seem nearly as dark having left the confines of the forest's ceiling.

The occupied stocks caught his attention. Bare arms and a cropped head hung limp through the holes. There she was. The cause of his midnight ride and apparently the cause of some other mischief. Amazing she hadn't talked her way out of her present predicament with her clever tongue.

"Bailiff!" His command aroused a snort from Old Black and jolted the girl awake. Her head bobbed up, though he doubted she could see him from her vantage point.

"Bailiff!"

"Hither I be. What cause have ye for a-callin' me from me own bed?" The fat man tottered through his door, rubbing at his eyes for want of sleep, but once focused on Colwyn, he dropped to one knee. "Oh, Sir Colwyn! I beg pardon. Pardon and mercy, Sir. I knew not 'twas you."

"Release her."

"But, Sir, she's to be tried for—"

"I said release her!"

The thick-headed man considered a moment before rising and producing a ring with a key. "Very well, Sir."

Once set free, Colwyn watched the girl straighten as an old woman might rise from a chair.

"Mount." His voice come out harsh, letting her know he'd not be trifled with.

Her large brown eyes blinked up into his with a look bordering on bafflement.

"Mount," he repeated, extending his hand for assistance.

She looked from him to the horse, then from side to side, and finally returned back to him as if she couldn't quite comprehend his meaning.

"Mount? You're not expecting me to—"

Before she could finish, he reached down to grab hold of her, and strained to pull her up in front of him. He didn't have the time or patience for her dawdling. Old Black bolted as his heels dug into the horseflesh. The girl clutched his tunic, almost as if she were terrified. Her? Terrified? An amusing idea. He hadn't thought her capable of that emotion.

"One would think you'd never sat a horse before."

"Horse? This isn't a horse. This is a monster." Her grip tightened and her fingers dug into his skin. "If I fall off here, I'll break my neck."

"And well met for all the trouble you've caused me. I'd like nothing better than to be rid of a scourge like you. Loose your hold of me, woman, or you'll have my tunic ripped from my back." He slowed the horse to a stop. "Put your leg over and straddle him. Hold to the saddle here, and my arms will keep you from tumbling aside. How come you to know so little of horses?"

She frowned up into his face but took his suggestion to change her position. Once set, he gave Old Black full rein to ride off into the night.

"Why did you come after me? Where are we going?"

He grunted. Nay, she'd receive no more opportunity from him to weave another spell of words that would let her go free.

"Why won't you answer me?"

He brought his head down so close to hers, his lips brushed against her ear. She smelled like a sleepy summer day, warm and inviting, her short curls soft against his cheek. The night air suddenly seemed stifling with her so near. "Cease your chatter, wench, or I'll stop it for you."

She jerked forward, smacking against the warhorse's neck, and issued the growl of a feral cat. So, he held a wildcat, did he? He laughed loud and long at that thought, pleased at how he'd brought the conversation to an abrupt end.

Prompting Black to a full gallop, he guided the horse into the dark cavern of woods. As night wore on, fatigue lessened his animosity. It must've had the same effect on the girl because the tenseness in her body slackened, though she never fully relaxed against him. This small wench held a lot of pride.

By the time Gallimore came into sight, pale pre-dawn light announced a new day. The horse went directly through the courtyard to the stables without lead. Colwyn dismounted and was about to assist the girl when she crashed down on top of him, knocking him from his feet. With a snarl, he shoved her off to stand and glare down at her. "What are you doing?"

"You were going to leave me by myself on that thing. I could've been killed!"

"And so ye might if you ever try to topple me again. Come along. I've not time to give you the sound thrashing you deserve."

An angry set of her jaw gave her single response.

"Can you not simply do as thou art told? A more disagreeable wench I've yet to meet."

"And a more demanding man has yet to walk the face of this Earth. You're a bully, that's what you are. An overgrown, overbearing bully." She brushed herself off while getting to her feet, then competed against him in a deadlock of fierce stares.

"Sir Colwyn?" A boy's voice sliced through the tension, releasing the stranglehold of stubborn silence.

Tired of exchanging barbs with this woman, Colwyn looked away to his page. "See that Black is cared for."

"Aye, Sir."

"And let Lord Tarne know the girl has been found."

"Aye, Sir."

Turning back to the girl, he continued, "Do you see the obedience of which I speak? That runt of a boy has more respect for position than you."

"Respect? For you? Hah! Right. Now let me go home."

"Home? What home? Where is this home of which you speak?"

"I keep telling you, I'm an American and if—"

"What foreign tongue is this? I know naught of what you say. Your bearing begs nobility, yet your dress and language are such that I have never known. Who has sent you thus and why?"

She sighed, whether from exasperation or resignation, he couldn't tell. He did know that he was somehow a source of frustration to her, and the notion pleased him.

"Come." He strode from the stable, easily outdistancing her. Had the long ride truly proved too much for her, or did she find purpose in lagging to further incite him? Not wishing to enter into another contest of wordplay, he doubled back and swept her up with little effort.

"Quit carrying me around!"

"Nay. Quit your obstinance."

"No."

"Then, my lady, we are at a stalemate, are we not?"

Further words did not pass between them, though he couldn't help but wonder at her thoughts as he delivered her to an unused chamber. He shut the door against her questioning gaze, letting the key in the grate lock soundly any chance of escape. He'd done his part. He'd brought her back. He wanted nothing more to do with her.

Let Tarne deal with this aggravating shrew.

Chapter 5

Jess sat up with a yawn and a stretch. A glance around the room sent any shred of hope into a death spiral. Fabulous. This was one persistent nightmare.

Edging off the crude skeleton of a bed, she explored what little the room had to offer—a cold hearth, a trestle table, and two narrow windows carved high into the stone walls. From the looks of the weak light filtering in, she'd slept most of the day. One large wooden door stood shut, but another gaped open, revealing a small, shadowy room the size of a walk-in closet. It held a large earthenware container, a few wooden pegs on the wall, and a scent reminiscent of a tuna can that'd sat too long on a counter. She'd find better accommodations camping at a state park. Didn't these people at least have outhouses?

A jangle of keys in the lock pulled her attention back to the closed door, and her heart rate increased. Maybe now they'd let her go.

She couldn't see the face against the glow from the corridor, but the strapping figure stooping to enter left her no cause to wonder. Didn't this man have anything better to do than badger her? Weren't knights supposed to be out fighting dragons and jousting at tournaments? A frown tugged down her lips. "You again."

He cocked his head and smirked. "Come. Lord Tarne summons you to table."

"Lord Tarne? You call your own brother Lord?"

Expression unchanged, he swept his arm in a grand gesture toward the door.

"And what if I refuse, Lord Colwyn?" Her jibe induced no response. This was one cool man. Too cool. "Colwyn is your name, isn't it? I've guessed that much, but not where I am. From the looks of things, maybe the question should be when I am."

He stood, blinking at her, not saying a word. His arm held steady toward the door.

She tilted her chin, hoping to appear as intimidating as him. "You don't talk much, do you?"

His smirk spread into a half grin. "There is no need. Your words are enough for us both. Follow me, or I'll make it known to the earl that you'd rather receive him in your chamber."

Not the response she was looking for, but at least a response. "Fine. Lead the way."

Accustomed now to the long-legged pace of the man she trailed, she paid keen notice to the twistings and stairwells of the route they took. As they descended yet another spiral staircase, baritone curses curled up to meet her ear. Two steps from the bottom, she froze, wide-eyed.

In front of her, a huge guard towered over a cowering boy. The big man raised an anvil-sized fist ready to strike.

Jess recognized the boy who'd served Colwyn in the stables, but her jaw dropped when Colwyn did nothing. In fact, he walked right on by, never slowing a beat.

"No!" She flew down the last stairs. With a wild snatch, she clutched the boy to her before fist met flesh.

Both men stared at her, mouths agape.

Raging injustice screamed inside her. "Are you people crazy? What kind of a place is this where children are beaten as casually as stray dogs?"

The boy did not return her embrace, but neither did he squirm away. His somewhat reluctant acceptance of her protection reminded her of her own son. When would she see her boy again? The freight-train of a question slammed into her heart, inflaming her all the more.

A scowl etched deep into the guard's pockmarked face. He lowered his fist, but he didn't unclench it. "Woman, stand you back. You've no right to—"

"Don't speak to me of rights. I haven't had any since I set foot in this Dark Ages sideshow, but this I won't let happen. No child deserves a beating. Now leave him be!"

The big man advanced, glowering as if he'd clout them both. Jess shrank back, tugging the boy with her.

"You heard the Lady. Leave off." Colwyn's words stopped the guard mid-stride.

A sneer distorted the man's mouth until Colwyn covered the hilt of his blade. His face paled, and he dipped his head before wheeling away.

The boy wriggled like a puppy in her arms. She loosed him to scamper in the opposite direction of his adversary. Tension from the face-off shook through her, and her shoulders sagged, but she set her jaw, defying Colwyn to say anything further on the matter. His mouth opened, about to meet the challenge, though no words came out. Instead, he shook his head. Rendering him speechless was a small victory to be sure, but a victory nonetheless. She'd take it.

"Shall we?" He arched a brow, and she followed him once more.

Down a broad stairway and across a foyer of immense proportions, a wide portal led into a huge room. Smoke from several hearths lent a spectral quality to the dismal glow of torches and candles, stinging her eyes into tearing. The affront to her ears was no less. Men bantering, dogs begging scraps, serving women bustling about with platters of food. Somehow, this didn't quite match the picture in her mind of a formal dinner in a nobleman's castle.

Colwyn led her over the rush-covered floor, past tables dotted with soldiers who could use a good scrubbing, all of whom took time away from their food to look her over. She did her best to pretend the stench of unwashed bodies didn't bother her and walked on.

Tarne sat centered at a table on a raised platform. Ignoring her arrival, he stabbed at an unidentifiable piece of meat, blood oozing out into a puddle on his plate. With repulsed fascination, she watched him bite into the raw chunk of muscle and chew, and chew, until a movement at the side of his plate caught her eye.

Perched on the table next to him, a bird with inky-black feathers bobbed to peck its stiletto beak into the same cut of meat. The creature ripped away a chunk of the flesh as if it were a fresh kill at the side of a road, a splatter of blood leaving a skull-shaped red mark on its beak.

Jess blinked, speechless. The raven from the dark woods? She'd bet any amount on it. Her hands turned clammy, and her mouth went dry. Perspiration tickled a dewy layer at the nape of her neck.

"Here is the girl." Colwyn's announcement was as nonchalant as if he delivered nothing more than a load of yesterday's stale bread. Without further comment, he sauntered to the far end of the table and seated himself, leaving her to face his brother alone.

Tarne set down his knife, then wiped the back of his hand across his mouth and scrutinized her from head to toe. "You are not dressed."

She gave herself a quick once-over. A little wrinkled and dirty maybe, but jeans and a tee-shirt were still in place. "What?"

"Henceforth you will present yourself before me in more suitable garments. Colwyn!"

"Aye."

She turned her head at the sound of his voice, hoping he could read the resentment she flashed at him. He ignored her.

"See to it." Tarne commanded with a flick of a limp wrist.

Colwyn nodded in-between bites. His dark, unbound hair fell forward, hiding his face from her view.

Tarne stood, planting his palms on the table, and leaned close to her. Even with his advantage of being up on a platform, he met her eye-to-eye.

"Do be seated my—hmm. Lady, shall I call you? For I have yet to satisfy my doubts on that account." With mock formality, he pulled out the high-backed chair next to him in invitation.

She glanced over her shoulder at the oversized doorway on the opposite end of the room, debating the prospect of making a run for it. She'd have a better chance if she bided her time and slipped away without an entire Great Hall of witnesses watching her. Besides which, the aroma of food caused saliva to pool at the back of her mouth. The primal need of hunger outweighed freedom for the moment. She'd stay and play along, for now anyway.

Without a word, she walked the length of the table to get around to the back side. Every so often her feet came in contact with something that crunched and crackled like a nest of June bugs squished beneath her heel. *It's just the rushes, girl, only rushes.* But what did they cover up?

She went past Colwyn, who fixed his gaze on a trencher of food.

Next to him, with chin to chest and a slight snore escaping on the inhale, sat the woman she'd seen the day before. The mother of these two men obviously had a drinking problem.

When at last she made it to Tarne's side, she wished she'd chosen to run away. He licked his thin lips while assessing her, as if she were a side of beef about to be butchered into bite-size pieces. "There are many things I would know, but let it not be said that the Earl of Gallimore does not offer impeccable hospitality. Sit. Eat."

She let him play the gentleman and push in her chair but did not allow herself to relax even one tensed muscle. Impossible anyway, especially sitting next to the fat, black bird who eyed her like a carcass to be picked clean.

None of the food looked familiar, except for loaves of bread so dark they might be burnt. Grainy sauces the color of mustard swam in pewter bowls. Thick slices of marbled gelatin jiggled on silver platters. Plump raisins and ground nuts adorned swirls of custardy mounds.

With deliberate selection, she tasted an amazing variety of flavors ranging from sage and cinnamon, to what she could've sworn tasted like the fragrance of roses. She raised a golden goblet to her lips and washed it all down with a strong brew leaving a bitter aftertaste.

"Now, M'lady, I'll be put off no further." Tarne leaned toward her, his face inches from her own. A fine spray of spittle landed on her cheek with his next words. "I would know how and why you spoke of the routing of King Edward."

Disgust tightened her throat, and she tried not to gag. "Well, actually, I'd rather know how and why I'm here."

He didn't answer, nor did he pull back. Wispy hairs dotted his chin, a failed attempt at a show of manhood. She'd do anything, say anything, to increase the space between his body and hers. "Look, I don't know that much about King Edward. I know his side loses, at least this time, if I remember right. That's all I know. Now, can I go?"

"How can you remember that which has not yet happened? You appear out of nowhere, proclaiming doom on the mightiest of men, yet presume to know nothing. A curse from a nymph of the forest? A curse of your own calling perhaps? Who are you?"

His eyes bored into hers, searching, delving for only God knew what. The urge to run filled her, and she scooted her chair back a few inches.

"No, a curse not laid by you," he answered at last.

Well, at least she wouldn't be burned at the stake, then. Whoa, what was she thinking? This place was starting to get to her. Hoping to clear the crazy thoughts, she reached for the goblet to down the rest of her drink. The bird's spiked beak darted out, puncturing into the soft, fleshy meat of her hand. Stabbing pain radiated up her arm as she jerked away.

With his own raven-like movement, Tarne snatched her wrist, pulling it close. He eyed the wound with avid curiosity. A deep-red droplet of blood welled up, and she watched in horror as he raised her hand to his mouth.

"No!" She wrenched from his grasp and rocketed to her feet, knocking her chair over in the process.

Laughter erupted from Tarne as if he'd been told a grand joke, so much that he pulled a frill of lace tucked in his sleeve and dabbed the corners of his eyes.

"You're sick! That's what you are." Her charge sobered his mirth and stilled Great Hall. No one spoke. No one moved.

Tarne rose, unfolding himself as a bat would its wings. "You will mind your tongue in my house, or find that you've no tongue to mind at all. Time will reveal King Edward's fate, and your own as well. You are restricted to grounds until further notice. Colwyn, she is your charge. Dismissed."

She didn't wait for a response from the knight. Not caring that every eye in Great Hall watched, she stormed away. Let them look. Let them all see her walk right out the door, for she'd not be stopped. Not by Tarne. Not by Colwyn.

Not by anyone.

•

Colwyn chased after the fiery wench, boots pounding to catch up with her. 'Twas a wonder indeed that Tarne had not struck her down for her show of disrespect. Obviously, his brother wanted to keep her alive and within his reach, but Colwyn did not relish the task of being the appointed guardian to accomplish such a feat.

She walked with purpose and speed, and didn't lose cadence even when stepping out into the chill of the night. He didn't reach her side until the gatehouse, where she threw her strength into trying to force open the mighty doors of Gallimore. Amusement lightened his dark mood as she battered her fists against the solid oak and screamed into the dark.

He leaned back, arms folded across his chest, and relaxed against the stone wall. Let the little pixie use up all her energy on such a fruitless pursuit. Mayhap she'd tire herself out, making his job all the easier.

Breathing hard and red in the face, she turned to him. Unwieldy springs of curly hair added to her frantic appearance.

"Open this door. Let me out!"

Amazing how appealing she looked in the glow of torchlight. Frenzy lent a deep flush to her cheeks and lit her eyes with an untamed brilliance. Her chest heaved, and even in her odd garments, rounded curves piqued his interest, making it hard to avert his gaze. It had been a long time since he'd given a woman a second glance. Why this one?

"The gates are shut for the night. They'll not be opened 'til cockcrow."

"I'm not staying here that long." She turned on her heel in a perfect military pivot and marched off.

He sighed, tiring of the game. Where could she possibly go? He trudged after her as she entered a stairway leading to the top of the walls.

An unseasonably cool breeze met them on the narrow walkway. He let her stop and peer over the edge at what appeared to be random intervals. "What are you doing?"

She glared at him but kept up her silly probing along the length of the entire battlement. As they came to the end at a tower door, he decided to save them both from having to walk the whole periphery of Gallimore. "The western wall bears a more treacherous drop than what you've already seen. There's no point in continuing."

The look in her eye made him glad she was but a woman. He'd not want to face that kind of hostility from a man.

"You enjoy seeing me squirm, don't you?"

The acidity of her voice and the desperation it conveyed gave him an unexpected twinge in his gut. "Nay. Not so. As much as you've been an irritant to me, I bear you no ill-will. I do not possess my brother's penchant for evil-doing. Truth be told, when his focus is on you, it is off of me."

"I see. All you care about is yourself."

"Is there anything else to care about?"

"Yes." Her tone carried conviction.

"What then?"

His question must've struck some chord in her, for she gave up her searching along the parapet wall and instead leaned against it. She stood silent, eyes vacant as if her mind roamed far away. She slid to a sitting position and covered her face with her hands.

Who could understand this woman? Fire and brimstone one minute, the next soft and almost vulnerable. She mystified him as none other.

"Come, M'lady. 'Twill be no benefit to pass the whole of the eve in the damp and dark. At least seek what rest you may in the comfort of your chamber, for come the morn, you'll no doubt want to renew your escape attempts with fresh vigor."

She let her hands drop to her lap and raised her face to him. Her cheeks lacked the tear stains he expected. How uncommon. He'd give much to know what raged through her mind to bring about such a change.

"I suppose you're right." She rose to her feet. "And I don't often like to agree with my enemy."

Suddenly tired, he sighed. Naturally she counted him her nemesis, but what might it be like to be this strange woman's friend instead of foe? He couldn't shake the renegade thought even as he stomped down the steps behind her to solid ground.

Racing footsteps and puffing breaths ended further speculation. "Sir Colwyn! 'Tis Old Black. I fear he'll go down!"

He turned, and the page plowed into him. "Calm yourself, boy. What happened?"

"You must come, Sir. There is no time." The lad tugged at his tunic.

"Nay. I must see to M'lady first, and—"

"Oh, go on." The woman pulled her gaze from the boy to meet his, the soft lines around her mouth hardening. "I paid plenty of attention when we came from my room. I can get back there. Tend to your horse. Maybe it'll keep you up late, and then you'll be the fuzzy-headed one in the morning when I make my getaway."

He hesitated, weighing her words. "Since when are you so accommodating?"

"I have my moments. Besides, it's not like I'm going to run out the gate or dive off the walls now, am I?"

True. She'd get nowhere tonight. "Very well. In the main foyer, get you a vigil light from off a hook. Use it to light your way, and mind you, make haste to your quarters. I will account for you before I retire this night, so do not think to scurry elsewhere. You cannot know all that skulks in the dark, nor should you seek to find out. Understood?"

She merely stared with her luminous brown eyes and remained silent.

"Hurry!" The boy pulled on his sleeve.

Colwyn scrubbed his jaw with one hand. Could he trust this girl to go to her chamber? Should he?

"I fear for Old Black, Sir." The lad's voice rose.

He narrowed his eyes at the woman. She didn't flinch. If Black weren't his prized destrier …

Exhaling long and slow, he stalked toward the stables, glancing over his shoulder now and again to see the woman pick her way toward Gallimore. For once she seemed to carry out his bidding, unless she toyed with some other unknown ruse.

He could only hope he hadn't made another serious mistake.

Chapter 6

Jess gave every appearance of heading toward the castle, but as soon as that infuriating man disappeared, she backtracked to the closed gatehouse doors. With one more good try, she might find a lever or a knob. Maybe the door's release had been right in front of her, but she'd missed it with that watchdog of a knight breathing down her neck—that same watchdog who expected her to be safely inside her room by now.

Well, it wasn't like she'd promised him or anything. She owed him nothing after the way he'd treated her. With new resolve, she explored every bit of the big, weathered doors—even the stone pillars on each side. Her fingertips rubbed raw in the process, especially when frustration sent her over and over the same areas. Defeated, she turned back to the castle. A little sleep might give her fresh insight, or at the least, leave her well-rested for an early morning getaway just as she'd told Colwyn.

Other words she'd said to the man mocked her as much as the stone fortress looming in front of her. Why had she answered yes so forcefully when he'd asked if there were anything else to care about in life other than himself? That was the very question she subconsciously wrestled with since Dan's death. This heathen knight went and voiced it out loud, shaking a response from her that she didn't know if she believed.

Was there anything else to care about? Deep within, buried under a mountain of grief, she knew the answer. An answer she wouldn't embrace, for if she did, it would change her life.

This would require more time to sort through. Time she didn't have right now.

Entering the echoing foyer, she couldn't imagine any place more foreign. Snatches of a bawdy drinking song carried out from the Great Hall, quickening her search for the lantern Colwyn had mentioned. She didn't want to run the risk of facing Tarne again tonight—or ever.

A carved table held a small lantern that would work as well as any vigil light—whatever that was. Retrieving it, she headed for the grand stairway. The glow of the candle she carried radiated out, highlighting fireworks of colors on a prominent tapestry. The sparkle of it drew her to a momentary standstill.

The craftsmanship of needlework on the piece cried out with magnificence. Golden letters burned like laser light against a purple velvet background. Easy to read, but hard to decipher. It looked like a sample of old English she'd seen before at the library. Knights. Castles. Old English tapestries. Of course. Why not? It fit right in with the décor of this bad dream.

Phonetically it read:

> *When night bends to kneel*
> *at the throne of the sun*
> *A new realm dawns westward*
> *bringing all wanderers home.*

A poor rhyme for someone to have put that much painstaking effort into preserving it with such beauty. What in the world did it mean?

Slurred voices grew louder from the Great Hall, rousing a sense of urgency and increasing her pulse. Time to move, but which way? It should be left, down the wide hallway, and turn left again into a narrower one. Up a stone staircase, spiraling past door one, door two, next door and down one more hallway.

But the door didn't open into a hallway. She stepped into a room she'd never seen before. A peculiar, acrid smell burned her nostrils, yet there was no hearth. There were no windows and no furniture, only stone walls and a stone floor. At her feet, a geometric pattern had been etched into the rock flooring—a Star of David inside a circle, each point touching the edge. That was all. Nothing else on the floor or the walls, yet something more lurked in this room, beyond the ring of light cast by her candle. Something she would not like to discover.

She whirled and smacked into Tarne.

"I see you've found my little sanctuary. What brings you here, and where is my lout of a brother?"

"I, uh—" She inched away. Being alone with Tarne was entirely different from being alone with Colwyn. Both were dangerous. One was evil. "I'm going to my room."

He pulled her to him, corralling her within his bony arms. Though frail-looking and petite, the strength of his grasp pressed her body to his, nose to nose. Her candle crashed to the stone floor, and the light spluttered out. A sickening cramp in her gut signaled she might lose her dinner, especially as his breath mingled with hers.

"I'll have you stay here, in my room, if you don't mind." He drew her farther into the center, away from the door.

"I do mind!" No one else had entered the room, but they were not alone. A chorus of rushing whispers swirled about them, and a frigid breeze blew like that of an October wind.

"She is the one. She is the one. She is the one."

Jess swallowed hard, trying to keep from trembling. The unworldly chanting and Tarne's suffocating embrace ratcheted her heart rate. Desperation coiled around her, squeezing the breath from her lungs. There'd be no talking her way out of this.

God, no. Please. Help me.

All sound stopped. The wind stilled. And Tarne released his grip.

Not waiting to find out how or why, she ran to the door and flew down the stairs. Though not certain which way to go and near impossible to see in the dark, one thing she knew for sure—locked gates or high walls would not contain her.

•

Tarne narrowed his eyes to slits, watching through the darkness after the disappearing form of Jessica Neale. With nothing more than a focus of his will, the door closed. He stood motionless, embracing silence and complete blackness as his companions.

His voice, like a taut wire about to snap, rose to a shrill whine. "She is the one? She is—"

A gust of air blew his hair back and took his breath as well. Only after it passed could he speak. "Then the time is nigh at hand. Cursed are those who stand in my way."

He walked the room several times, each revolution increasing in speed. After the seventh pass, he stopped circling and went to the center of the room. Stretching out his arms to a human cross, he lifted his head to the ceiling. "Reveal to me my enemies. Reveal to me my victory. Reveal to me the kingdom of my realm."

A convulsion threw him to the floor, writhing and rolling about on the cold stone blocks, foamy spittle running past his lips. Not until later did he lay still, curled into a fetal position, baring his teeth in a feral smile.

Power would be his. He would be master of much. And somehow the girl would help him accomplish this—willing or unwilling.

•

"Cease your fretting, boy." Colwyn paused long enough to ease the page's mind before leaving the stable. The lad's fussing, though warranted, still irritated him. He kneaded the muscles at the base of his neck in vain attempt to ease the tension. "I'll not be long. I'll see M'lady has safely gained her chamber, then I'll return."

The boy's frantic look eased. Why couldn't Jessica of Neale be as predictable? Would she be in her quarters, or wouldn't she? As he headed across the courtyard, he couldn't help but wonder. He'd not wager a heavy bet either way.

When he entered the keep and passed Great Hall, no sound met his ears. The night hours must be well advanced indeed, farther than he imagined. He must've spent more time with the downed horse than he'd realized.

The first sign of trouble presented itself as he neared the open door of the girl's dark chamber. Though her behavior was most often perplexing, would she not have closed the door if she slept inside? The thin light his candle offered confirmed his worst suspicions.

The little sprite. And after he'd warned her to go straight to her quarters. A more disagreeable wench he'd yet to meet. Where would she have gone? Though he couldn't pretend to understand the workings behind that pretty face, an inkling of her whereabouts rose to the top of his mind.

He shut the door behind him, then stopped cold. Creeping toward him from the opposite end of the corridor, his brother advanced like a cockroach from a crevice.

"I told you to guard the girl, not bed her."

Colwyn let the accusation go unchallenged. Let Tarne think what he would, better than knowing the truth of her absence.

"You're up late, brother."

"If I trusted in your competence, I'd be asleep as a babe even now. I came to assure that this time you did not let the wench slip through your fingers. Obviously your firm grasp entertained firm flesh as well."

Tarne's assumption rankled, and the sudden rush of fury surprised him. Why should he care if Tarne presumed he'd lain with the girl? Yet the thought of her slandered virtue involuntarily curled his hands into fists at his side.

"Every now and then, Colwyn, you surprise me. 'Tis no better way to subdue a wench. I should have thought to suggest it."

Teeth on edge from the comment, Colwyn managed to smirk as if in affirmation.

"Perhaps I should share the same pleasure. Step aside."

Colwyn's heartbeat increased ten-fold as he took a reluctant step away from the door. Tarne's skeletal fingers reached out. His heart would surely stop once his brother discovered the truth.

The door gave way against the pressure of Tarne's hand, but he never fully opened it. He paused, then retreated to the center of the corridor. Colwyn wondered if his erratic pulse would ever return to normal at the fright he'd received.

"Nay. Not yet. She'll have less spirit after her tussle with you. I would have her fresh and fighting. Perchance later, or on the morrow, I will seek her out. See that she's available at my summons."

"Aye." With a controlled exhale, Colwyn watched his brother slink down the hall. He waited, assuring himself Tarne wouldn't change his mind. When a sufficient amount of time passed, he snapped into action. He had to find that girl and with haste.

By now the occupants of Gallimore had long been abed, allowing him to set an unhampered course toward the front gates. Not wanting to attract the guard's attention, he extinguished his light and let his eyes adjust to the dark as he traversed the courtyard.

Sure enough, at the base of the massive doors, torchlight from the pillars flickered onto a slight figure lying curled into a tight ball. Would he forever be pursuing this girl in the dark of night?

He crouched and studied her as she slept. Tousled brown curls blended with the dirt where her head rested. Without a frown of anger lining her face, her full lips looked soft and inviting. Desire to reach out and touch the smoothness of her pink cheek pulled his hand closer until her warm breath caressed against his skin. He closed his eyes to ward off the unexpected hunger she aroused from deep within. Nay, he would not own that feeling—never again.

He stood and nudged her with the toe of his boot. "Awake, woman."

She rubbed her sleepy eyes like a child who'd been called from a nap. The unguarded moment didn't last long before she shot to her feet with a scowl. "Go away. Leave me alone."

"I told you to go directly to your chamber. Why do you sleep here?"

"I am not sleeping under the same roof as that brother of yours. I don't trust him. I don't even trust you."

What could've possibly happened to her during the time he'd spent in the stables? "Has the earl harmed you?"

"Not yet, and I'm not giving him, or you, the chance. Keeping me here against my will is a crime, and you know it. I told you I'd be leaving as soon as the gates open, and I mean it. I'm staying right here."

Her obstinacy cooled any heat of desire that remained. "Your resistance is most tiresome. Have you not come to realize you have no choice? You have no say whatsoever in what is required of you. You've tried the gates, you've tried the walls, and you've tried my patience to the end. It is late, and I am in no mood to argue. You will do as I say or—"

Her grumble interrupted him. "I know, I know, or you'll carry me off, or pull a knife, or whatever. Fine. I won't give you the pleasure this time. Let's go."

She stomped off of her own accord toward the castle and didn't slow a step, nor look at him, as he caught up with her. She did not say one more word all the way to her chamber, and likely wouldn't have if he hadn't stopped the door from slamming in his face. He planted his foot in the opening, and she whirled, bristling to confront him.

He cast a precautionary glance down the hall, then lowered his voice. "Take that trestle and brace it against the door for the night. Do not remove it until I come for you in the morn." His words visibly drained the fight from her.

Confusion edged with fear wrinkled her brow. "Why? Why tell me to do this?"

Not wanting to relate Tarne's intentions, he simply said, "Do it."

With a step back, he waited for the door to shut and listened to the scrape of wood on stone. When the bump of table met the oak of door, he turned to leave.

He wanted to feel relief that for once she'd obeyed him. He wanted to be convinced she'd be safe for the night. The only thing he knew for sure was that if he did not keep a good watch over her on the morrow, Tarne would have his way.

And even if his guardianship proved faultless, there was no guarantee her virtue would remain intact.

Chapter 7

"That is way too tight. I can hardly breathe." Jess's ribs squeezed together until she feared her lungs would implode. The pain made her regret anew that her planned flight from Castle Gallimore had failed before it even began.

Colwyn had wakened her from a sleep wrought with frightening images of Tarne and the windowless room. She'd been spooked by the events of the previous evening, but most of all by Colwyn's insistence to barricade her door. Only at his voice had she dared to drag away the table cocked against whatever unknown had threatened her in the night.

If the knight had given a moment's thought to her comfort, he would've brought a plate of food with him. Inconsiderate man. Instead he'd hurried her off to meet Traline, a servant who didn't seem to mind his barking orders, and demanded Jess stay with her until he came back. Traline's deft hands had cinched and pinched her into a common medieval torture known only to womankind— A dress.

"Hold still, M'lady, I'm nearly finished." The woman tugged the laces at her back. "There. Now hold your arms up and we'll slip this on over your head."

Miles of scarlet damask descended over the snowy white kirtle she'd been forced into. "I can't believe I'm putting this on. Why would anyone wear this?"

"You want to look pleasing now, don't you M'lady?"

"Just call me Jess, and no, I don't care if I look pleasing."

Traline's brow furrowed. "Care not?"

"Oh, never mind." The effort to try to explain probably wouldn't be worth it anyway. Her eyes burned from lack of sleep, her stomach growled for its emptiness, and her heart ached to hug her own little boy. The desire to go home wrapped around her like the fabric Traline fussed with. But where was home, and where was she? "Tell me about this place. Tell me about Gallimore and its people. Maybe you can help me sort out where I am and how I got here."

A puzzled look crossed Traline's face. "Why do ye ask me, M'lady?"

Jess let out a long, low breath. "I want to go home, that's all."

"All right, then," she said, apparently accepting Jess at her word. "I know what 'tis like to be far from your people."

"You're not from around here?"

"No, M'lady, but it's not me you were asking about. The people of Gallimore proper are a fine lot. A more hard-working people ye'll not find the likes of anywhere else."

"How about Colwyn? What do you know about him?"

Traline frowned. "You mean Sir Colwyn."

"Okay, Sir Colwyn." She fought the urge to roll her eyes.

"He's a fine man, that one. Never predictable, but always trustworthy."

"Fine? Trustworthy?" She held back a snort. Were they talking about the same person? "He's a big bully. Arrogant, annoying, unfeeling. I don't think I'd trust him with my cat."

"He's a troubled man, that's all. He's learned to hide his true self."

"Right."

"There's much more to Sir Colwyn than he allows to show."

"Whatever." She would've shrugged if the dress weren't so constricting. For all Traline's defense of Colwyn, maybe she had a thing for him. "So, what's the deal with Tarne? Is he always such a jerk?"

Traline cast her eyes to the floor. The frown she'd worn earlier returned ten-fold. "Keep your distance, M'lady. He's a man much feared and rightly so."

"Yeah, I think I've figured that out. If the people fear him, how did he get to be in charge in the first place?"

"When Lord Haukswyrth, second Earl of Gallimore, passed on, the title went to his first-born son, who was Lord Tarne's sire. After his demise, reign went to Lord Tarne himself. 'Twas a sorry curse Sir Colwyn could only claim that of second son. But, there is hope of a new realm some day." Traline stopped her explanation to guide Jess to a small, cushioned stool. With yards of fabric draped on her, sitting became a whole new experience. She doubted larvae in a cocoon could feel as trapped.

"What happened to your hair, M'lady?" Traline ran her fingers through the short brown locks.

Not to be sidetracked, Jess ignored the question. "What's the new realm all about?"

"'Tis not much more than a hope really. A hope sprung from a daft old woman. It's said the first Lord Haukswyrth took possession of his title and the Gallimore lands by deception and murder, though the truth of it went to the grave with him. After his death, Lady Haukswyrth took to roaming the castle halls by day, loony as a skittering titmouse. By night, it's told she shut herself up in a room with no windows to work on the finest tapestry ever to grace the wall of the castle."

"Yes, I've seen it," Jess interrupted.

"It is a beauty, is it not?"

"The tapestry, yes. The room, no."

Traline's hands stilled. "What say you, M'lady?"

"The tapestry is amazing. The room with no windows, well … that place is just plain scary. I'm never going back there again."

Traline set the brush down and backed away.

"What? What's the matter?"

"Nothing, M'lady. I'm finished now. If that's all ye'll be needin', I'll take my leave and good day to you m'um."

Traline flew to the door and it slammed shut before Jess could even answer. Stunned, she retrieved her bundle of clothes and waistpack heaped in a corner, all the while keeping her eye on the door, half expecting it to open again.

She paused in front of a full-length mirror of burnished metal. The image reflecting back startled her more than anything. She looked like something out of a fairy tale. Except for the short hair, she fit right in with the rest of the castle motif. For some reason, the thought brought the sting of tears to her eyes, but she would not cry. She didn't belong here. She didn't even want to belong here. Time for answers, and time to go home.

Instead of waiting for Colwyn to return, she set off in search of him, clutching her pack of clothing. He must've been the one she'd seen the night of the accident. He had to know something, some bit of information. She'd put his supposed trustworthiness Traline boasted of to the test.

A quick glance around the courtyard turned up nothing but a few lewd stares from some loitering guards. She couldn't stand the idea of looking through the castle corridors with the possibility of finding Tarne. If she could remember which building housed the stables, she might find Colwyn there. As a bonus, she might even discover an unguarded door or gate that could lead to her freedom.

Dusty, dirty, hot, the pounding sun beat on her layers of clothing. She considered turning back to change into her tee-shirt and jeans, but it'd taken an extra person to lock her into this fabric cage. She wouldn't get it off by herself.

In her search, a cool length of shadow from an overhung roof called to her. Walking in the shade next to the stone walls gave some measure of relief, until flapping black wings and a jagged 'caw' halted her. The possessed raven landed in a puff of dirt, twitching its head and leering at her. This time she wouldn't even dare to walk around it.

With a quick turn, she smacked against Tarne. This was turning into a nasty habit. She bolted sideways, but iron fingers clawed into her shoulder, forcing her to remain stuck between the creature and the man.

"I've been looking for you, M'lady." His foul breath bore testament to his character.

Determined not to lose her balance and fall into his arms, she fought back the material swishing against her legs and wrenched from his grasp. "What? What could you possibly want from me? Let me go. I'm of no use to you."

"Oh, but on that account you are mistaken. I am sure, M'lady, that I can use you in ways you cannot fathom." His eyes fondled her in places that hadn't been touched in years. She turned her head, quaking from the lust he emanated.

"Come now. Colwyn might satisfy in the basest sense, but what I offer will affect your very soul."

She turned cold even in the heat of the day. His suggestion carried more than sexual overtones. *Lord, please.* She swallowed, fear tasting like vomit.

"M'lord!"

She could've flung her arms around the servant who interrupted. Tarne looked as if he might slay him on the spot.

"M'lord, a scout's ridden in. The men return to Gallimore this day. He would report to you now."

Conflicting emotions rippled across Tarne's face, a spectrum ranging from rage to resignation.

"Very well. I'll finish with you later, M'lady."

Jess picked up her skirts to free her feet and broke out in a run. She would've liked to race full-speed through the gates of the outer bailey, but that was the direction Tarne went. Colwyn and the stables seemed the next best choice. He'd shown rare moments of softness, and she had talked him into letting her go once before.

A rich, musty odor of hay and shoveled manure met her nose inside the low-ceiled timber and earthen shelter. Many people relished the ancient smell, but to her it seemed sour and decaying. Close-quartered stalls lined one next to the other like a stack of horsey dominoes. Old Black had to be here somewhere, and hopefully with his master nearby.

"M'lady?"

She turned from the whinnies to the voice of a boy, Colwyn's page. Pangs of longing for her own son made her want to reach out and brush back the unkempt hair that rebelled over his forehead and shaded his eyes. "Hi, um, what is your name?"

The boy took a step closer and peered at her unafraid. "Me name's Tagg, M'lady. Or boy. I'll answer to either. What are ye doin' in the stables, m'um?"

"Actually, I'm looking for Colwyn. Do you know where he is?"

"Aye, m'um, that I do. My master is down fetchin' fresh creek-bed mud to mix a poultice for Old Black."

Jess batted at a bug that landed on her cheek and noticed Tagg took a step back from her. How many times had the poor boy been struck by such sudden movements? "He's going to put mud on a sick horse?"

"Aye, M'lady. 'Tis his favored horse, and Sir Colwyn's fairly worried. Old Black took to the colic last night. In all his thrashing about, his foreleg got cut wide open. Now a fever's set in, m'um. "

"Could I see?"

"Aye, M'lady."

He led her down several stalls. What was she doing playing vet? She couldn't tell a piebald from a palomino. Still, a peculiar urge nagged her to take a quick peek.

Tagg used a soothing voice to calm the big horse, then produced the foreleg in question. The gash itself didn't look deep, but the flesh puffed up around it. With that kind of infection, no wonder the horse had succumbed to fever. Colwyn intended to make it all better by slapping mud over it? No, she had a better idea. "Go get a pail of water and a clean cloth."

"But, M'lady, we should wait—"

"Look, I think I can help Old Black right now. Wouldn't that be a great surprise?"

He moved into action. Meanwhile, Jess rifled through her clothes bundle to reach her waistpack. She'd kept half a small tube of an antibacterial cream in the back zippered pocket, leftover from a scrape of her own.

When the boy returned, she had him wash the wound and pat it dry as best he could.

"Put a little of this on your finger and dab it all along that cut. Then we'll rip a strip of cloth to tie around it, and repeat this procedure every six hours or so. I think by tomorrow, Old Black will be much better."

"You really think so, M'lady?" His voice carried a hope she could only pray would be well-founded. She did not want to see him disappointed.

"I do." She smiled at him.

And he smiled back—a crooked-toothed grin that bore resemblance to her own chipped-tooth son. His greasy hair needed a good scrubbing and she reached out, brushing it back from his bright eyes. She longed to hold him as she might her own boy but he looked away. He'd reached his limit of motherly affection.

"Boy!"

They both flinched. The unmistakable bark outside the stables could only be Colwyn.

"Remember now, do as I've said." She winked at Tagg and set out to find the man she'd been looking for.

She saw him, but she didn't go to him. Not right away. Twenty paces from her, Colwyn bent over a huge bucket, straining to stir with an oaken paddle the size of a small oar. Stripped to the waist, he exerted all his strength into churning the concoction in the barrel. His hard-packed muscles flexed and bulged in as fine a specimen of manhood as she'd ever seen. Brawn and scars from past battles attested to the fact that he led a life of vigorous training. His broad chest glistened from the sun's glare, tanned, strong. Actually, kind of inviting. It might be comforting indeed to be protected in his embrace. What would it be like if he gave her a warm smile? A knowing smile?

Wait a minute. What was she thinking? If he caught her looking at him, what would she do?

She waited in the murky shadows of the stable's opening, glad he couldn't see her gaping like a moon-eyed schoolgirl. What had gotten into her? She was no better than those empty-headed females who spent their time ogling construction workers.

Blinking away from the sight, she concentrated on why she'd come. He'd been there—in that storm. Surely he must have some ideas of his own about what had happened. Maybe instead of trying each others patience, they could work together to solve the mystery.

A simple enough concept. How hard could it be?

Chapter 8

"I've been trying to find you. Could we talk?"

The voice of the wench plagued Colwyn even here at his own stables. "Not now woman, can't you see I'm—" His words trailed off as he straightened to look at her. The glare he'd intended turned into astonishment. Catching him completely unexpected stood a woman, no, a lady. A grand lady. Soft fabric, much more tightly fitted than her previous strange attire, molded against her well-rounded curves. His gaze traveled the length of her, and his mouth went dry. A jolt charged through him that he hadn't felt in years. He cleared his throat, but even so wondered if words would make it past the tightness in his throat. "M'lady?"

She looked over her shoulder as if to see what he gawked at.

Fie. He'd let too much emotion show. Like a sudden winter wind, his face froze into a stoic mask. "Why do you seek after me?"

"I wondered if we could call a truce, so to speak, and just talk. I've got so many questions and no answers. I thought maybe you could help?"

"I help no one save myself, unless there's gold to be earned." His answer came out stern and rough. Many a lesser woman had trembled at that tone, teared up or simply fled. This woman merely offered him a cool stare. Much to his annoyance, a growing respect for her took hold deep in his belly.

He set aside the paddle and reached for his tunic to conceal his nakedness. Even with the cloth over his shoulders, this chit of a woman made him feel strangely uncovered—as if she could see past the wall he lived behind. Nonsense. He didn't have time for this tomfoolery.

Hefting a wooden pail to his shoulder, he gave her a nod. "Very well. Come along and ask your questions, though I promise no answers."

"I thought I was supposed to be restricted to castle grounds." She crossed her arms, which served to enhance the cleavage he'd been trying to ignore.

A slow fire burned through his veins, and he swallowed. The longer he stood gaping at her, the harder to maintain his cool façade. He averted his gaze, willing away the rogue emotion she elicited. "You'll find I don't always listen to 'little brother' as you call him." With that, he headed toward the gates standing open in the light of day. Rustling skirt fabric swished behind him.

The rocky trail leading to the creek did not lend itself to conversation. He heard her stumble several times, but she didn't cry out. As the path steepened near the water, he turned to tell her to wait where she stood. Too late. Her slippered feet were no match for the grade, sending her crashing into him. For the second time in as many days, she toppled him, and they both rolled one over the other until landing at the water's edge. Though she bore the brunt of his weight, a sharp rock stabbed him in the knee, and any remaining desire washed away with the stream's current.

He growled in outrage. "You are a plague worse than any I've ever known."

"Well you could've warned me this little jaunt required hiking boots instead of satin slippers." She squirmed from underneath him to stand and brush herself off.

"What think you I turned around to say?" Fighting the urge to strike her, he snatched up his fallen pail and waded into the biting water. How could one small woman push him to such extremities? As the river rushed past his legs, the shocking cold did much to soothe his throbbing knee and raw anger.

He bent and dragged the bucket along the bottom for a load of dripping muck. Lugging it to the banks, he found the woman nested atop a large rock. Sunlight glinted bronze highlights in her brown hair and lit her skin with a creamy glow—nay. He would not entertain more of such thoughts. Setting down the heavy pail, he went straight to the point. "Your questions?"

She turned her face from him and remained silent.

"I've not got all day, woman. I've a horse to tend. Either you ask your questions now, or—" he stopped as she looked back at him. The distress in her gaze captured him.

"Can I trust you?" she asked.

Odd question. Could she? At times, he didn't know if he could even trust himself. "Rather you might ask if you should trust me." Her eyes bore into his, and he got the distinct impression he didn't measure up. Not a new feeling, but the sadness settling in his gut surprised him.

A frown tugged her lips into a pretty pout. "I think I have no other choice. What is today's date?"

His mouth dropped open before he could think what to say. "What a half-wit! You tread to the river to ask this of me? 'Tis the sixth moon, twenty-seventh day."

"I know it's June twenty-seventh, but it's the year I'm concerned about. What year is it?"

"Why ask me these ridiculous questions? Perhaps you hit your head in the fall." He reached to see if she bled, but she ducked away. Fine. She could bleed to death for all he cared. "'Tis *anno domini* thirteen fourteen."

"Right."

Her look of disbelief fueled his fire. "You would brand me a liar?"

"It can't possibly be thirteen fourteen, and you know it."

He narrowed his eyes. "I've more to do than stand here and argue trivialities with a woman."

She stared him down as if searching every nuance of his face for falseness. "You really believe it's thirteen fourteen?"

"There is naught to believe. 'Tis truth."

At that, her face grew ashen, and her questions suddenly ended. She slid off the rock and grabbed at roots and brush, making a futile effort to climb the vertical embankment. What had he said to cause this kind of reaction?

"I have said it before, but it bears repeating, you are a curiosity Jessica of Neale." Offering his hand, he managed to get them both, along with the muck bucket, up to solid ground. She collected her bundle of belongings, scattered in the dirt from the earlier tumble.

"Here." She produced a small leather-bound book.

Looking it over, he found numbers inside the front cover. Lots of them, and small. Very small. He squinted. It appeared to be a calendar of sorts, but the digits at the top were all wrong—in the two-thousands. Shaking his head, he gave it back. "This means nothing to me."

Rummaging in that black pouch of hers, she offered him something else. "Look at my date of birth."

He took into his hand a harder, thicker paper than he'd ever touched. No. It couldn't be paper. Light reflected from it, smooth and shiny as a thin piece of glass, yet it did not cut. Words he could not understand or even read met his eye, but most incredible, a perfect likeness featuring Jessica of Neale looked back at him. So small! How did the artist render an exact portrait in such tiny proportion?

"Right here." She pointed her finger at some numbers. "This is when I was born."

Nineteen hundred what? Nineteen hundred? It made no sense. "What say you?"

"I'm saying that I was born in the twentieth century, but you're telling me it's only 1314."

"You did hit your head in the fall. Let me look." He reached to examine her once again, but she ducked away in obvious frustration.

"Remember that storm? The one you said threw you from your horse? The one you claim sent you days off track in an instant?"

"Aye." Uneasiness shivered through him at the mention of it, for as yet he could not account for that strange incident.

"I was there, Colwyn, in that same storm. I'm sure I saw you. You crossed the road in front of my car right before I hit the tree."

"Nay. My men were there. The horses. The blinding light—"

"You must've seen my headlights, and you're wrong. There were no horses, no other men."

Though he had no recollection, he would not stand for being contradicted. He'd tolerate it from Tarne, but no one else. He stepped to within inches of her face.

"I know nothing of lights on a head or of you." His voice rose. "Explain to me how a man travels two full days to the Northern borderlands to be caught in a tempest, and at once is returned alone to his homeland. Tell me how an entire contingent of armed men disappears. Then clarify how I've come to be saddled with a burr of a woman like you."

"I don't know." She met his glare head on. "But yelling at me like a big bully is getting us nowhere."

He grabbed her with rough hands, hoping to impress by force that he'd not accept such impertinence from a woman. That was a folly. Her soft skin beneath his hands muddled his thoughts. He dare not let his eyes travel lower than her face, nay, nor rest upon her inviting lips.

"Let me go. You don't know any more than I do. I was hoping you'd give me explanations, not more questions, and certainly not violence."

He dropped his hands, hating the uncomfortable twinge of shame lodged in his chest. Why did she bring out the bully in him?

"You know I don't fit in here. I'm as foreign to you as you are to me. Half the time I barely understand what you're saying, and even though you won't admit it, I know you don't understand me. You're telling me it's the 1300s and I'm saying it can't be. I live and breathe in the twenty-first century."

Taut muscles kinked the back of his neck, and he began to pace. To believe her would mean she'd been sent from the future. Impossible. Preposterous! His underlying suspicion was to accuse his black magic-working brother, but no motive presented itself at the moment.

He stopped and faced her. "Then speak to me of the future. Who rules Gallimore lands in your time?"

"There's nothing to rule. Gallimore doesn't even exist except as a pile of rubble."

"Gallimore razed?" He might almost laugh. "And who reigns as king?"

"There is no king. Parliament makes up the rules. England isn't exactly a super power anymore."

He could feel his eyebrows meet his hairline. "In truth, the authority of Parliament does grow, but no king? You speak of anarchy, woman."

She sighed and looked away. "It seems like that sometimes."

"What of King Edward's battle? The one I should be fighting in even now?"

Her eyes sought his before she answered. "Good thing you're not. The English troops are pretty much massacred, as I've told you before."

He shook his head at the solemn expression she wore. "Surely you must know I believe not one word you speak. Why this falsehood?"

"Here, look."

She offered him the pouch he'd seen her wear wrapped around her waist.

"Why give me this? 'Tis nothing but a pocket."

"No, look closer. See?" Her fingers pointed as she spoke. "This is called Velcro, and the buckle there is plastic. Now watch."

Between her forefinger and thumb, she tugged at a metal tag that followed along a jagged track, revealing an opening. "That's a zipper. You've never seen this before because in your time it hasn't been invented."

He let his frown envelop his whole face as he ran his finger along the toothy line of the opening. Delving deeper, he pulled out of the pocket a shiny bit of parchment. Again, a perfect likeness smiled back at him like the one Jess had shown him of herself, but this was a young boy.

"Give me that back!"

He held firmly to the miniature image and the pouch. "Whose portrait is this?"

"None of your business. Now give it back."

"M'lady, everything about you has been made my business. The boy is obviously of great import to you. Who is he?"

Her chest heaved, and he might burn from the sparks in her eyes. 'Twas a wonder her voice managed to breach her clenched teeth. "He is my son. Please. Give it back."

He pursed his lips and raised a brow. This woman thrust more surprises at him than he could parry. "A son? By whose sire?"

Like a mussel's shell, her mouth pinched together.

"If you've a son, then it stands to reason there is a father. Who might that man be?"

Her fists clenched at her sides and she shook, making her other outbursts seem like casual disagreements.

"Don't question me about my personal life. I came to you for answers, not an interrogation."

"If indeed you are from the future, M'lady, then surely you already know the outcome of everything. Why ask me?"

She whirled away and raised her hands to the sky, fists still clenched, her voice distorted by choked-back tears. "God, do you hear me? What am I doing here? Get me out. Get me out now!"

Never had he seen anyone so bold as to address God without a priest present. Crossing from head to heart and shoulder to shoulder, he lifted his eyes, expecting at any moment the clouds to split apart, rent by a lightning bolt sent to strike Jessica Neale dead.

•

"See to the horses, men, then see to yourselves. You've earned a bed, some food and a wench, in whatever order you see fit." At the resounding whoops and hollers, Faulk dismounted, his heavy boots landing on the solid ground of Gallimore's courtyard. The hot sun heightened the smell of sweaty, lathered warhorses snorting around him as soldiers led them to the stables. Nailing the ground with a wad of spit, Faulk wished he could go with them.

Only one man remained at his side as the others dispersed. Faulk heard the man delegate the care of their own over-worked mounts to another. "You're a good man, that you are, Geoffrey."

"Aye, and well I know it."

Faulk turned to him with half a grin. "Know you as well we might both be a-swingin' from the gallows before this day is spent?"

Geoffrey nodded, but did not retreat. Faulk admired that about him. Brave. Loyal. Trustworthy. Rare traits that he'd seen in only one other man besides this one—and where was that man now?

Scratching at his growth of beard, Faulk tried one more time to piece together the words he'd have to say to the Earl. A more distasteful task than the one at hand he could not imagine. The memory of the last bearer of ill-tidings he'd seen Lord Tarne deal with made his skin crawl to this day. This might well be his last—

"Faulk!"

Instantly both him and Geoffrey bent to one knee, bowing their heads. "Lord Tarne."

"Quit your show of fealty and come with me. I've been waiting for your return, and waiting pleases me not."

They rose to follow the scarecrow nobleman. Life had dealt Faulk some bitter blows, but he wagered servitude to this tyrant outweighed them all. He'd much rather be at the mercy of Sir Colwyn who, though harsh and aloof, more often than not was at least fair.

And what of Colwyn? The mystery of his disappearance could not be unraveled. Where had he gone? After the night of the wicked storm, Faulk had rallied the men to search for him. No one unearthed a clue. Not a trace of the man was revealed. The earth must've simply swallowed him up. How could he possibly put that into words, as Lord Tarne would surely inquire the whereabouts of his own brother? Rather, how would he give an account of the disappearance and live to see another day? Grim determination alone led his feet into the mock throne room in which Tarne liked to enshrine himself.

A snap of the earl's bony fingers sent a servant running to fetch a flagon of wine as he set himself upon a pedestal with an ornate chair. "Speak."

With a quick glance at Geoffrey and a deep breath for courage, Faulk began. "My Lord, I regret to lay sorrow at your feet, but Sir Colwyn is—"

"I'll hear naught of him!" Tarne slammed his fist onto the arm of his fancy chair. "The king, the battle, our victory of conquest is what I wish to hear."

Faulk didn't dare make eye contact. "My Lord, the king's men did but know defeat. Victory belongs to Robert the Bruce. By the time we drew near the battlefield, the stench of the dead kept us at bay."

"What?" Tarne stood, his voice rising as well. "We outnumbered the Scots. I personally assured the king the stars were in his favor. I should've known something was afoul when my worthless brother came crawling home. Guard!"

Faulk noticed Geoffrey's eyes widen, but he remained at attention as Tarne ordered a Lady Jessica and Sir Colwyn to be summoned. The woman's name he did not know, but Colwyn? Here? How?

The last he'd seen of his captain had been by a flash of lightning. His body had arced through the air from the buck of a crazed horse. He should've been killed from the impact, and his remains found in the dawn of the next day. He hadn't. It didn't make any more sense than discovering that Colwyn was here.

Relief and disbelief waged a tug-of-war, not that he'd let his expression give any hint of it away. Thankful to not be the center of attention, he watched as Tarne jumped down from the dais and paced the floor, mumbling all the while in an incomprehensible tongue.

The guard returned with a boy in tow. Fear etched into the lad's features. This would not go well for him.

"What is this? I asked for my brother and the lady, not a sniveling child." Tarne reached up and backhanded the towering guard. "Report to the post for a lashing."

"But, My Lord," the man stuttered his defense, "this is Sir Colwyn's page. He can tell you exactly—"

"I did not ask for a page. Report at once or it will be the worse for you."

Without further argument, the guard left the room. Faulk swallowed. Would that he himself might be so lucky as to escape with only a whipping.

"Boy, where is your master?"

Tagg looked at the floor. Faulk held his breath.

"He's down at the creek, M'lord."

Tarne grabbed hold of the boy's shoulders, shaking him so that his head bobbed back and forth. "He's to be guarding the Lady Jessica, not off cooling himself at a creek!"

"Nay, M'lord," Tagg said through chattering teeth. "M'lady is with him."

"What?" Tarne threw the boy, and he sprawled in a heap against the far wall. "She is confined to the grounds yet he disregards my orders to romp in a river with the wench?"

Turning wild eyes back to Faulk and Geoffrey, Tarne gave a new command. "You. Take some men and bring them in. I'll suffer disobedience from no man. Dismissed."

"Aye, M'lord." Their voices answered in unison.

Faulk left the fuming little man, glad to have escaped his wrath, but disturbed at this new commission. If Colwyn were entertaining a woman as the boy had said, he'd not take kindly to an intrusion. What if Colwyn didn't want to come willingly with his second in command? He'd crossed Colwyn only once before, and he bore the jagged scar to prove it.

Chapter 9

Jess stumbled over her slippers as a sweaty guard clutched her arm and hurried her across the inner courtyard. He yanked her up the steps to Gallimore, following close behind Colwyn and the man named Faulk. Breathing through her mouth, she tried to keep from inhaling the ale and urine stink of the guard.

They whisked past Great Hall and entered a corridor with tapestries she'd never seen before. At the end of its length, a door stood ajar. Colwyn's page slumped against the wall near an arched doorway. Even from a distance, she could see his thin shoulders shudder from sobbing.

With little more than a glance, Colwyn and Faulk passed by the sniffling boy, but Jess planted her feet. "Please, just a minute."

The guard kept up his pace, dragging her along. Fresh blood covered the boy's sleeve where he'd been wiping his nose, but no one seemed to care. Her heart swelled until it ached, as only a mother's could. She'd never leave her son to cry alone, nor would she leave the hurt little page. She wrenched away from the stinking guard and knelt before the boy.

"Hey, Tagg, you okay?"

He brushed away tears with a grubby fist and sniffed one last time. "Aye, M'lady. You best not keep Lord Tarne waiting."

"You're more impor—"

"Move this baggage from my path." The voice, sharp as gravel, made Jess cringe. "I would know what transpires without impediment or delay."

A painful jerk on her arm pulled her up and out of the way of the puffy-faced woman swishing past her. Great. Now she'd not only have to deal with Tarne but his mother as well.

The guard hustled Jess into the room where Colwyn and a

handful of soldiers waited at attention.

Tarne stood on a dais, bringing him eye level with Colwyn. "Faulk confirms your pathetic story, brother, but the tale does not explain how you ended up here at Gallimore days before the rest of your men. Neither does it excuse your absence from aiding the king. If we fall from favor, I hold you responsible. I ought to lock you up here and now."

Colwyn merely set his eyes on a distant point, as if being locked up meant nothing to him. Why did he let his own brother treat him this way? He towered over Tarne in every respect, yet he submitted as if he were the weaker one.

All of her speculations came to a screeching halt at Colwyn's next words.

"I believe Lady Neale can account for the time difference."

Every eye turned her way, and her mouth dropped open. "What?

"By all means," Tarne said, "enlighten us."

She ignored him and stormed over to a granite-faced Colwyn who refused to look down at her. "You know I can't answer that. I came to you for answers. You don't want to get yourself in trouble, do you? Whatever happened to chivalry?"

Tarne's feet tapped against the stone flooring, and she clenched her jaw when she realized he stood behind her. No way would she turn around. She'd rather face the knight of cold steel in front of her than the pulsating evil at her back.

"Ahh, brother." Amusement edged Tarne's voice. "Now you've gone and angered the wench. Is there no end to your charm? You'd do well, my lady, to bring your questions to me. As you can see, Colwyn is not half the man that I am. I can provide you with so much more."

Tarne's cold finger stroked the length of her bare neck and trailed the curve of her shoulder. Colwyn, though inches in front of her, did nothing to stop his brother's touch, and that sent her over the edge at last.

She whirled around. "Stop it! Don't touch me, and you can quit with all your innuendos. I'm not interested, and I never will be."

Tarne's eyes narrowed, and he leaned so close that she had to step back, smack against Colwyn's solid form. He didn't budge. Not one person in the room broke the silence, except for the matron of the castle. The woman's laughter must've increased the intensity of her rejection, for Tarne began to shake. Fear pumped her heart into a staccato beat so powerful, she wondered if Colwyn could feel it as well.

"So be it." Tarne turned back to ascend the dais, bony knuckles clenched into fists at his side. "'Tis doubtful my brother's presence would've made a difference in the battle's outcome. I believe 'twas you, Lady Neale, who spoke in prophesy the downfall of Edward when you first came here. That divination was in direct contrast to my personal assurances of the king's victory. I've my own suspicions, M'lady, that you are a conniving witch woman. Therefore, you will be the one to remain locked up until I am assured I remain in good stead with the king. If so, perhaps I shall release you. If not—"

He fingered a jeweled dagger at his side and ordered Colwyn to see to her confinement. What if Tarne did lose favor with the king? As if it was her fault. Before she could think any more on it, strong fingers bit into the flesh of her upper arm, and Colwyn hurried her out of the room.

She struggled in his grasp, twisting, turning, spitting out words with malice. "What a jerk! How could you do that to me? You knew I couldn't answer him. Why make me the scapegoat? What kind of man are you? Let me go!"

She wrenched with such force, they both stumbled, and Colwyn yanked her all the harder to the top of the grand stairway. He stopped and turned to her, a flash of danger lighting his eyes.

"You will come along peacefully, or I'll heave you over my shoulder—and you of all people should know I will make good on that threat."

She knew, and she had no intention of letting him have the pleasure. She didn't ever want to feel his hands touch her. "You are a living, breathing contradiction. Sometimes I get a glimpse that you just might have a heart, and then at times like this, you're downright cruel."

"Cruelty is oft' times born of necessity, M'lady. I do what I must."

"You do whatever your brother tells you, and I don't understand it. You let him order you around like a dog on a leash. Why? Why do you stay in this horrible place? Why don't you leave? Let me go, and then get out of here yourself."

An unreadable expression descended like a cloud over his face. "Do not try to hypnotize me with words conjured to gain your freedom. It will not work this time."

She planted her fists on her hips. "Ahh, so you believe I'm a conniving witch woman as well."

"I believe in nothing. Nothing save my own wits and strength."

She stilled at his words, letting her hands fall to her sides. He sounded so hollow. Empty ... and familiar. Had that not been her same creed for the past few years? And to what end had her own wits and strength carried her? Isolation and aching loneliness, that's where. She almost preferred when this man yelled at her than when he pricked her soul. "You must be very lonely."

He narrowed his eyes and cocked his head. "Why must I?"

"I know, Colwyn. I know what it's like to live that way. Holding everyone at arm's length. Always keeping your guard up. Never being honest with anyone—especially yourself. There is more to life than loneliness. It doesn't have to be that way."

The green of his eyes bore down on her with such intensity that she knew she'd struck a chord in him, but not only in him. She spoke as much to herself.

His eyes widened and his mouth dropped. "Why do you say such things to me? Who are you, and why have you come? And don't give me any more babble about the future. You speak of honesty. Tell me the truth."

Frustration clenched her jaw and she looked to the ceiling. "I've told you all I know. My only hope is that maybe I'm really not awake and this is all a dream."

He grasped her by both shoulders and pulled her close. Close enough to feel the warmth of his breath on her cheek. Her heart thudded, and a traitorous quiver low in her stomach tingled as he whispered in her ear. "Am I a dream?"

He nuzzled her neck, and she swallowed back the vulnerability rising in her throat. "No."

He released her and a rogue grin spread across his face, reminding her of her earlier wish to see him smile. A slow burn worked its way through her entire being until she exploded. "I cannot wait to be rid of you. A more presumptuous man I've yet to meet. At least I've got the guts to admit I don't have a clue of what's going on. You don't know any more than I do."

"Exactly," said Colwyn, "Which is why 'tis better for you to be confined than me."

"What?" She staggered mentally at the arrogant statement. Had he really said that out loud?

He took firm hold of her arm once more and continued on his mission, dragging her along, but she would not give up. "You are the most vain, pompous man I know. Have you ever once thought of anyone besides yourself? Did it cross your mind that maybe I don't want to be here? You're a knight, for heaven's sake! Aren't you supposed to be rescuing damsels in distress, not be the one locking them up? Shouldn't you have the urge to protect me?"

The second she said it, embarrassment at her wayward tongue made her cheeks sting and her throat screw up into a tight knot. Undoubtedly, those words would come back to haunt her.

"You would have me as champion?" He turned to look at her, and for once she saw she'd astonished him. "Do you put yourself into my care, M'lady?"

"No! I'm in no one's care. I don't need anybody's care, least of all yours."

He grinned, obviously enjoying her discomfort, and she wished she'd never had the urge to see him smile.

"Good," he said. "Then I'll not feel badly about doing this."

"Doing what?"

He answered with the opening of a door off the side of a flight of spiral stairs and a rough shove to her back. The door slammed shut behind her. Its resounding noise echoed with sickening finality.

"Hey!" Her stomach lurched in a reflex of panic. "This is worse than the last room you locked me in. Do you hear me? You can't leave me here. Colwyn? Colwyn!"

She paused, hoping for an answer. Nothing. Not one word.

How long would she be locked up this time? Pounding her hands against the thick door, she found it as immovable as the gates of the night before. "Colwyn, don't leave me here. Come on. Listen. I'll admit it … I need you. Let me out! Colwyn?"

No answer. Just her racing heart throbbing in her temples. She let loose a cry and flung herself down on a cot with no mattress. Two years worth of ignored emotions rose like bile. She'd lost her husband, she'd lost her entire world, and now she'd lost her hope as well.

•

Colwyn stomped down the stairs in a foul mood. He'd not listen to the girl's cries. He'd ignore every last word chasing after him.

Perhaps Tarne spoke truth, and the girl did practice witchcraft. Of course. She must be a witch. She deserved to be locked away. She deserved even worse.

Then why did a conscience he hadn't felt in years suddenly kick him in the gut? He'd rather take a beating than suffer the churning and burning hammering in his chest, and all because of a snippety woman.

He took the last of the stairs three at a time as he spotted Faulk in the main foyer. "Faulk!"

"M'lord?"

Colwyn put every ounce of the tension that filled him into a good cross-hook, sending Faulk staggering backward. Then he garnered a bent-kneed stance, posturing for retaliation. A good brawl would do much to improve his disposition, and Faulk would no doubt deliver.

With a hairy forearm, Faulk swiped away the dribble of blood at his mouth and sized-up Colwyn's position. True to his expectation, Faulk met him head on. They went at it, raining blow upon blow, until his muscles screamed and breathing took more effort than he cared to admit. Even so, he pinned his second-in-command to the foyer floor.

"Do you yield?" Colwyn asked, harsh and hoarse. The remainder of his strength ebbed with the sweat trickling from each pore.

"Aye." The answer came between heavy breaths.

He rolled off the big man and stood, wiping a backhand across his forehead. "Then let us drink away what's left of us." Clouting Faulk on the back, he led the way into Great Hall. After acquiring two jugs and two tankards, they hunkered down on a bench in a quieter corner of the big room.

"Tell me true, Faulk. What happened the night of the storm? Spare no detail for there is much I do not know."

Faulk drank deep and long before he answered. "I would ask the same of you, Sir, for I cannot explain away the events of that wicked eve. 'Twas as if the earth swallowed you up. Perhaps if you'd ridden Old Black, you'd not have been thrown. In a flash of light I saw you fly into the air, but never did I see you land. Truth to tell, I did not see you again until this day here at Gallimore. I thought you were dead. Why did you leave us? Where were you?"

Colwyn flexed his empty hand into a fist and slowly released it, only to repeat the action again and again. He could not answer Faulk's questions any more than he could answer the girl's. "What then? What happened the next morn?"

Faulk frowned and took another swig. "Very well. Keep your secrets. A noble's mind is one I'll not claim to know. Before the sun cleared the horizon, we tore the woods apart in search of you. We found not a sign. You yourself have trained the men in tracking and can cast no blame on their skill.

"I knew we'd lost many valuable hours and that we were hard-pressed for time. I pushed the men as much as I dared, and then some.

"We made Bannockburn by nightfall, intending to marshal with the rest of the king's men to attack the next morn. We found the king's men all right—what was left of them, anyway. Butchered, the lot of them." Faulk looked away with a curse, and drained his mug. He refilled, drinking down another full draft of the brew before continuing.

"Butchered," he repeated.

Faulk raised his eyes, the red rims speaking of more than strong drink. Colwyn gave a slow nod of affirmation and understanding of what the wordless stare communicated.

"I should have been there. We should have been there." He threw his mug to crack against the wall and shot to his feet.

Faulk reached for balance on the tottering bench. "What will you do?"

His chest swelled and deflated before he answered. "I will go to London. I will see the King."

"It could mean time in the tower," Faulk paused, "or your life."

He needn't have voiced his concerns. Colwyn knew what it meant. He knew the implications of meeting face to face with a sovereign who could be flightier than a summer's breeze. He was as likely to find favor as not. He knew all right, but it wouldn't stop him from going.

Jessica of Neale was wrong. He did sometimes think of someone other than himself. If King Edward indeed carried a grudge, Colwyn wouldn't be the only one who suffered. Blood would be spilled at

Gallimore. Blood of innocents. And for that reason alone, he must try to persuade the king of his family's loyalty.

He hated to order the haggard Faulk back out on a journey, but time had become a precious commodity. "Ready fresh horses and pack our needs. I'll meet you before the hour is done."

Faulk stood, stumbling under the ale he'd consumed. "Aye, Sir."

He watched his second-in-command shuffle a trail through the rushes on the floor as he made his way out the door. Only then did Colwyn turn his head and scan the Great Hall from table to table. Men in various states of consciousness dotted the big room. Some clustered around tables, gaming and betting away their few coins. Others guffawed around tankards of drink, or lay stretched out and snoring upon backless benches. Several claimed shadowy corners, a wench filling their arms and their attentions.

One soldier stood near a display of weaponry adorning the northern wall, casually taking in all the revelry the Great Hall had to offer, but he did not participate in any of the vices. Colwyn approached this man.

"Geoffrey."

"Sir Colwyn."

He offered his hand and they clasped forearms in greeting.

"'Tis good to see you whole and sound, Sir."

"'Tis good to be such. I would ask favor of you, Geoffrey."

"Favor, Sir?" Trustworthy brown eyes met Colwyn's. "Of me?"

"Aye." He nodded once. "'Tis no man I'd trust more, save Faulk, yet for now I require him by my side."

Geoffrey didn't answer, but Colwyn could see his words pleased the soldier standing before him. "I must needs journey to London, but I am uneasy at leaving behind the Lady Jessica."

"Say no more, Sir." He bowed, fist to one shoulder. "I swear she will be in my charge until your return."

Colwyn smiled at the man's eager acceptance. "This is no small task I ask of you, so think well on it before you pledge your vow. Tarne plays a cat and mouse game with her, and she herself is part lioness. Either of them could eat you alive."

The man answered without hesitation. "To you have I given my service, my life. If this is what you ask of me, consider it done."

"Then see no harm befalls M'lady, nor any to yourself."

The young soldier lifted his chin. "Daily shall I put the matter into God's hands, as well as for your own safety, Sir."

Colwyn clapped him on the shoulder. "You're a good man, Geoffrey."

"So I've been told, Sir." He flashed a grin.

"You know I share not your reverence for God, nor am I a man of prayer, but so might I become for the saving of your life—and the Lady Jessica's."

Chapter 10

"My lady?"

The voice caught Jess unaware, and she turned her face toward it. The sound came through a narrow slot in the door that slid open with a complaining screech. So, that hadn't been a mail slot after all.

"My lady, I've brought your supper."

"Tagg?" She left the cot she'd been lying on and peered through the opening. Sure enough, the boy's bright eyes glittered at her from the other side.

"Aye, M'lady. I'll be bringing ye whatever ye'll be needin'."

Through the slot, she saw him add a proud tilt to his head, much the same way she'd seen Colwyn respond at times. This boy took on the role of consoler like one years beyond his age.

"You probably shouldn't get caught hanging around me. I'm not on the best of terms with Tarne right now. Not that I wouldn't mind the company, but you don't want to get yourself locked up."

"Not to worry, M'lady. As I've said, I've brought your supper."

A flat, stale piece of bread came through, laden with an unrecognizable cut of braised meat and cooked root vegetables. The aroma reminded her it'd been a long time since she'd last eaten.

"And here, M'lady." He pushed through a wineskin filled only enough so as to fit through the slot.

"Thank you, Tagg,"

"I've got something else."

Little by little, a rough-woven blanket poked through the door's hole. "You're wonderful." She hoped he could read the gratitude on her face and in her smile.

He grinned at the praise. "Oh, M'lady, I almost forgot. Old

Black's fever, it's breakin'. The wound is still somethin' fearsome, but the best part is, he's taking water now."

"See, I told you." She bit off the end of a carrot, and it tasted wonderful even without butter and salt. Between bites, she continued, "Let that master of yours know it was you who pulled him through and not some disgusting mix of mud and who-knows-what else."

"Oh, but Sir Colwyn's gone, m'um."

"Gone?" What a snake, leaving her to bear all the blame Tarne had to dish out. "Gone where?"

"I know not. He rode out with nary a word to me, and Faulk went with him."

"Is that unusual?"

"He always lets me know, M'lady, so I can pack up his gear and saddle his horse. Not this time." A scowl hardened the boy's face for an instant, then disappeared.

So, was he ratting out on both her and the boy? "You're a very patient young man to put up with such a conceited master."

"Why he's not so bad, m'um. If I grow to be half the knight he is, well, I couldn't ask for more." His tone dripped with hero-worship.

She gritted her teeth. "There are better men than Colwyn to model your life after. All he cares about is himself."

"Nay, m'um." A frown creased the boy's smooth face. "You're wrong about him. You just don't know it yet."

"Then why would he leave me here, alone, to face Tarne by myself? Does that sound like something a man of integrity would do?"

"M'lady, I know naught of such fancy words, but I do know Sir Colwyn must have a good reason. Sometimes I don't understand why he does things, but in the end, it always works out. You'll ne'er go wrong by putting your trust in him."

Such childlike faith in a man—and an unpredictable one at that. "I hope you're right."

"You'll see."

She wasn't so sure, but this boy didn't deserve to bear the brunt of her cynicism. "Where are your parents? Do they know how hard you're working and how poorly you're being treated?"

"Poorly?" His nose twitched like a rabbit. "M'lady, I've got it better than most. Sir Colwyn sees to my needs, and Traline clucks at me like me own mum."

The reality of the boy's situation dawned bright and clear in Jess's mind. "You never knew them, did you? Your parents, I mean."

"Nay, M'lady."

She strained her ears, but she didn't detect much sorrow.

"Traline says my mother weren't strong enough to live after bearing me, and my father, well … Traline said the man left the day I was born and she's not seen him since."

"Oh, sweetie, I'm so sorry."

"Don't fret, M'lady. Like I said, I've got it better than most."

"How can you say that? I've seen the guards treat you like a whipping boy, and Colwyn acts as if you're his slave."

"Oh no, M'lady. I'm in training is all. Right now I'm but a page. Sir Colwyn teaches me to care for his armor and his horses that one day I may care for my own. When I turn four and ten, then I'll be a squire and learn the use of swords and lances and the ways of war. Gallimore's not much on manners and the arts, but nowhere could I train to be a finer soldier. And all this only because of Sir Colwyn's good graces, for he could've had a nobleman's son. Instead, he chose me. I am honored indeed."

Would her own son be as content in such a cruel situation? "You're an amazing boy, you truly are."

He glanced away, and she realized he'd had enough of such serious conversation.

"Well, you keep up the good work. I'm sure Old Black will be better soon. I'm glad you came and told me."

"I'll come back tomorrow, M'lady. I'll come by whenever I can."

"Thanks. You have no idea what that means to me."

With his apologies for having to shut the slot, he bade her good night. In the quiet of her room, she heard his light trot down the stairwell and wondered where the pat-patting of his feet would take him. Where did he lay his head each night? Did Colwyn provide amply for the boy, or only for his most basic needs? Glancing around the darkening, barren room she occupied, she decided on the latter.

And what of her own son? Physically he lacked for nothing like the little page did, but since Dan's death and the grief that imprisoned her, she hadn't really been there for her boy, not emotionally. It was so hard to look at him and see Dan's eyes staring back. More often than not she withdrew and busied herself with work. Would she ever get the chance to make it right again?

She choked down the rest of her cold dinner and wrapped herself in what warmth the thin blanket offered, hugging herself against the damp air. She had plenty of time to reflect on the generosity of a young boy, the coldness of a grown man, and the regret that stabbed her in the heart.

Plenty of time.

•

"Fie!" Colwyn brushed the burning ember that shot out from the fire, lighting on his knee. The pain darkened his black mood.

"Mayhap," Faulk paused, flinging the last of a gnawed rabbit carcass into the inky depths of the forest, "mayhap you're cursed, Sir."

"Aye." He looked from Faulk to follow the orange flames reaching to mingle with the night sky. "I've been cursed from the day of my birth. That's nothing new and so hardly accounts for the wench. She says she's from the future. How can that be? Why would she make such a claim?"

"Perhaps she truly is a witch as Tarne has said."

Colwyn chewed that thought as one who eats with a sore tooth. The accusation didn't sit well with him. For all her bluster, he saw in her a purity that would not consort with such evil. "Nay, not a witch. But what then? Think you she's daft? Be she a liar?"

"You've spent time with her. Is she half-witted?"

"Nay." Pinching the bridge of his nose, he tried to ward off the headache that threatened. "She's got more wit about her than many a man I know, and a good measure more courage."

"She lies then." After a stretch and a scratch, Faulk wrapped his cloak tight and bedded down on the ground next to the fire. Obviously he'd finished the conversation.

But Colwyn would not rest, nor would he allow his second-in-command such luxury. "Why? What does she stand to gain by telling such an outrageous tale? And why tell only me? She's not spoken a word of this to Tarne."

"Perhaps," An enormous yawn didn't do much to clarify Faulk's already mumbled words. "Perhaps she fears him."

"Again, nay. That little wench isn't afraid of anyone. Which leads me to believe she is capable of lying, but for what purpose?

She could have spouted any number of falsehoods to prevent being locked up, yet she did not. She should have made up a reason. She should have concocted some kind of fabrication. 'Tis her own stubbornness that's gotten her into such difficulty."

"You begin to sound, Sir, as if the wench matters to you."

A fierce frown tugged down the corners of his mouth. He'd allowed a woman to matter to him once—but never again. "She is naught to me. She's a nuisance and a plague." The words came out a little too forcefully, and he stretched himself out on the damp dirt wishing now he'd have let Faulk gone to sleep.

"Methinks she's the reason you're out here, is she not?"

He turned away and let the question curl up like a spiral of smoke into the indigo sky. His quest to clear Tarne's name with the king was not because of a short-haired, scrappy girl. Tarne commanded it, and he followed orders. He always followed orders. That was it, plain and simple.

Then why could he still hear her calling out after him, though it'd been nearly two days since he'd left her? *Colwyn, don't leave me here ... You're the only one who can help me.* He'd tried not to listen, but even now he could not forget the desperation in her voice.

He turned over and attempted to mold his body and grind his thoughts into the bumps and hollows of the uneven ground. He wanted to sleep. He needed to sleep, but there'd be no way he could until he admitted to himself that he did not believe Jessica Neale was a liar. Irksome and shrew-tempered, yes, but far too vulnerable to be a liar though she tried to disguise it.

What if all she claimed were true? Dare he believe she'd come nearly seven hundred years after his time? How could that be possible? A scholar of science would be hard-pressed to explain it, much less a simple man like himself.

Understand it or not, his gut instinct told him she spoke truth. Too much truth. *You must be very lonely.* She had been right—more than she could possibly know. He'd experienced love for less than a whisper of time, and it left him haunted and empty.

Jessica Neale seemed so sure that life had more to offer, more to believe in, more ... what? What did she know, what had she experienced, to create such conviction? He could ask her, but would he be brave enough to listen?

Flipping like a beached fish, he tried once more to claim sleep.

I'm in no one's care ... I need you. The disturbing words would not be silent.

He sat upright, ignoring Faulk's snores, and poked at the dying fire with a nearby stick. So be it. He'd remember it all then.

She said she'd been, what was it? Driving? Aye, that was it. Driving. The storm, and then light, and then nothing. It'd been the same for him. What did it mean? *Think. Think!*

He picked apart each possible solution as quickly as his mind could concoct one. No explanation held sway other than what she'd said. I don't have a clue of what's going on and neither do you. Right again. As far-fetched as it sounded, and though comprehension of why or how was beyond him, he believed she spoke truth. God help him, he actually believed she spoke truth.

That single, stunning belief meant he'd left an innocent woman, locked defenseless and alone, to the whims of his unstable brother. And more than anything, that's what kept him awake long into the deepest darkness of night.

•

Heavy boots pounded up the stairs—the hard-soled footwear of a man. The resolute steps stopped at the other side of Jess's cell door.

She knew the next sound to meet her ears would be the door slot opening. If she cared to turn over on the rope-gridded skeleton bed, she'd see a pair of dark chocolate eyes staring at her. The slot would shut, the footsteps retreat, and game over.

She wouldn't play this time.

The curious eyes came around mid-morning and again in late afternoon, as near as she could tell from what little light the high-set slit windows offered. The first visit had occurred on the second day of her captivity. She'd been spooked, thinking Tarne had come for her, or maybe someone else watched with harmful intent, but the owner simply blinked back at her as if making some kind of assessment. She'd put all her skill into pleading and demanding to know who looked at her and why, but success eluded her.

Even Tagg couldn't tell her. He'd not once been there when the eyes had come. The amount of description she could give was minimal. The slot never stayed open long enough for her to run over and get a good look. A few times she'd lain in wait near the opening when she heard the footfall coming, but he kept his face so close to the door, she could only see long lashes beneath dark brows and a pair of well-defined cheekbones, nothing more.

It'd been four days of this silly routine now, and she'd moved beyond caring about who persisted at this ritual. Let him look. She had nothing to hide. Boredom and loneliness fatigued her to the point of lying on her cot and staring at the rough edges of each stone block comprising the wall.

The slot didn't close as quickly this time, and when it finally did shut, no footsteps tromped down the stairs. Instead, she heard the same sound as when a chambermaid came to empty her pot—the sliding of a heavy draw bar and then the grating of hinges pushing open.

But the chambermaid had already been there this day.

Before she could roll over and get herself off the cot, a soldier towered over her. Genuine concern wrinkled his brow and she couldn't help but furrow hers in confusion.

"Who are you?" She attempted to gracefully get herself off the rope framing, but she had yet to master the full fabric of her skirts.

"I beg pardon, M'lady, but allow me."

Immediately, mighty arms hoisted her to her feet then released her just as quickly, leaving her tottering.

"Does it go well with you, M'lady?"

Light-headed and slightly disoriented from blood rushing down to her feet, she scrutinized him to see if he joked. He merely gazed back in all seriousness.

Apparently, grooming mattered to this guard. He wore his hair pulled from his face and fastened in a stubby pony tail, its color reminding her of a pie crust baked too long in the oven. Except for sideburns framing his jawline, he kept his face clean shaven. His eyes held the warmth of an old friend's, and her immediate reaction was to trust him, though she took a step away from him anyway. "Who are you? Why do you come to look at me every day but never say a word?"

"Be at peace, M'lady. I mean you no harm. If 'twould ease your mind, I shall leave you, for I am fully satisfied you fare well."

He retreated, but as he neared the door, she took a step forward. "Wait."

Glancing over his shoulder, he paused. "Aye?"

"You never answered me."

He turned around but stayed close to the only exit in the sparse room. "I am called Geoffrey, M'lady, one of Sir Colwyn's men. I am charged to look after you, nothing more. I entered only because I feared you might be ill, but I am pleased to see naught is amiss with you."

"Yeah, right, I'm just fine." She scratched at a nagging itchy spot behind her ear before continuing. "Nothing's amiss with me, not a thing. I'm locked in this chilly room for days and days, but I'm doing great. I miss my home. I miss my son. I want to leave, but other than that, life couldn't be better."

His calmness annoyed her. She wanted a reaction, any reaction, not a blank stare. She lifted the wrinkled skirting of her gown. "This dress is the most uncomfortable thing I've ever worn, and there's not even any toilet paper. The food's usually cold by the time it reaches me, and you should try sleeping on this contraption without a mattress."

Her agitation increased with each complaint she lobbed at the silent man. She took to pacing the length of her bed and back. "I don't know where I am, or when I am. Technically speaking, I shouldn't even exist yet, but here I am in all my glory. Nobody would know or care if I dropped dead in the fourteenth century. I live in fear that the next person to walk through that door will be Tarne, and I'm just plain old mad at Colwyn for locking me in here. My teeth feel nasty, I want a bath, and to top it all off, I'm pretty sure I've got lice. Now, does that sound like everything's just wonderful for me? Does it?"

Spent, she stopped pacing and flopped down on the solid edge of the bed frame, chin in hands, not caring if this Geoffrey character stayed or left.

"It pains me to see you in such despair, M'lady. 'Twould do you well to commit your concerns to prayer."

"Right." She let the word float on a sea of cynicism.

"Surely God will hear you and answer."

She lowered her hands and raised her eyes to his. "Don't talk to me about God. I don't want to hear it."

"Earnest petitions are always received by God's ear, M'lady."

The gentleness in his voice hinted at sympathy. *Oh, no. No way.* She'd suffered enough pity during the days following Dan's death.

She'd not take any more. "You're wasting your time. I know first-hand that sometimes God answers, sometimes He doesn't. That's the way it is."

Geoffrey paused and shifted his weight before responding. "I mean to dishonor you not, M'lady, but you are mistaken. God always answers, though oft' not in ways we might expect or favor. Think well on this, and do not doubt. If Sir Colwyn intercedes on your behalf, and him a mere man, how much more so the God of your creation?"

"What?" Her jaw sprung open and she shook her head. No. It couldn't be true. That made no sense. "What do you mean? Colwyn's the one who locked me in here and left me to rot."

"He must have good reason for his action. He does care for your safety, M'lady. 'Tis by his charge I keep watch over you."

She let her mouth shut in slow motion, flabbergasted into silence.

"'Tis not truly my place to converse with you further, M'lady. Know I will ever be watchful on your behalf, and bear in mind that bidden or unbidden, God is always present." The deep brown eyes peered at her a moment more before Geoffrey quietly left the room. Hinges groaned shut, oak sealed against oak, and bootsteps faded.

She wished now that those eyes had remained silent.

Chapter 11

The stench of London met Colwyn's nose as he and Faulk neared one of the city's outer wards. He'd hoped to enter on a cloudy day. The sun's heat would sizzle the nauseating smells to unbearable levels. He swiped a bead of sweat trickling down his neck and his hope died a quick death.

Small houses crowded together in the narrow streets with a channel running down the middle. He held tight rein on the lively palfrey who sidestepped the open sewage. He could lay no blame at the horse's skittish prancing. Refuse of all kinds fouled the public thoroughfare from excrement to bloated animal carcasses. The need to escape the stench almost stopped him from inhaling.

His ears were as battered as his affronted lungs. Beggars pleading alms, merchants barking their wares. Dogs, and poultry, and children added to the noise until he wanted nothing more than to stop up his hearing.

A crowd blocked the crossroads they approached. He lifted his forearm in signal for Faulk to draw up alongside him.

"Know you another route that we may avoid this mob?"

"Nay, Sir."

He rubbed at the stubble on his chin with one hand while keeping grasp of the reins in his other. "Then we press on. Follow close. I'll cut a path."

Giving pressure with his knees, Colwyn urged his mount forward. He directed the mare into the crowd, keeping to the outer edges, until he saw what held the crowd's attention.

In the space where the two roads crossed, a wooden framed stage had been erected. A red and gold fringed banner skirted the bottom of the platform, decorated with symbols of the church embroidered in the middle. On the stage, a play depicting the trial of Christ entertained the people.

A theatrical Bible scene typically held no interest for Colwyn. He'd seen them before and had not been impressed. 'Twas nothing but a priest's money-making scheme to collect more coin than could be extracted during mass. This one, however, drew him in—not the performance in and of itself, but the expression on the man portraying the Christ.

He prompted his horse into the thick of the crowd, disregarding the angry protests and curses at his bold move. When close enough to see the actor's face clearly, he yanked the reins.

Pain, hurt, incredulity at the wickedness of humankind, all this and more emanated from the actor's clenched jaw and determined set of his shoulders. Oh, how he could relate to the resigned look on the man's face as he stood trial, allowing evil men to have their way. He knew that feeling. He'd felt this way his entire life, trapped into serving his brother, who on a whim could have him executed at any time.

He'd seen enough.

With a sharp jerk of the bridle, he pivoted the horse, heedless of who might meet with a crushed foot from his mount's trampling hooves. Faulk had remained at the edge of the crowd and cocked his head in inquisition. Colwyn met his eyes, but offered no explanation. Instead, he veered right and continued on his course without comment.

They rode on, longer than he would've liked, until at last he spotted a placard bearing a painting of a scarlet hand. The wooden sign announced they'd reached their lodgings for the night—The Red Glove Inn. What a small measure of happiness indeed to finally extract his backside from the saddle. He dismounted, flipping his horse's tether into Faulk's care, eager to trade the stink of the streets for a smoky hearth and a bowl of fragrant stew.

Colwyn stepped over the threshold while ducking to avoid the doorframe's short lintel. The small public room sported two windows coated with layers of grime that allowed for a dim grey light. Rough hewn tables and benches filled most of the room. Several men sat with tankards and looked up from their conversation at his arrival.

"Innkeeper." His voice boomed louder than the underlying hum of chatter.

A ferret-faced man, short of stature and painfully thin, ran to his call. "Welcome, welcome, Sir. Sir Colwyn, is it not? Why, 'tis been much too long since you've graced the likes o' the Red Glove with your presence. How might I be of service to you, Sir?"

He didn't necessarily like the nervous little man, but he had no complaints against the level of care at this particular lodging. "Two rooms, one for me and one for my man. Send a boy out to see to the horses."

"Aye, Sir." Immediately the man whistled for a wiry boy, obviously one of his offspring, to carry out his wishes.

"How long might you be staying, Sir?"

"I am unsure, though not for long. Know you if the king resides at court?"

"That he does, Sir." The innkeeper wavered from foot to foot, looking like a chipmunk unsure of which tree to run to for safety. "Pardon my asking, Sir, but might you be about the king's business?"

He evaded the question with one of his own. "What know you of the king's business?"

"I only ask, Sir, that I may be of aid to those sleeping under my roof. If 'twould aid, Sir, I know that the king's called a parliament of representatives from all shires and burroughs to raise funds to pay for the astounding loss at Bannockburn."

"Then counselors and ministers currently attend court as well?"

"Aye, Sir."

Satisfied with the information, Colwyn ordered a substantial meal for himself and Faulk, accepting a mug of ale from a serving wench. Though he didn't relish the idea of sitting again, at least the bench he sank onto wasn't trotting or cantering.

Faulk plopped down as well, eyeing him over his own flagon of brew. "You look like a ratter who's caught himself a fine, fat bagful."

"I am well pleased the king is in residence. He could've been at any number of landholdings or hunting lodges and our journey would've had to continue. I am happy for a roof, a bed, and some cooking other than yours."

Faulk lifted his mug in mock salute. "There's still the matter of gaining audience, especially when the king will likely not forget your absence at Bannockburn."

"True, but Counselor Aedmund is sure to be at court. He holds the king's ear. He'll see I meet with Edward, and that I'll not do so alone."

"'Tis a comfort, then, that if sentenced to the tower, you'll have someone to watch you go?"

Faulk's jest deflated his optimism. He was right. Simply because he might gain easy access to the king was no indicator that the outcome would be as successful. Though he counted Counselor Aedmund as his friend, that virtue alone would not assure Edward's good will.

•

An unholy alliance bound Tarne as securely as the girl he had imprisoned. For the past seven days, he'd sought after and consorted with a union of powers better left undisturbed. He'd used every skill, all he knew of the darkest crafts, yet a vision of the future remained in the shadows.

With a long fingernail, he pushed entrails about on a tin pan, hissing his displeasure. The first augury had not gone well. He'd never seen a trinity of kidneys from one animal before. So, he'd tried again, and now this.

Scooping up the offending omen, he went in search of Gallimore's matron. Perhaps with her past experience in the arts, she could tell him what this meant. His spirit guides had refused to elaborate, no matter what sacrifice he offered.

He suspected where to find her. She spent most of her days in drink, talking to people whom no one could see. Entering her chamber, he saw her, sitting at table, wine glass in hand.

"Mother, look."

Lady Gwynneth Haukswyrth tried to focus her bloodshot eyes on what he offered, but he noticed it required too much effort. "What is it?" Her words slurred and her head bobbed.

"Oh mother, for God's sake!"

"God?" Her shrill laugh turned into an unpleasant wheeze. "Strange to hear that name come from your mouth, my boy. You pay God no more homage than do I."

"Pay attention, old woman. Your future is linked to mine, and this does not portend well. Look closely."

She squinted into his outstretched palm, and he gave her time to look it over carefully. He held what appeared to be a heart, gray from lack of life. No, there were two hearts, uniquely two, but bound as one. Tarne detected a sudden diminishing of his mother's stupor, though she remained silent.

Her veined eyes burned into his. "The voices? What do the voices say? Tell me all you have heard, all you have seen."

"They say 'she is the one,' but that is all. They do not say the one for what purpose, nor how the purpose is to be accomplished. Somehow, 'tis by her hand that power is shifted, but I cannot see beyond that."

"The new realm." Lady Haukswyrth pinched her lids shut and murmured words that could not be understood. White spittle collected in the crease of her mouth. Just as suddenly, her eyes bulged open and held his gaze. "The new realm is at hand then. But why name a woman as 'the one'? It begs the question as to whom the new realm will belong. Could it be her?"

He jerked back his hand and slammed it onto the table. Bits of clotted blood and tissue splattered from beneath his fingers. "To me, mother. It belongs to me! You have groomed me in the arts and ways of power, and it is I who will reign. Who is to stand in my path?"

"You've said it yourself. She is the one. Know you who that woman is?"

"Aye." The answer barely made it through his clenched teeth. "The insolent wench Colwyn dragged home."

"Then take care of your problem. You need me not to tell you how to go about it."

"You don't understand." He paced a small circle, all the while inspecting the pointed toes of his shoes. "There's something different about this woman. I've sensed it from the start. She's not one to be controlled like all the other simpering serving wenches or mindless noble ladies."

"Stop your grousing. At least Colwyn keeps up a manly pretense, which is more than I can say for you."

He stopped dead still and angled his head. "You would favor him?"

"I would favor neither of you. You've both been a disappointment."

He raised his hand to slap her, but she closed her eyes, and instantly he felt his arm forced down to his side as if squeezed by a vice. This was too much to be borne, even from his own mother. "You dare try that with me?"

Her jowls jiggled as she laughed, further inciting him. "I came to you, old woman, not for child's play but for a solution to this crisis that affects us all. I see you've no wisdom left to impart. You've outlived your usefulness."

"Why come to me? Resolve this yourself. If the woman cannot be controlled, then eliminate her."

"Of course I've entertained such action, but the voices give me no further guidance. What if I eliminate the very one who holds the key to my reign?" He reached for the bottle of wine and drained it carelessly, blood-red liquid dribbling a stain onto his tunic.

Ever calculating, she would not let it pass. "You fear her."

"Fear? Me? I fear no one. Nothing."

"Mayhap you should."

He looked at her as if regarding a cadaver. Aye, there was a thought to savor. "Perhaps your mentoring days are through, old woman. You speak nonsense."

"Is the student greater than the master?" The sneer pasted on her lips soon uncurled into an open mouth gasping for breath. Her fat, jeweled fingers clutched at her neck, frenzied in trying to pry free from an unseen choking grasp. But Tarne would not relent from his trance, not until he'd more than proven his point. The fear in her eyes fed his soul.

She slumped, limp and lifeless, in her cushioned chair. Before entertaining satisfaction of victory, he bent close, assuring himself that all corporal functions had ceased. Closer still, until the skin of his lips touched wisps of her hair drawn up at her ears.

"Yes, mother, I do believe the student to be greater than the master." He whispered as a lover might bestow an endearment.

Standing tall, he brushed his surcoat to straighten any wrinkles. He didn't give her a second look as he stalked from the room and went straightaway to Great Hall. Once through the doors, he paused, taking mental tally of who inhabited the big room and which man might best suit his needs.

"Rollo!"

A rotund guard, three tables adjacent to where he stood, turned a head the shape of a malformed cabbage. A past battle lent him an uneven gait, but he stood and attended Tarne without hesitation, dropping to one knee.

"M'lord."

"Rise. I have need of you."

The man rose like an ancient oak, the trunk of his body, thick and solid. "I am none but yours, M'lord, able and ready to do your bidding."

Tarne didn't like having to look up at the monster guard, but no doubt this fool would carry out whatever he commanded. "I've a delicate matter of, how shall I put this—disposal, I suppose. One I'd like kept quite confidential. Meet me in Lady Hauskwyrth's quarters within the hour. Dismissed."

Tarne pivoted and hurried to the tower stairs, then climbed the turret's narrow passage to a closed door. Sliding open the heavy bar, he entered the cell where the girl slept. She didn't stir even as he drew the dagger from his side.

The wench didn't look as if the fate of a new realm could be tied to her. Small and defenseless, actually. No matter. Ill omens or not, he would not allow her the chance to prove otherwise. He'd given too much of himself, too much of his soul, to be defeated now.

He crept toward her, and though she lay on her side, he could see the rise and fall of her chest as she breathed. She was a comely wench. Dark ringlets of curls crowned her head and her lashes lay against rounded cheeks, curved and soft as no doubt the rest of her would feel beneath his hands. Physical desire began to build the longer he stood and looked at her. He could bed her, take his fill, then let his blade finish the deed. The thought intrigued him, and he toyed with it until he could contain it no more.

Reaching to touch her creamy flesh, he stopped when she rolled over, lying flat on her back and facing him. What if her eyes snapped open now?

You fear her. You fear her. You fear her.

No, he didn't fear anyone—and he'd prove it. Dagger poised over his head, he aligned the tip to strike her throat.

•

Colwyn emptied his gut onto the side of the hard-packed street outside the Red Glove. He wiped the rancid taste from his lips, then straightened, willing his head not to explode. Five days. Five long, aggravating days he'd spent drinking what ale the inn had to offer.

His disposition transfigured from veiled patience, to agitation, to outright brooding ugliness. The few other guests, the innkeeper, and even Faulk had learned to make themselves scarce once he returned from his morning pilgrimage to court.

Daily, Colwyn petitioned to see the king, and daily he retreated in defeat. He had yet to set foot past the soldiers posted at the front doors. Persuading the gate guards of the importance of his mission proved easy enough, but without a summons bearing the king's seal, he would not be allowed into the palace housing King Edward and his nobles. He was free to roam the pebbled front courtyard decorated with sculpted topiaries and marble statuettes. He could hike around and inspect the royal livery, admiring the display of fine horseflesh if he wished. He might even join in some rousing gaming with the men stationed at the garrison. But, he could not gain access to the only building he wished to enter.

Even his messages to Counselor Aedmund remained unanswered, which did not bode well. Something wrong was afoot.

He retrieved his mount from the mean stables behind the inn and resolved that this day would see an answer to his quest.

The streets gave off a putrid odor as he directed his palfrey toward the palace. No good could come from people living in such filth, and Colwyn yearned to leave it all behind for the fresh air of Gallimore.

He dismounted at the palace gates, nodding to the guard he'd come to know.

"Having another go at it, Sir?"

"Aye, and I vow I'll not leave until the king grants me audience. See that my horse is stabled for I can't be sure how long this will take."

"As you wish. Tether her and I'll see she's looked after."

Colwyn went through the routine of securing his mare to the hitching rail and tramped along the same graveled path his boots kicked at day after day. It would be different this time. He'd make it so.

Up the polished stone steps, he fixed his course with single-minded purpose. Either he'd gain entrance, or become a permanent presence stationed at the front door. The plan lacked ingenuity, but for now it was all he had.

With a tug on the bell-pull, he waited, and waited. The two soldiers on either side of the wide marble landing ignored him, and he wondered if the doorkeeper inside did the same. He pulled again.

The massive paneled and painted door opened, and to his surprise, he encountered a servant he'd not yet met. Mayhap the time had come for a new tactic.

He bowed from the waist as if the doorman were of import. "Good day to you. My apologies for my late arrival as I was expected nigh on a week ago. I am the newly appointed representative from the shire of Kensingham, and have endured many a mishap on my long journey to court. My baggage, my men, even my last coin has been lost to highwaymen, but I am proud to say that I have persevered in my oath and duty to the king. Long live Edward."

A wave of perplexity washed across the doorman's face. "Kensingham?"

"Aye, you've heard of us then. A newly acquired burgh skirting the farthest reaches of the northern moors. I am Lord of Kensingham. Come now, you'd keep me outside after all my turmoil?" The doorman puckered his brows, overtly trying to recollect Kensingham, and Colwyn took the opportunity to shove past him into the grand foyer.

"Hold, hold!" The befuddled servant swooped after him. "I must see your summons. No one may enter without a summons."

"I've told you, my good man, I lost everything on the road. Everything, do you understand? 'Tis by God's hand alone that I stand in front of you now. But I know how formalities must be regarded and properly adhered to. You are only carrying out orders, and a fine display of competence do you present. If you could request after Counselor Aedmund, he would put this whole affair to rights. And, I'll see to it attention is brought to your loyal and proficient service." Colwyn paused, hoping he'd mixed the proper amount of flattery with enough morsels of what could be truth to make it a palatable plea.

The doorman's mouth opened, then closed, then opened once more. "Follow me."

Light of step and spirit, he stuck close behind the blue velvet jacket of the servant. He'd made it. He'd made it in. The victory enhanced the beauty of the arched hall, exaggerating its opulence.

The doorman entered a smaller sitting room and motioned for Colwyn to do the same.

"You may wait here, M'lord. I'll have Counselor Aedmund notified of your presence."

Colwyn beamed at the man. "You will be well rewarded for your hospitality. Let it not be said that the Lord of Kensingham does not honor those who honor him."

As the doorman left the room, Colwyn shook his head at the whispered mutterings of the servant. "Kensingham. Kensingham?"

He collapsed into a finely upholstered chair. The strain of the past few days had been building, but he hadn't realized how much until he allowed himself to deflate into the embroidered cushions. He would see the king. He'd see him this day. He'd plead his case and renew his pledge of undying service. Surely Edward would see no ill will was meant by his absence at Bannockburn. Trouble would be averted, and he could return home—return home to see what kind of mischief Jessica Neale had gotten herself into.

Or worse yet, what kind of depravity Tarne might've instigated.

Chapter 12

Tarne plunged the dragon-hilted dagger toward Jessica Neale's bare neck. Inches from contact, his arm diverted off course as if parried. Great beads of sweat formed on his brow as he tried to force the knife once more. His hand was stayed each time and from every angle, as if an invisible shield cloaked her.

An uncontrollable shaking started at his shoulder and rippled down his arm. His fingers splayed and the dagger flew, skittering away to spin on the floor. He reached to retrieve it, then recoiled. His flesh singed from the glowing heat of the metal.

And still the girl slept.

What kind of sorcery was this? Something was at work here that would not be governed. He retraced his steps and locked the door, then set off at a dead-run to his round room. Whatever protected this girl would be no match for him when he returned.

He entered the murky darkness and flung his body to the floor, sliding across the inscribed star to the center of the circle. The moment his body lay spread-eagled, the engraved image took on an eerie incandescence. He couldn't move if he wanted to.

A whooshing wind arose, lifting his body along with it, levitating him into the air.

"Why?" He screeched to be heard. "Why was I denied her blood?"

Strike at the heart, not at the flesh. Persuade. Coerce. Deceive.

Wham—he slammed to the floor as suddenly as he'd been raised. Dazed, he lay a long, long time, semi-conscious.

As his senses returned, he thought on what had been revealed. Yes, indeed. Properly applied manipulation and coercion might prove to be all the more sweet than a quick kill. A cat toying with a mouse often honed the predator's skill in the exercise. He'd spent years sharpening his claws. Time now for hunting.

He'd woo her. Give her time to appreciate all his fine attributes. Show her his immense wealth and noble position. Every man, and especially each woman, had a price for which they could be bought. He'd simply find out what passions tempted Jessica of Neale and then offer them to her. She'd be his for the taking, thus ensuring that all power of the new realm would be his.

That settled, he stood on tentative legs, woozy as if he'd imbibed overmuch on ale. Leaving the crypt of his round room, he snagged the first servant he encountered. "Find my steward. Have him draw a bath and lay out my finest garments. Go."

He would primp and powder and preen until he looked his best. The woman would not be able to resist him.

•

A ruby-eyed dragon mesmerized Jess. The dagger's hilt had been crafted by a master, and though it wouldn't have been a design she'd choose, it still inspired appreciation and wonder—like wondering how it appeared on the middle of the floor when she woke up this morning.

The comforting sound of the slot sliding open interrupted her uneasiness. Perhaps either Tagg or Geoffrey could give her a reasonable explanation for the appearance of the knife.

She hurried to the door, intending to ask, but as she brought her face close to the opening, she jerked her head back. Her heart faltered and she gasped a sharp intake of breath that ached in her chest.

A singular shiny, black eye, round and moist, looked back at her with a stare so intense, it reached deep into her soul. The insatiable gaze locked onto hers, and she couldn't look away.

No wonder she hadn't heard any footsteps preceding the opening of the slot. There hadn't been any. But how could a bird possibly open a sliding door slot? Who else, or what else, waited on the other side?

As suddenly as the slot opened, it slammed shut. She tried to control the wild beating of her heart as she strained to hear retreating footsteps. Nothing. Not a sound. Not even flapping wings. Terror snaked around her spirit and squeezed. She gripped the dagger, waiting for the door to open.

She'd protect herself with the blade the best she could, but what did she really know of fighting with a knife? And against whom or what would she be fighting?

How long she crouched there, poised for defense, she couldn't say. Her breathing eventually resumed its normal cadence, though her inward level of fright hardly diminished. The door did not open, but there was no guarantee it wouldn't. Tarne would come eventually, and she was as helpless to stop his return as she was to keep the possessed raven from appearing.

What to do? Fear gripped her, and the heat of its monstrous breath made her face hot. Two options presented themselves, and she didn't like either—embrace or retreat. She shrank from the thought of living every minute in dread, but exactly how could she release it? Ready, set, quit being scared?

She pulled herself off the floor and walked the perimeter of the room as her mind swirled. In that eddy of thoughts, Geoffrey's words resurfaced. He'd said out loud what she'd been taught growing up—that God would hear and answer her prayers. She could sure use that belief right about now, but she'd extinguished her faith long ago. Yet Geoffrey's words blew like an incessant wind, coaxing to flame a hidden ember buried deep in the ashes of her heart.

She'd assumed God had ignored her request that day she'd pleaded for Dan, but maybe God had answered her after all—and it had been no. An answer she hadn't wanted to accept, but nonetheless an answer. What a stunning, simple thought.

Yet even in her denial, God had answered her few meager prayers since—her cry for help in the round room and again when she'd faced Tarne in the courtyard. She could ask God to be her protector and ease this fear of Tarne, but it might not flesh out as she would expect. Could she accept that?

She lifted her eyes to the stone ceiling, then knelt on the cold, stone floor. When the door slot next grated open, she flicked a wary look toward it, but noted that her heart didn't jump to her throat. She tensed alert, but overwhelming fear didn't wash over her. The most overpowering sensation she experienced was the tingling in her legs from the knees down as she stood. She must've been kneeling quite some time indeed.

"M'lady?"

Both feet asleep, she willed more than walked herself to the door. "Hi, Tagg."

His smudged face looked pained, from what little she could see. "What's the matter? Is it Old Black?"

"Oh m'um, it's Traline. She's got the ill-humors again, but this time it's worse. I fear for her. Without Sir Colwyn, she's the only one here who treats me right, besides you I mean. I can't lose her, I —" His lower lip trembled.

"Okay, sweetie, slow down. Take a breath. You're going to be a knight someday, remember? Knights remain calm even when facing danger. I'll try to help, but I'm not understanding. What exactly are ill-humors?"

"She hides herself in the dark of her chamber, curled up and moaning. When I enter, she clutches her head and wails at me to shut the door. She retches and retches till nothing is left. It's frightening."

Ill-humors? Sounded more like a nasty migraine. "I think I have an idea, but I'll need your help. Here's what I want you to do. Are you listening?"

His lip still quivered, but she had his attention. "Remember when I went with Colwyn to the river? I had my clothes and my waistpack with me. They got left behind when Tarne's guards came for us. You have to find my pack and bring it here. I know you can do this. And, if you find my clothes, I'd love to get out of this dress. Tagg?"

He turned and left with such speed, he forgot to shut the slot. And if that slot was big enough for a meal, an arm would surely fit.

Securing the fabric of her sleeve up around her triceps, she tried one angle after another until her forearm felt like rubber—thick and numb. If she could stretch an inch more, only an inch, closer and so near and—ouch!

A long wooden splinter jammed deep into her skin. She should get it out now before the pain reached her senses or a nasty infection set in. But how? No tweezers, no needle.

Only a dagger.

She gritted her teeth and worked until blood dripped a line down her arm. Unsteady from the sight, but pleased to remove the jagged piece of wood, she ripped a piece of fabric from the hem of the hated dress to stanch the flow.

What a stupid escapade. She should've thought before trying that lame escape attempt. Didn't people in the Middle Ages die from minor cuts and abrasions? As much as everything within her cried against the reality of her living in medieval times, the ache in her arm and the blood seeping from the wound could not be denied. She reprimanded herself and resolved to be more safety-oriented in the future. Future. Right, as if that concept meant anything anymore.

She waited a long time before Tagg returned. Maybe someone had pilfered what she'd been forced to leave behind.

"M'lady? Here I am. I searched well and long, but this 'twas all I found."

Her pouch came through looking weathered and worn, dirt-embedded and practically growing moss. It didn't matter though. The familiar sight and feeling filled her with warmth. In the waistpack, beneath the berry-stained nature journal, she removed an amber-colored pill bottle. No stranger to headaches, she fingered through the ibuprofen layered on top to the prescribed triangular pills at the bottom, then pushed one through to Tagg.

"Bring this to Traline along with a drink. Tell her she must swallow it. Try not to let a lot of light into her room. After a while, she will relax and then sleep."

"Are you sure M'lady?"

"Didn't we get Ol' Black put to rights again?"

At the mention of the horse, hope dawned on the boy's face followed by a look of awe. "Oh, M'lady, you must be an angel! You must be—"

"Stop it, Tagg. Ask Colwyn. He'll tell you I'm no angel. Now, are you going to help Traline, or stand there gawking at me?"

"Thank you. Thank you, M'lady."

"Get going."

The slot slid shut, leaving her no chance to mangle any other body parts in an escape attempt. It did, however, give her privacy to rip yet another strip of fabric from her dress to fashion a kind of sheath for the dagger. She'd conceal the weapon beneath her skirts, attached to her leg. Like some cold, strange growth, the touch of the knife would take a certain amount of getting used to, but it belonged to her now. This blade could prove to be her salvation, or the death of her. Either way, she'd be free of this place.

•

"Bull-headed! A more bull-headed man I've yet to meet. You will sit and hear what I have to say, or spend some time in the tower until you're more compliant."

"Counselor," Colwyn folded his arms against his chest and shifted his weight on firmly planted feet, "as I've said, I have come to court to see the king. On this matter, I will not yield."

An open-mouthed sigh punctuated the old man's weathered face. "Very well. I see you are determined to stand there and be obstinate, but allow my tired bones some rest."

Counselor Aedmund settled into the upholstered chair Colwyn had vacated the instant the older man had first entered the receiving room. If anyone could claim the respect and allegiance of Colwyn's heart, it would be this grizzled and gruff individual sitting before him. Over the years, Counselor Aedmund had come to represent the father figure that had been denied him since childhood. For reasons unknown, the counselor harbored a fondness for him and an intense dislike of Tarne. Colwyn never thought to question it for fear that this single source of acceptance might disappear.

"I've known you from birth, and what I have to say brings me no pleasure. You'll do well to heed my words." A grim frown blended into the man's wrinkled countenance.

"Go on."

"Here's the way of it then, and you can be very glad I caught sight of your sorry carcass before the king did. Edward has decreed swift and complete destruction of any and all nobles who did not give aid at Bannockburn. His pride is wounded. He's a lion who's taken a painful swipe. What little pretense of manhood he tried to cling to by winning that battle has been ripped from his frail grasp. He'll no longer listen to reason from me. I still hold the queen's ear, but the king, well …"

A raw nerve of fear rippled up Colwyn's back.

"Colwyn, you know I'm fond of you and always have been. 'Tis you who should have been first born. I can't say I'll miss that scoundrel of a brother of yours, but—"

In two strides, he bent to kneel at the counselor's side. "What are you saying?"

Watery eyes, pale from age, focused on his face. "I'm saying the king's men will march on Gallimore. Lord Tarne's life, and all that is his, will be taken. The king's mind is set and will not be swayed. On that day, Colwyn, you must choose between fealty and family."

"I have no love of family."

"I thought as much, but know this. Even in choosing fealty, there will be nothing left for you. You will be a commoner at best, an outcast at worst. Though your life be saved, your noble standing and all that entails will be forfeit."

Colwyn stood to pace the small room. Running his fingers through his thick hair, he attempted to straighten out the mad onslaught of what the near future might hold. No home to call his own, but neither a master to claim him either. A future outside the walls of Gallimore, without fighting other men's battles, without duty or obligation—without Tarne.

He returned to the counselor's side, then nodded with a slow, exaggerated movement. "I will be free, old man."

"Are we ever truly free, my boy? What value does freedom hold if your soul is wrapped in chains? You and I have lived our lives as nobles, and though it's brought us certain comfort, I daresay it's not brought us peace."

Colwyn jerked his gaze to pierce through the old man's cloudy eyes. "Peace? You might as well speak to me of love. I know not the meaning of either."

The counselor raised his leathery hand to rest with surprising lightness on Colwyn's head. "I see much in you that is reminiscent of me. Learn from my errors, boy. Do not turn your back on love when it is offered to you, and when the way of peace is revealed, seek it with all your strength. Do not allow your pride to hinder you."

Had anyone else dared to utter such words to him, he would've flattened them on his way out of the room. Instead, he tucked the wisdom away, unwilling to consider it at the moment.

"Leave now. Do not return home nor wait for the day of attack. Find a far-off country. Start a new life."

"And you?"

"Me?" The wizened counselor snorted his amusement. "I'm too old to heed my own advice. And, as I've said, the queen's ear is still mine. I've a feeling that therein lies the hope of England. God be with you, my boy."

"Thank you, Counselor. I owe you much."

"You owe me nothing. Now get your ugly backside out of here."

A rare smile tugged at Colwyn's mouth. "You know, old man, you're nearly as ornery as I."

"Coming from you, I shall take that as a compliment. Now go, and take care. Godspeed my boy, or should I say, Lord Kensingham?"

Colwyn smirked at the jibe and rose to his feet, anxious to put into action the Counselor's suggestion. He opened the door and took great care to assess the corridor in both directions. Satisfied, he marched as if on an important errand toward the grand doors leading out of the palace.

All the while he monitored his route from palace to livery, his mind jumped from plan to plan. Steal into Gallimore, take as much gold as he and his page could carry, and leave in the dark of night. Nay. Why even bother with the trip? Send Faulk back while he arranged passage on a ship. Have Faulk and the boy meet him with as much gold as they could manage. Nay. Not likely to succeed. They had no access to his brother's wealth, and Colwyn had precious little stored away in his chambers.

He could simply leave. Now. Leave behind everything and earn his own keep. Make his own way. No ties to the past. No ties to anything. The thought of freedom intoxicated like a sweet, heady wine, but a bitter aftertaste lingered at the back of his mind. What? What nagged him? As he walked his horse out of the royal stables and onto the graveled road leading to the gates of the palace, he pondered over the elusive dark cloud looming over the horizon of the freedom that he intended to pursue.

He rode into the crowded streets and peasants parted to avoid his mare's lively step. So many people, but none gave him more than a cursory glance. That's when he knew.

He'd be lonely. He'd hardly acknowledged that emotion before until someone had pointed it out to him. He came to a dead stop the moment he remembered who that someone had been.

Jess.

A low growl rumbled in his chest. She plagued him even here in London. What a bother! Could he leave the country knowing he'd locked her up for his brother to abuse? And what would happen to her once the king's men arrived? He knew her to be far from defenseless but the odds were stacked high against her, and it'd been by his own hand. He'd have to go back and release the little wild cat so she'd at least stand a fighting chance.

Having decided that much, he set his mare at a clipped pace to track down Faulk. He'd observed Faulk's patterned behavior of vacating the Red Glove for the better part of the day ... and night. His friend had often shown a penchant for riverside pubs, so that's where he began. Lusty drinking songs and boisterous men reeling in their revelry were all that he found. Not one of them resembled Faulk.

Until long after sunset, he searched from pub to pub. Catcalls from women of the night added to the city's background noises tickling his ears. He cast them a brief look, but their wares bulging above low-cut bodices did not bring even a tingle of enticement. Only one woman occupied his mind while he searched.

All the bleary-eyed, ale-sodden men began to look the same from inn to inn. Each door he opened let out a blast of lewd lyrics and the stink of unwashed bodies until he despaired of ever finding Faulk. Could he have called it an evening already?

Heading back to the Red Glove Inn, he went over again and again a plan that would be feasible. Set the girl loose, then steal away with what he and the page could take. That could work. He'd leave for Gallimore this very night.

Dim yellow light barely escaped the sooty windows of the Inn. He dismounted and tethered up his horse near the door, then pushed against the slab of weathered wood. It swung open with surprising ease, leaving him nose to nose with Faulk. The odor of stale spirits hung over him like a brewing cloud.

"I've been looking for you, Faulk. We leave tonight."

"Aye, Sir." And with that, his friend fell forward onto Colwyn in a drunken stupor.

The weight of Faulk was no small matter, especially a limp Faulk. Colwyn set his teeth against the strain, then heaved and dragged the drunken man over to a solid bench where he could sleep it off. Faulk would be in no condition to ride tonight, but that didn't have to stop him.

"Innkeeper!" Colwyn rubbed his fingers against his tired eyes. It'd been a long day. Maybe he should wait until morning. He mulled the idea over until the proprietor came to answer his call.

"Aye, Sir. What'll ye be needin'?"

"I'll be needing my account settled at once. I leave tonight."

"At this hour, Sir? I daresay the roads are not safe. And your friend there—" The little man pointed an accusing finger toward Faulk. "Is in no condition to ride."

Colwyn tapered his eyes to slits in challenge. "Are you saying I'm not able to protect myself?"

"Oh, no—oh, never, Sir. No, no, I'd not say such a thing, not me." He began to wring his hands much the way squirrels fondle acorns. "At once, Sir. I'll figure the cost for you at once."

As the innkeeper scurried away, Colwyn mounted the steps to his tiny room. It didn't take long to roll up his few belongings and shrug on a warmer surcoat. He left the room as he'd found it—a single bed and a worn bench that could serve as chair or table.

Faulk snored from the corner and Colwyn nudged him with a shove. No response. Even the snoring stopped. It would be a long while before Faulk caught up with him.

"Innkeeper!" He didn't even try to hide his impatience.

The nervous little man came immediately but ducked his head as he apologized, "I'm still figuring, Sir. Many pardons, but a moment more is all I require."

Colwyn scowled as he untied a small leather pouch secured at his waist. With a flick of his wrist, he let it fly. "That should be all you require, and then some. As soon as my man awakes, see that he's provisioned with two days food for each of us, then send him after me."

He marched out the door to the jabbering sound of the innkeeper spouting his gratitude and undying service. Relieved to shake the dust of London from his feet, he mounted his horse. Throngs of people no longer crowded the street, and none but evil-doers of the night darted in and out of shadows. He made good time in reaching the city gates.

"I wish to pass," he shouted at the gatekeeper using his most authoritative voice.

"Who hails and what be you about?" A guard twice his size came at his call. He wondered at where such a mammoth of a man might've been reared.

"I am Sir Colwyn Haukswyrth, Knight of Gallimore Castle, brother to Lord Tarne Haukswyrth who is Earl. I am about royal business and expect not to answer to you."

"'Tis no fitting hour to be outside the safety of the gates, Sir. Be your business so pressing as to risk your life?"

"'Tis not your concern but mine."

Colwyn watched as the big man signaled his cohorts stationed as lookouts atop the gatehouse. They verified no one waited in ambush outside the city gates to shove their way in. At the guards' approval, the huge soldier released the lock of the smaller door in the gate, and Colwyn urged his mount through.

Trading the stench of the city for the rush of fresh, damp evening air gave him a surge of energy. Even the overcast sky obscuring the moon could not darken his spirit. He hadn't felt this good since … dare he remember? It'd been so long ago. Saris, Traline's older sister, had been the only light he'd known in all his dark days. She'd been dead nigh on ten years now.

Kek-kek-kek. A sparrowhawk jabbered, but Colwyn shoved aside the sound, choosing instead to focus on a new life far away. He would take the counselor's advice. A small glimmer of hope built inside him. No more rejection from his mother. No more humiliation from Tarne. Life could be very good. He might even learn how to smile again. He'd free Jessica Neale, and then he'd free himself.

Kek-kek-kek. The annoying bird called again. Closer. Louder. But nay, sparrowhawks do not call in the dead of night.

A sharp, burning jab stung his back. He reached to rub at it, but his hand encountered the stickiness of blood and the shaft of a protruding arrow.

Highwaymen! If he'd been on Old Black, no doubt he could outrun them, but this horse was new to him and untried.

Digging in his heels, the horse bolted, but Colwyn did not.

The next arrow had found its mark.

Chapter 13

After releasing the heavy draw bar, Tarne shoved open the door and strode through the opening into the center of the tower cell. He'd give the girl full opportunity to view his magnificence, for he'd taken great pains in his choice of attire.

The upper half of his powdery blue tunic cut closely to his figure, flaring out to give a wide effect at the skirting. Sleeves of fawn colored silk buttoned tightly from elbow to wrist, which displayed quite handsomely the fine, white flesh of his hands. Pink woven hose, seamed back and front, clung to his legs, revealing every muscle. He'd seen to each detail, large and small, right down to the forking and curling of his short beard.

Jess sat on the edge of the bed frame wearing a cool look of apprehension. She didn't appear impressed.

"M'lady, I've come to release you."

She got to her feet, but she didn't take a step toward him or the door. "Why?"

Arrogant wench. He offered her freedom, yet she thought to question it? He'd see her broken, that's what. He'd see her broken and—*persuade, coerce, deceive.*

Remembering his directive, he used his most charming intonation. "I am shamed at my poor treatment of a lady such as yourself. I most humbly beg for your forgiveness and for the opportunity to make amends."

"Huh."

A stranger to self-control, he bit his lip until the saltiness of blood soothed him. "My dear, I am pained indeed to realize what monstrous behavior I've demonstrated. I've allowed you to suffer behind this locked door and have taken advantage of your good graces."

"Oh really? That's interesting, because I'm pretty sure that last time we spoke, it wasn't grace that you championed as my hallmark. I believe the words you used were 'conniving witch woman.' Have you changed your mind about me then?" She crossed her arms and set her chin.

How could he possibly carry this out? Woo this creature? He'd sooner spawn with the devil himself. *Nay, don't think of it. Just do it.*

He bent to one knee and bowed his head. "I am a changed man. Please forgive me, my lady."

For once, she held her tongue.

He stood, and in doing so, offered his hand. "I've had a fresh chamber prepared for you with warm bath and new garments. Would you consider dining with me this eve?"

She narrowed her eyes and drew back. "I'm guessing Colwyn has returned, and you've found out I really am innocent of all you've accused me. Is that the news he brought?"

"Nay, M'lady." He let his arm drop back to his side, seething at her impertinence. Nonetheless, he allowed nothing but pleasantry to shine from his face as he continued. "Colwyn's not yet returned. I've simply come to my senses of what a crime I've committed in keeping you here against your will."

"Are you saying I'm free to leave?"

"Of course."

She paused and frowned in deep thought. "I can walk out the door, at any time, without you or anyone else stopping me?"

"You have my word."

"Really?"

"Truly."

"And if I choose to leave now?"

She might think leaving the gates of Gallimore meant her liberty, but his reach extended farther than she could imagine. After stepping aside to let her pass if she chose, he bent from the waist. The act of deference almost gagged him, but at least she didn't bolt out the door.

He straightened. She hadn't moved a bit. "Will you allow me to show you to your new quarters?"

Her hesitation prompted him to wonder what war waged inside her pretty head. At last she nodded assent, but did not speak. The conquest was not yet over, but this battle belonged to him.

He led her from the barren cell and down the turret stairs. As they wound through several corridors, he listened to detect if she continued to follow or attempted to leave the castle. Her footfall remained steady, though at a distance.

Their journey ended outside an open door of one of the more elaborate bed chambers on the east wing. "I hope this will make up in some small way for the dismal surroundings you've endured."

She asked nothing though her brow raised in question. He let her pass into the elegant room that contained every accoutrement a woman could want. Careful to avoid making her feel skittish, he remained at the door.

Her eyes darted from the brocaded bed curtains to the ivory inlaid vanity covered with cut glass bottles and various cosmetics, and finally rested with longing on the wooden tub filled with steaming, herb-scented water.

"It is pleasing, is it not? All this room holds and more is yours. Refresh yourself. I'll see that a serving girl meets your every need before you can think to ask her. I shall receive you, at your convenience of course, in my antechamber for a quiet dinner, away from the coarse loudness of Great Hall. Would that suit you, M'lady?"

Even from across the room, he heard the growl of her stomach at the mention of dinner and noticed she struggled to draw her eyes away from the bath. His lips parted in a slow smile as he watched temptation whisper in her ear. He'd give her all the time she needed to let the appeal of creature comforts tantalize her.

She scratched long and hard at a spot behind her ear, and then turned to him. "This doesn't mean I trust you, but I do appreciate the amends you're trying to make. I suppose I could stay one more night, but I'll most likely leave in the morning."

Instinct told him she waited for him to object. He didn't.

"And, I'll have dinner with you, but not alone. I'd prefer if the guard Geoffrey were in the room."

His smile tugged up to his ears. "As you wish, M'lady. Any accommodations within my power are at your disposal. I will have Geoffrey posted at my door to await your arrival, if that be your desire. Now please, partake of that which has been prepared for you."

He took care to close the door with a gentle touch, not wanting to interrupt her confused state of mind. Let her wonder at his miraculous change in manner. A warm bath, clean garments, and a hot meal might be enough to soften her toward him. If not, 'twould be a small matter to send the guard Geoffrey away and use more persuasive means. If the power of the new realm, boundless wealth, and expanded lands lay wrapped within Jessica Neale, he'd uncover her part in it and snatch it away for himself. An enjoyable prospect indeed.

•

Jess relaxed on the squat stool in the wooden tub until a shiver reminded her that the water had long since cooled. She shrunk from leaving the comfort of the bath, but soon it would be too chilly.

A young serving girl named Anne offered drying cloths at her movement, and she wrapped herself snugly. Anne could hardly have been more than a teen with her pimply complexion and deferring personality, although her reserve might be attributed to her station. Nevertheless, she had a certain bubbly quality that could not quite be contained and a perky sparkle to her blue eyes.

"I'll see to your dressing now, M'lady, if it pleases you."

No, it didn't really please her, but she'd never manage getting a dress on by herself, and who knew where her jeans and tee-shirt were. She remembered the layers and intricacies the last time Traline had dressed her. Which reminded her, she really should check on Traline. "All right, let's get this over with."

The undergown smelled of lavender, an improvement over the garments she'd worn for nearly two weeks. While the upper half didn't lace up as tightly as before, still the softness of the fabric fit well against her curves. She appreciated the overdress to keep Tarne's prying eyes from leering at her, but the armholes were so wide and long, it didn't completely hide her shape. The rich color of the gown reminded her of her favorite crayon in a new box of Crayolas—midnight blue.

"I'll see what I can do for your hair, M'lady, if you'll sit over here." Anne indicated the padded stool in front of the vanity. Jess sat and let the girl begin trying to run a comb through her unruly locks. Anne leaned closer and the comb parted here and there, tickling the base of her neck and ears.

"Oh, M'lady, please don't think me too forward, but I do know of methods for ridding lice other than shearing your head."

She tensed with the affirmation of what had been a creepy crawly suspicion of hers up until now. Lice? She swallowed what she wanted to scream, and instead met Anne's eye in the polished metal looking glass. "Please, do whatever it takes."

The girl rummaged through bottles on the table top and uncorked a squat, amber container. As she massaged the contents into Jess's scalp, the aroma of crushed olives filled the room to blend with the leftover rose scent from the bath.

The hearty scrubbing relieved any remaining stress not soaked away by the bath, save one. Tarne. The sudden change in his behavior was unexplainable. True, she had turned her fear and protection over to God, but a miracle of such proportion? And so quickly? Astounding. Had the Israelites felt the same way when walking between the rolled up walls of the Red Sea?

"There, M'lady. We'll do this each day and soon your hair will be put to rights. Now for a head covering."

Anne retrieved from the wardrobe some kind of gaudy, over-sized hat with at least two full yards of gossamer material attached. Just looking at it gave Jess a headache. She stood, and made a hasty move toward the door. "That's okay. I'll skip the head thing. I think I'll run and check on Traline now."

Protests followed her out the door, but she wouldn't turn back. She'd put up with the poofy dress, nothing more. Now which way to go?

To the right, the hall dead-ended at a door. She decided on going left, and reward came three-fourths of the way down where the main stairs intersected the corridor. Descending two flights, she stepped into the foyer which Great Hall adjoined. She went down one more set of stairs to the front doors, hiking her skirts to travel the last set of steps. Her slippered feet finally reached the soil of the inner courtyard. Outside, the warm air of early evening smelled sweet and fresh.

She scoped the grounds and saw pretty much the same scene as the first day she'd arrived. Random guards, a servant or two carrying out some mundane task, horses tethered near a water barrel. She picked her way along the edge of the courtyard toward the servants' quarters.

A rumbling thunder of hooves soon roared past and she stopped her mission to see what the commotion might be about. The man she'd seen before with Colwyn halted his horse at the foot of the castle stairs. Was it Frank? Or Hulk? Or—

"Lend some muscle!" The stocky man's shout reverberated in the courtyard as he dismounted. Another body yet remained on the lathered horse, draped in a limp heap, and a vague familiarity called to her from the slack shape.

"What is this?" The nasal-pitched voice of Tarne carried on the air. He stood at the top of the stair, disdain written on his features. "Highwaymen, M'lord, outside of London. They got the better of Sir Colwyn. He'd been bested before I got to him. I fear for his life. I shall fetch a physician straightaway."

"Bring him to his quarters," Tarne said, "but there'll be no physician. Either he lives or dies by his own merit."

A low murmur went through the crowd of gathered men, but not one dared defy the earl's orders. In compliance, they reached to retrieve Colwyn's body.

The pathetic group of grown men inspired a raging contempt to bubble up inside of Jess. In her short time here, she'd witnessed many selfish acts—the harsh treatment of Tagg, the rude actions toward herself, even Colwyn's verbal admission of caring only about himself—but no one deserved to be laid out to die.

Not even Colwyn.

Why did no one stand up to Tarne? How could these people stumble through life allowing injustice to reign, turning a blind eye and deaf ear to the needs of their fellow human beings? What an ignorant lot of men, fearful and selfish.

Sickened, she turned her face away and saw the open gates leading to the outer bailey—leading to freedom. A sudden rush of yearning to leave these horrible people behind welled within her. She could leave, like Colwyn had left her. Go, and never give this place a second thought.

But if she walked away, she'd be no better than those men she despised.

Could she live with herself knowing she'd willfully turned her back on someone, even someone as undeserving as Colwyn? After all, it'd been Colwyn who'd locked her up. And Colwyn who'd ... released her from the stocks hours before her hand would've met the chopping block. Colwyn who'd urged her to barricade her door to protect herself. Colwyn, who'd had many a chance to force himself on her, but for the most part, played the gentleman. Yes, he aggravated her, but that hardly constituted a death sentence.

Deep within, a layer below logic, she knew the right choice. As much as she ached to escape this fairy-tale-run-amok, a gut-feeling that something bigger, something beyond her frail humanity, cried out for compassion even when undeserved. Or perhaps, especially when undeserved.

A string of curses from two guards within earshot interrupted her mental debate. "He's as good as dead. That wound will take him all right. 'Tis a shame, that's what. Sir Colwyn knew how to treat his men right."

The words bulls-eyed her conscience. Colwyn should be treated right himself, and if nobody else would see to it, then it would be up to her.

She cast one last glance at the gate, then set a resolute course back across the courtyard to the castle. Up the stairs and through the door, the bleak shadows of monotone gray swallowed all color and light as she went.

Tarne stood in the foyer, arms folded, almost as if he expected her. "Are you quite ready now to accept my hospitality? I see you are—refreshed."

His eyes traveled the curves her dress accentuated and rested on her bodice, his tongue darting out past thin lips. Had she made the right choice? "Yes, I am, but I think you should allow a doctor to tend to Colwyn first."

"Really?" He raised his hand to toy with the curl of his beard. "And of what concern is the welfare of my brother to you?"

"The same concern I would show for any other injured person."

He took a step closer. "Even for myself?"

She paused. Could she answer that honestly?

"Yes, even for you." She nearly choked on the taste of those words.

"How very interesting. You are quite the puzzle, Lady Neale. And should I refuse to send for a physician?"

Exactly. What could she do about it if he refused? Not much. She raised her eyes to his and spoke with much more bravado than she felt. "If you refuse, I'll look after him myself."

"In essence—" He paused for dramatic effect as if that would change her mind. "What you are saying is that whether I send for the physician or not, you will be staying at Gallimore."

Her stomach roiled. She hated being backed into a corner. "Yes, I suppose that's what I'm saying."

To make matters worse, he laughed at her. A gurgly, chirpy sort of laughter that smacked of one who'd never truly felt an honest expression of mirth in his life. "Oh, Lady Neale, if nothing else, you are entertaining. I enjoy diversion, and you provide me with so much. Go and use your healing powers, if indeed you have any. But know this, I await you in my antechamber. Understood?"

Her gut heaved at the thought, but nothing worthwhile came without a price. She hadn't realized that being a good Samaritan would be this costly. "Yes, I understand."

"Good. Then allow me to escort you to your invalid."

"No, really," she stalled. "I'm sure I can find Colwyn's quarters. I wouldn't want to trouble you."

"I insist. That's a command, not a suggestion." He held out one of his stick-figure arms for her to claim.

She closed her eyes for a moment to draw on some inner strength she hoped to discover, then reached out her hand to rest as lightly as possible on his arm. The fabric beneath her fingers spoke of the coolness of death. He led her up one flight of steps and down a dim corridor, lit sporadically by flickering wall sconces. The second Tarne's feet stopped before a closed door, she removed her hand and exhaled. She hadn't realized she'd been holding her breath most of the way.

"You may see to Colwyn, but do not dally overlong. Your chamber is directly up one level, only a door away from my own at the end of the hall. I've had Geoffrey summoned and he'll attend us while we dine. If you like, we can discuss your request for a physician."

Her heart pounded in warning as he leaned closer. His mouth brushed against her ear as he whispered, "I can always be persuaded."

And then he was gone, his legs carrying him spider-like down the hall.

She shuddered at the queasiness he left behind and wiped at the spot he'd defiled. Maybe her noble idea of returning to Gallimore hadn't been so wise. *Lord, why am I here?* The short prayer brought comfort, until an answer followed.

Love him.

Her blood ran cold. A jerk of her head from side to side revealed nothing but empty corridor. Who said that? It'd been so clear— love him. Love who? Tarne? Colwyn? She recoiled at the thought of loving either of them. Wow. She'd heard of stress causing freak reactions in some people but this? Hearing voices? Sure, why not. She'd heard voices in the round room, and if she was back in the fourteenth century, why would hearing voices in an empty hallway be so strange?

She squared her shoulders, took a deep breath and entered the lair of the knight of Gallimore. Inside a rather Spartan antechamber, she paused. The sound of weeping issued from an open door across the room.

She hurried and peered in at a scene that wrenched her heart. Rays of dying sunlight shone through slotted windows and touched gently on the page crying bitterly at his master's bedside.

Unwilling to disturb his grief, she took a stealthy step behind him to get a better look at Colwyn. One glance and she understood why the boy cried. The knight's proud cheekbones and jawline were now a disturbing shade of mottled purple, puffed and contorted. One eye, the green of which had startled her the first day she'd met him, swelled in alarming degree—distorted by angry red flesh. A jagged crust of dried blood mingled with the growth of unshaven beard along his chin. The severe beating left him almost unrecognizable.

"Oh, my." Her words came out shaken and shivery.

Tagg turned and plowed into her. Without considering, she held him close, murmuring consolation. His thin body shook as his sobbing soaked her gown.

What had she gotten herself into? Basic first aid seemed a far cry from what this man needed, yet those were all the skills she had to offer. What had made her think she could possibly help in the first place? What an idiot. She should've left this place behind when she'd had the chance.

Just then, a tear-streaked face looked up at her with all the earnestness a ten-year-old boy could possess. "You'll help him, won't you M'lady? Like you helped Old Black and Traline?"

His pleading eyes held onto hers, willing her to answer.

"Yes, Tagg," she heard herself say. "Of course. We'll help him together. You and me. We'll help your master get better."

She hoped she'd convinced him. As for herself, she didn't believe a word of it. Setting Tagg aside, she knelt at Colwyn's bedside, which took quite some doing in the full fabric of her skirts. "Colwyn?"

She reached out and brushed back the hair matted on his forehead. The heat of his skin burned against hers. She'd never felt such a fever before.

Sinking back on her heels, she blinked away a pool of unshed tears, and her stomach clenched into a tight ball. As much as she'd disagreed and argued and fought with this man, she didn't want him to die. His had been the first face she'd seen in this foreign place, and she was loathe to let it go. "Oh, Colwyn."

He needed a doctor, and he needed one now. Her mind made up, she stood to leave.

Through sniffles, Tagg's alarmed voice cried out, "Where are you going, M'lady?"

"Don't worry, Tagg. I'm going to have Tarne send for a physician."

•

Rushing wind or relentless waterfall? White noise droned on and on, *shhh, shhh.* Whooshing, unending, eternal. Colwyn longed to feel a wet spray or bathe in a cool breeze, but flames consumed him. Heat, like the blast of a blacksmith's furnace, radiated and throbbed. Had he ever been so hot in all his life? If fire indeed raged around him, no light accompanied it. He floated somewhere in a sea of voidless black, skimming the bottom of an ocean of night, unable to rise to the surface. He could let go and sink. The miry depths would accept his weight, but once entombed, would never let him go. It would be easy. A release. Permanent.

Colwyn. Beyond the shushing roar, almost imperceptible, someone called to him. His name was a bird dancing from leaf to leaf in the treetops beyond where he could reach. It hovered on wings of love and comfort. He knew the voice, but from where? And how?

Though the blackness held him firm, he knew a choice lay before him. A path must be chosen. Down or up, which direction should he take?

The noise stopped, leaving behind a fragile silence—one that might shatter to sharp-edged particles at the slightest provocation. It hurt the ears. He wanted it to end, to return to the constant gusty whine.

A whisper. Nay, a shout. Nay. Nothing at all but words shifting shape in the darkness.

Do not turn your back on love when it's offered to you.

Where was the offering? Where was the love?

Oh, Colwyn.

The one speaking his name would surely know. He'd seek the owner of that voice and learn of things he'd never understood.

Later. For now, he could do nothing but tread the dark waters of oblivion.

Chapter 14

Tarne drained his fourth goblet of wine, enjoying the ethereal aura it left on his tongue. Setting the chalice to rest on the feast laden table, the swish of a gown came from the doorway, and he looked up. The graceful form of Jessica Neale edged toward him and he stood to greet her, steadying himself with a hand on his chair. Had it been four cups, or five?

"M'lady, you are resplended, resplendive, ah, you are radiant. Come closer, my dear, and allow me to greet you properly."

"Look, Tarne, I really need to talk to you about—"

"Nay, nay." He shook his head side to side and decided not to do that again lest he lose his balance. "I'll not hear a word 'til proper decorum has been carried out."

He reached for her hand and brought her palm to his lips. His tongue explored the saltiness of her skin. Her soft warmth tingled through him as the five cups of wine had, or was it six?

She snatched her hand from his as if she'd touched a live coal.

Tarne laughed. "You are a great beauty, Jessica of Neale. Sit at my side, for I would feed you with my own hand if you would allow."

"We don't have time for this!" She took a step back but didn't run away. "Don't you understand your brother is dying? He's burning up with fever. He needs a doctor, right now, and—"

He maneuvered himself to within inches of her, stopping her words with his finger against her lips. "I am much more apt to be agreeable if you will but humor me, M'lady."

She turned her head from him, glancing toward the door. At the opportunity, he let his hand stroke against the soft curve of her bare neck, to her shoulder, then lower—

She jerked from his touch. "Why is Geoffrey not in the room

with us?"

"He is posted outside the door, my dear, guarding and ever vigilant. Be assured no harm will befall us in here with his watchful eye out there. Shall we sit?"

He enjoyed watching her fine, white teeth nibble at her lower lip as she stared at the chairs. Before night's end, he'd enjoy his share of nibbling those lips as well, and then some.

"Fine," she said at last.

He offered her a high-backed chair set close to his own. She sat on the farthest edge of the seat. No matter. If she wanted a physician badly enough, she'd relent and be in his arms shortly.

Seating himself, he proceeded to fill her goblet, then lifted it to her mouth. She hesitated at first, then sipped, fixing her eyes on him as a doe might on a predator. After she drew her head back, he brought the cup to his own lips, finishing what she'd left.

"Tarne, can I— "

"Nay, do not call me such. I would have you call me M'lord, for it would sound so delicious rolling off your pretty tongue."

She pressed her lips together, defiance lighting her eyes, and stood.

"You did want me to send for a physician, did you not, my dear? Do, let's discuss."

He watched her breasts rise and fall with a great inhale and exhale before she resettled herself in the chair.

"All right, fine, M'lord. I'll stay. We'll discuss." She smiled sweetly at him. "Why don't you refill my glass, and yours, and we'll have a nice little chat together."

Ahh, sweet vanquish. He twisted his mouth into a smile to match the curl of his moustache.

"Your beauty is only surpassed by your wisdom, my dear." As he raised the bottle to the chalice, a pool of the purple vintage spread out to stain the white linen table cloth.

"M'lord, Colwyn needs a doctor right away. Tonight. Maybe you didn't realize how bad off he is, but I'm sure your mother would agree—"

Her words went on, but Tarne lost track of them, picturing the delightful look of horror that would cross the lady's innocent face if he should chance to tell her of his mother's recent death. A bubbly giggle escaped him, which made it even more hilarious, and he chortled until the world around him swirled.

"My mother is, ah, indisposed for a time. We won't need to be bothering her with such trifles. I'm sure you and I can come up with a suitable agreement concerning Colwyn's care." He snaked his arm behind her shoulders, pulling her close to him. With his other hand, he reached up to caress her cheek. Her heady smell of lavender filled his nostrils. He leaned closer, nuzzling his face against the curve of her neck, and let his hand roam lower. His breeches, his tunic, nay all his garments suddenly felt much too constrictive, and he fumbled to loosen the belt at his waist.

"Please," she whispered.

"M'lord," he commanded, running his tongue along the length of her neck.

She tensed and pulled away. "Please ... M'lord."

"Ahh, yes, my dear. Beg me some more."

•

"More! I must have more." Faulk dismissed the soldiers who'd set down sloshing buckets of water in Colwyn's antechamber. He tumbled a pile of clean rags into the wooden vessels, then quickly wrung them out. Loading up an armful, he carried the heap of cold material into Colwyn's bed chamber.

"Remove the old wraps, boy."

Tagg pulled away the damp cloths surrounding Colwyn's body, and Faulk replaced them with the fresh, cool rags. As soon as they touched Colwyn's skin, the fabric heated through, but the first shock of coolness would lessen the fever raging through his captain.

The fever had set in halfway between London and Gallimore. Faulk had sought to outrun it by getting Colwyn to the castle for healing care, but time had run out—just as surely as time would run out for Colwyn if his fever didn't break soon.

Cloths in place, Faulk stomped out to the antechamber and dropped to the one small bench against a wall. He scrubbed at his face, willing himself to stay awake. The ride had been torturous and he'd hoped to find some relief upon reaching Gallimore, but no one seemed to care. Only the sniffling page dared help him after the earl's refusal to send for a doctor. A pox on Tarne. A curse on him. Resting his head against the stone wall, he let his eyes close. A soldier of many years, he'd learned long ago to rest without sleeping. But this time, after so long on the road, his senses dulled.

He jarred awake when someone entered the room, then shot to his feet, battle ready. "Halt!"

The authority of his command, or perhaps the sharp edge to his voice, caused the intruder to stop. There stood the woman over whom Colwyn had fretted and troubled many a time. He crossed his arms against his chest, feet planted, unsure what to think. The short doze had left a bit of a fog in its wake. "What seek you here, M'lady?"

"I came to see Colwyn."

She sounded genuine enough, but he'd take care not to let her vex him as thoroughly as she had his captain. "For what purpose?"

"I came to see how he's doing."

"You'll see more of him than you might wish to if you continue your course. I've stripped him, and he lies bare with wet cloths to cool the fever."

The pink of her cheeks deepened. "Oh, uh, good. Good thinking. Hopefully that will hold him over until Geoffrey gets back with the doctor."

"But Lord Tarne said—"

"I know what he said. He's since changed his mind."

"What say you?" He let his bushy eyebrows merge together. "The Earl's not one to take back what he's declared publicly, and I heard him vow there'll be no physician."

"I told you. He changed his mind."

"But what would've influenced him to—" His words trailed off as he searched her face. Fully awake now, he noticed much more than he'd seen before. Her hair, half pinned up, but half sprung loose and askew as if someone had taken rough hold of it. Red marks, raised and angry, finger-length, wrapped part way around the bare skin of her neck. Bare also, her shoulder, gown ripped and hanging. Her lips puffy and chafed, as if someone forced—

He nodded in sudden understanding. "'Twas your doing. You persuaded Lord Tarne, and I daresay 'twas no easy task." What she'd endured by the hands of Tarne for the sake of Colwyn, Faulk could only imagine. A hearty respect for the woman replaced his wariness.

He unfolded his arms and stepped aside, offering her the bench. "'Twill be some time before a physician can be fetched, and there's naught more we can do for M'lord until then. Sit ye down,

M'lady."

"Thanks, but no. I think I'll go change into something a little less, uh, ragged, and then I'll come back and relieve you. You look like you could use some rest."

He let a wry grin spread across his face. "You speak truth, M'lady."

She smiled back at him, and a wave of warmth flushed through him. No wonder his captain was so taken with this woman.

She walked to the door, but paused before passing out of sight. "You know, Faulk, you are wrong about one thing."

"What is that, M'lady?"

"There is something more we can do for Colwyn."

He angled his head. More? What more could he possibly do besides cool rags? "What is it, M'lady, for I swear I would do all that I could for my captain."

As if daring him, she tipped her pert little chin and stared him down before she answered.

"Pray."

•

Jess's head bobbed from fatigue. The past three days she'd slept little and eaten even less. Now she sat at the quiet of Colwyn's bedside, letting the candle's flame mesmerize her into contemplation with its dance of orange and yellow.

It had made her ill to grovel before Tarne, first for a physician, and then for the continuance of Colwyn's care. Like a vulture with raw meat, Tarne enjoyed her begging. She endured his advances until her teeth ground into a permanently clenched position whenever she needed to be with him. Thankfully, she'd discovered that the best way to keep Tarne at arm's length was to finagle him into drinking too much wine. A drunk Tarne was a sleepy Tarne. She'd kept him from going too far, but how much longer she could keep this up worried her.

After all this effort, she hoped it would be worth it. Watching the display of fourteenth century medicine left her in doubt. When the doctor had finally arrived at Colwyn's bedside, his medical procedures sent her running out to the antechamber to vomit in the corner.

He'd used maggots. A large pouchful of fat, glistening white maggots applied directly to the infected arrow-wound on Colwyn's back. She could not bring herself to observe their miracle-working power, but she had to admit that when they'd been removed, the affected flesh appeared much improved.

Not that Colwyn had regained consciousness. That worried her as well. The fever had long since broken, but still he did not wake up. She spent much time praying for him to live, surprising even herself at the fervency for which she asked God to spare his life. She put as much passion into her pleas as she had when she'd begged for Dan's life. But this time, she noted a difference. She prayed honestly for the man to live for his sake alone, and not for the sake of her being left behind.

"M'lady?"

She pulled away from her thoughts and the hypnotizing candle flame. "Hey, Tagg."

"'Tis Lord Tarne. He asks for you in Great Hall."

How long could she keep this up, indeed? She exhaled long and slow. "Okay. Isn't Traline supposed to have the next watch?"

"Aye, m'um."

"Could you let her know to come now? I don't think we should leave Colwyn alone yet."

"Aye."

She smiled at the retreating boy. What a gem. Eager to please. Always willing. A rare find in a boy his age.

When she turned back to look at Colwyn, her smile froze. He lay, not moving, but eyes wide-open and staring at her.

"Colwyn?"

She went to his side in a heartbeat. Yes, he still breathed, but the terrible glassy gaze would not let her go.

"Leave." His words were not more than a whisper. "Take—"

She gathered her skirt, leaning over him, and rested her fingers on his brow. "Don't talk. Not now. It's okay, Colwyn, we're taking care of you."

His eyes burned into hers, but not from fever, from something more. She drew as near as she dared, closer than her comfort zone normally allowed, as he struggled to rise.

"Leave this place. Take—" The effort of speaking drained his face of color.

"What? Leave for where? Take what?"

Determination sent his breaths out in shallow puffs against her cheek as she leaned her ear toward his lips.

"Go now. Take my—"

The strain was too much. His body went limp beneath her as unconsciousness claimed him.

"M'lady? Is everything a'right?" Traline asked from the doorway.

Slowly Jess rose, trying to make sense of what'd just happened. "Traline, did you see that? He woke up and warned me. He seemed pretty insistent about getting out of here and taking something with me. Do you think that fever affected his mind?"

Traline looked past her to where Colwyn lay in the same position he'd been in for days. Her lips puckered and her gaze wandered over Jess's features. "I didn't see a thing, m'um, nor hear a word spoken. Maybe you should go rest yourself, M'lady."

Jess rubbed at the tension in her temples with her fingertips. "No, no. I'm sure he was awake. I'm sure he tried to tell me something, something that seemed pretty important to him."

She looked back at Colwyn's sleeping figure, unchanged and unmoved. Was she starting to imagine things? Maybe Traline was right. With little sleep the past four days, she did feel out of sorts.

"I'll send word to Lord Tarne you're not well, M'lady."

With a last glance at the unresponsive Colwyn, she dismissed the whole episode to nerves worn thin by fatigue. "No, don't send word. I believe it will be less restful for me if I keep Tarne waiting."

"As you wish, M'lady."

"But Traline," she said before leaving the room, "if Colwyn does wake up, send Tagg for me right away, no matter the time of night. I have this feeling that—"

"That what, m'um?"

She shook her head. "I don't know. A strange feeling. I can't really explain it. You'll send for me?"

"Aye, M'lady."

Leaving Colwyn to Traline's care, she stretched her neck from shoulder to shoulder as she walked the grim corridors of Gallimore. The oppressive atmosphere weighed heavy on her spirit, making even the most cheerfully lit rooms look bleak. She craved air, light, space—none of which would be found as long as she stayed here. At the very least, she would get herself outside after dinner. A short walk would likely do wonders for her spirit, even if only in the confines of the inner bailey.

That much decided, she entered and paused in the doorway of Great Hall, assessing the big room. Soldiers guffawed on several benches, a greyhound snuffled through some rushes in a corner, and Tarne sat at his raised table, dead ahead. At least tonight they'd dine in Great Hall instead of his antechamber, and she might have an easier time fighting off his inquisitive hands.

She set her shoulders straight and tall and walked the length of Great Hall toward Tarne. As she went around to the back of his table, she passed by Faulk, who ate at the far end. Being second in command, he filled his captain's place while Colwyn lay in bed. He nodded at her in friendly acknowledgement and gratitude filled her, for she knew both Faulk and Geoffrey could be counted as allies.

Tarne stood and seated her at his side. He touched his lips to her ear and whispered before he sat down, "This eve we shall get the formality of dining out of the way before retiring to my chamber."

Jess pasted a magazine-cover smile on her face. "Great. Let's drink to that." With satisfaction, she watched Tarne swig down all that his goblet held.

He raised his cup for a steward to refill then inclined his head toward her. "I hope you don't mind, my dear, that I've taken the liberty to have our usual libations replaced with water. I fear too much wine has gotten the better of me these past days, and I don't intend to leave you disappointed one more night."

Her smile remained, but her heart froze. Tarne eyed her with a smug look on his face. Now what tactic could she use? Glancing away, she noticed his mother's chair remained empty. Probably off on another drinking binge. Ahh, drinking?

"Uh, M'lord." The title churned in her gut like a dinner of meat gone bad. "It would please me to first honor your mother with a short visit. She hasn't stopped by to see Colwyn yet, and I could give her a quick update on his condition. I'm sure she's concerned."

"Very, very thoughtful, but nay. I think not." Tarne examined her as he sucked gristle from between his teeth.

She looked away, disgusted. A man with a fixed gait entered from the main door of Great Hall and marched straight up to the front of the table. He bent to one knee, and then stood. She'd use this distraction for what it was worth.

"Please excuse me," she said as the man addressed Tarne. She stood to leave, but didn't get far. Before she could step away, Tarne grabbed hold of her wrist with a grip more powerful than she expected.

"You are not excused," he said, while still looking at the messenger. "Your report?"

"Lord Tarne," the messenger said, bowing his head in deference. "I've been about your business and stand ready to report."

"Then do so."

The man's eyes shifted to Jess, and then back to Tarne. "Here, M'lord? Now?"

"Here and now." Tarne's grasp tightened, pinching like a cobra's jaws.

Jess winced, as did the messenger, at Tarne's harsh tone.

"Very well, M'lord. I took great care in following your instructions, but the sources to which you sent me had no knowledge concerning a Lady Jessica of Neale. She is not known to be an ally of King Edward. She is not known to anyone."

"You were thorough? You are certain?"

"Aye, M'lord." The messenger stepped back, fear in his eyes.

Her heart rate increased as Tarne dumped the contents of his glass with his free hand, and then cocked his head to look at her.

"I fear, M'lady, that my patience has neared its end. I will have the truth, one way or another, and I will have it now. Who are you, and why have you come to Gallimore?"

The Great Hall fell silent at his raised voice. Hot and jittery, Jess tried to pull away. How could she answer those questions when she didn't know herself?

Seconds ticked by in dreadful silence as the deadlock between her and Tarne would not be broken.

"Very well," he said with eerie calmness.

He turned her hand palm-side up and slid his eating knife diagonally across the entire length. In slow motion, a thin line of red appeared and soon welled into a wine-dark handful of blood. He tugged her nearer and reached for the goblet, then tipped her hand, slowly filling the chalice with her own blood. She wobbled light-headed at the sight.

"There is truth in the blood, and as I've said, I will have the truth. Good evening, M'lady."

She stood dumbfounded as he released her and stalked away with the cup. She had no doubt he'd be going to that horrid room of his and with a goblet of her own blood. What a sick and twisted man, sick and twisted like her stomach which wrenched at the throbbing pain in her hand.

"M'lady, are you well?"

The voice next to her belonged to Faulk, but she couldn't see him. All she could see was the terrible sight of her hand covered by slick, red drops raining from each fingertip. Funny how it looked fake, almost like paint, dripping and dripping.

"M'lady?"

Sound and sight receded to quiet and dark.

Chapter 15

The riot of voices in Tarne's head would not cease, and he paced back and forth, back and forth, like a hound locked too long in the kennels. All night and half the morning, he'd not been allowed to rest. Unseen forces pricked and prodded, so that he roamed the castle with endless steps. When Jessica Neale's blood had been poured onto the floor in the windowless room, the truth of who sent her sickened him. He'd suspected all along, but now he knew. And the knowing set his teeth to gnashing.

Destroyed. She must be destroyed. Why had he not ordered her throat slit the day she appeared?

The pain in his head clamped its jaws tighter, and he chanted to soothe the discordant whine in his mind. "Murder and death. Murder and death. I will reign. It will be so. She must go. Light be night. Dark will rule. Murder and death. Murder and death..." At the door of Great Hall, he stopped.

"M'lord."

Someone bent a knee in submission and then rose, towering in front of him. Of course. Rollo. Faithful, stupid Rollo. "I've a task for you, Rollo."

"Aye, M'lord. Ask, and it shall be as you wish."

She must go. It will be so. Light be night and dark will rule. Murder and death, murder and death ...

He screwed his eyes shut and pressed both palms to his ears. A howl rang, whether ripped from his own throat or elsewhere he did not know, but the sound filled his ears.

"M'lord?"

Slowly, he opened his eyes to fix upon the giant man with concern written across his huge features. Concern? Hysterical! Laughter rippled through him until his mind clicked like a snapped bone. Reality returned, clear and sharp. "I will have the wench, Jessica Neale, alive or dead—it matters naught. Do what you will, but do not disappoint. Bring her to me."

Rollo blinked, mouth agape, but didn't move.

A vein throbbed behind his eye, signaling more torture. Nay, not now. Not yet. "Bring me the girl!"

•

Pain. Sharp and unending. The muscles in Colwyn's back screamed. He opened his eyes to the light of day, then as quickly shut them. His throat parched, his stomach growled, and oh how his body ached.

"I thirst." His voice came out a rasping croak.

"Master!"

"Boy?" He scrubbed a hand over his face, then thought the better of it as tender skin above his cheekbone stung.

Tagg fairly jumped at his bedside. "'Tis me, Sir. I'd never leave you. Why, me and M'lady and Traline, we've all been seeing to you.   Even Faulk and Geoffrey ask after you.   'Twas Faulk who brought—"

He raised his palm. "Enough. How long? How long have I been here?"

"Nigh on four days now and . . ."

He let the boy chatter on. Four precious days. King Edward's men could come at any time. He had to get out. Nay, they all must.

"Help me up."

"Oh, Sir, 'tis too soon. You cannot."

"I said, help me up!"

Sweat trailed his temples as he rose into an upright position. His back seared in agony and he feared his head might burst.

"Drink," he said between breaths.

The lad raced to retrieve a mug and returned, spilling most of it over the stone floor in his haste. Colwyn drained the rest, then held the mug out for more. After several rounds, life seeped back from fingers to toes. "Tell me truly, boy, all that has happened."

"As I've said, Sir, Faulk brought you in. Lord Tarne said you could lay here and rot, but Lady Jessica, she stood up to him."

"Tarne released her?"

"Aye, Sir. He even said she could leave Gallimore if she wished.

But she didn't. When M'lady saw you, why, she stayed right here at your side. It was her that got the earl to send for the physician. She's here most all the time except for sleeping and when Lord Tarne summons her."

Colwyn grimaced, then pressed his palm lightly against his battered face. So the girl had been freed, and yet she stayed. Why? Hard to think with the boy chattering.

"Oh, Sir, I know she's an angel sent from above. First she healed Old Black, then Traline, and now you."

"What say you?"

The lad told of the warhorse and the serving girl, all in a tone of worship. Colwyn held back the smile that tugged his lips. "And the earl, what has he to do with M'lady?"

"He summons her every night. She's very brave, master, much like you."

Colwyn grunted, thinking hard. Had the little firebrand survived or succumbed to Tarne's advances? If Tarne had touched her—his jaw clenched, and he winced at the pain.

"Help me stand."

"You sure, Sir?"

With a nod, he swung his legs to dangle over the edge of the bed. Leaning heavily on the boy, he pushed up to a near stand, then dropped back, shaky and breathless. He'd not be leaving today.

"Get me Lady Neale."

"Aye, Sir." But the boy didn't move. "You shan't try to stand while I fetch her?"

"Think you I can?"

With a last glance over his shoulder, Tagg disappeared. Alone, Colwyn shifted against the pillows so that his weight would not press against his shoulder blade. What a simpleton to have ridden alone. His pride would exact a high price indeed if the King's men slaughtered him in his bed. Fighting, blood, strife ... Would he never know peace?

"Colwyn?"

Jess stood framed in the doorway, and he understood why Tagg called her an angel. A blue gown edged with silver embroidery defined her shape, and the rich color suited her creamy skin. Never had he seen such compassion in her eyes or heard such softness in her voice. Or had he? The dream voice from the fever had carried such a tone.

He sat straighter, fighting the torment stabbing his back. "I owe you a debt of thanks."

She smiled, and warmth radiated from every pore of his body. How could a fever return so suddenly?

"And I imagine your being in debt to me is not a comfortable feeling." Her smile changed to a smirk.

"Aye, comfort is not what I'm feeling at the moment." Nay, more like jittery and shallow-breathed. Why had he never noticed the golden glints highlighting the soft curls at her forehead, or the matching gilded flecks lighting her mahogany eyes? How would it feel to have her regard him with love instead of sympathy?

What? The fever must truly have addled his brain to muse in such fashion. He closed his eyes to stop the wild thoughts.

"Colwyn? You all right?"

Unsure, he said nothing, but allowed himself to look at her once more.

"You know," she pointed her finger like a scolding mother, "you scared your poor page half to death. He didn't think you'd make it. I had my doubts as well."

She had? He'd pay a king's ransom to know if those doubts had caused her grief or joy. "Then your wish to be rid of me would have come true."

"Yes." Her brow knit into solemn lines. "But I didn't mean to be rid of you in that way."

"I see." He wanted to smile at her seriousness, but his bruised face wouldn't cooperate. "Come near. I would speak with you."

She nudged a chair closer with one hand. The other she favored, being wrapped in strips of linen.

He nodded toward the bandaged palm. "You've hurt yourself?"

"No, not really. I've got your brother to thank for that."

He ground his teeth, then flinched at the smart of it. A flame of anger burned deep within. "What has he done? What harm has he brought you?"

"Well, other than being annoying and difficult to keep at a safe distance, I don't suppose he's brought any."

A flood of relief cooled his fire. What would he have done if Tarne had taken advantage of her? What could he have done?

"You know, you're the one who left me here alone with him.

Why the concern now?"

An honest question, but one he couldn't answer. "I cannot say."

"Cannot," she raised an eyebrow, "or will not?"

He exhaled as much as his sore ribs would allow. "Suffice it to say I know not, and leave it at that. I've not the time or energy to banter a game of words with you, though 'tis a pastime I've come to enjoy. You have told me you are from the future. What is Gallimore's fate?"

"Great topic for when you're feeling better, but now you should lay back and rest. You were—"

"I cannot rest until I know."

She paused and brushed a stray curl from her brow. The urge to reach out and touch that downy hair tingled in his fingers.

"Well, I know someone who knows a lot about Gallimore's history, but not me. Sorry." She shook her head, emphasizing her point, and the curl bounced back to dangle on her forehead. "Now rest."

"Think, M'lady. Please. 'Tis important."

A sigh signaled the end of her patience. "All I know is that this castle is nothing but a rock outline in a goat pasture during my time."

His own patience ran thin, but a sigh would hurt. "You must know more."

"I don't!"

"Very well." He was right. A sigh did hurt. "What I tell you now, I say with grave intent, and I would have you obey me for once. Take Tagg and Traline. Leave Gallimore immediately."

"But where? And why?"

"Tarne's been branded a traitor. The king's men could arrive here at any time. No one will be safe on that day, and I'm useless to defend you. Do you understand?"

"Not that I'd mind leaving Gallimore." She batted the curl back and leaned forward. "But what about you?"

"No time. M'lady—Jess—the king's men are more dangerous than the earl."

He reached for her wounded hand, cradling it in his own. "This injury is but a trifle compared to what those men would do. I know not what method of torture they use in your day, but you have no idea the horrors you would suffer should you be taken."

If the king's men got a hold of her and the boy—a sour taste burned at the back of his throat. "Tell Traline Boar's Head Hollow. She knows the way. Make haste. I'll meet you as I am able."

"But, what if we got Faulk to help you and—"

"Nay!" Stubborn woman. Stubborn beyond fault, matched only by her outbursts of anger.

Anger?

He dropped her hand and skewered her with a mask of malice. "Get out. I never asked you to take care of me. I do not want you in my chamber. Go! Take the boy and Traline and leave here at once. Do not come back. I don't believe your pack of lies, and I'll have nothing more to do with you."

Her face took on a hard edge as she stood and shoved the chair aside. "Fine."

That one word hit him like a well-aimed lance. So be it, if it meant her safety. With any luck, it would. Otherwise, well, he would not consider the nightmare that would be hers.

Chapter 16

Faulk ignored the formality of a knock and smacked open the Lady's door. No movement. Not a sound but his own disappointed grunt. If Rollo found her first … nay. The chase was on, and by God, he'd be the victor.

He sped to Colwyn's quarters next. Raising a fist, he thumped on the door. Unconscious or not, he daren't enter his master's chambers in the same manner as the woman's.

"Come." A faint reply, unexpected and familiar.

"Sir?" He entered and crossed the antechamber, a mixture of hope and dread prodding him.

At the bed's edge sat Colwyn, worse for the wear, but upright by his own strength. "Your face bears surprise."

"Aye, Sir. I've seen you knocked about before, but never so grave as this. I did not know you to be awake. You fare well?"

Colwyn gave a nod. "I owe you my life."

"Nay. We are but even. I'd not have found you on the road had your sword not slain Sir Guy two summers ago. His dagger would have been my end were it not for you."

"'Twas nothing. He was a fly to be swatted."

"Aye, that he was." He smiled at the memory, then let it go. "The Lady Neale, have you seen her?"

"Why do you ask?"

"Lord Tarne seeks her."

The muscle along Colwyn's jaw twitched. Not a good sign.

"For what purpose?"

Faulk's mouth went dry.

"I said for what purpose?"

He studied the floor rather than his master's granite face. "The answer will please you not."

"I thought as much. I knew he'd not suffer her willfulness for long. Yet you would bring her to him? You would bring M'lady to harm?"

He jerked up his head. "Never. I did but seek to find her before Rollo, to see her safe passage out of Gallimore."

"Rollo?" Colwyn's face contorted, burning a deep shade of red.

"Calm yourself, Sir. I will see her safely away before Rollo or Tarne bring her to ruin."

"If you do this thing and are caught," he paused, the silence unnerving, "your life will be forfeit."

Faulk clenched his jaw. Curse it all! He knew, but how could he do otherwise? He cared for the fiery wench who faced all the earl had to give, and then some. "Aye."

Half of Colwyn's mouth raised, lopsided from the beating. "She's smitten you as surely as the boy, has she not?" His smile faded, and a cold, green challenge lit his eyes. "Then find her, for if Rollo chances upon her first, 'tis me you will answer to. M'lady is likely in Traline's quarters by now. See they leave Gallimore undiscovered this day. Agreed?"

"Aye, Sir." He turned, but Colwyn's words followed. "Do not think to consider Tarne's wrath, rather mine, should you fail."

He fled the room and sped down the corridor, taking the stairs two at a time. A sour curdling in his stomach told him someone would pay with his life before this day was spent.

•

"You're hurting me!" Jess winced as Faulk forced both wrists behind her back with a grip as secure as any handcuffs. Her heart raced, and a rush of adrenaline shook her, as if she'd mainlined a full pint of espresso.

"Where are you taking M'lady?" Traline's voice came from behind.

Faulk remained silent as he forced her across the dusty courtyard. Murmurs and whispers from bystanders met her ear, but only Traline dogged Faulk with a plea for her safety.

Maybe the king's men were already there as Colwyn predicted. He needn't have warned her of their cruelty. She remembered her history and the awful way Edward II had been murdered. And if they did that to a man, what might they do to her? A cold sweat rained between her shoulder blades.

She struggled to keep pace as Faulk breathed down her neck, barely managing to climb the stairs of Gallimore. The pressure he exerted kept her moving, or she'd be bowled over.

What a nasty cycle. As soon as she set her hope on leaving, something always propelled her back through the dark doors. But this time, she was shoved down a corridor she'd never seen before—straight into the castle's heart and then down toward the bowels.

She'd read descriptions of dungeons, even seen graphic pictures, but nothing prepared her for the smell once the door grated open. Pungent, putrid, rank, but so much more—like meat that'd sat too long on the counter, slowly rotting and decomposing.

The stench of death.

They stepped past the threshold and stood on the landing of a wooden set of stairs leading to where light and sound wouldn't go. "No!" Panic pooled in every muscle. Writhing against the iron bands of Faulk's grip, she broke free, but lost her balance. She tumbled headlong down the stairs, feet tangling in her skirts, and skidded to a stop at the bottom.

"M'lady!"

She could hardly hear over the rushing sound in her ears.

"M'lady, I meant you no harm."

Faulk's voice. What? The rushing turned to buzzing.

"M'lady?"

"I ... I—" Arms lifted her and she focused on Traline's face, who stood with a torch in front of her. "I guess I'm okay."

"M'lady." Faulk's voice broke, or was that her hearing? "'Twas but a show for prying eyes. None who saw could say that I did not bring you in. But I swear, I meant you no harm."

"I don't understand." Her mind refused to wrap around all that had happened or what Faulk tried to say. "Why bring me here?"

"This morn, all in Great Hall heard the earl's order to bring you before him. 'Twas admittedly an unorthodox way for me to exact your escape, but one I hoped would go unchallenged, as it has thus far. Any who saw would think I carried out Lord Tarne's wishes, but we must hurry. Are you steady?"

Steady? So, that was Faulk's arm holding her up. She stepped away, confused and disoriented, and glanced around the large, dark room. Being near the torchlight gave the rest of the dungeon the illusion of an endless cave. There were no separate cells to suffer in private torture. Instead, chains dangled like knobby tentacles at intervals around the walls. Underfoot, a thick layer of straw hid the floor, adding to the fetid smell.

"Be ye daft man? There's no way out." Traline stamped her foot, but the effect was muffled.

Frowning, Faulk grabbed the torch from her. "Hold your tongue, wench. Over here." He went to the backside of the stairs and scraped his boot. Traline edged closer to investigate, but no way would Jess go any farther from the exit.

Faulk squatted. With surprising ease, he lifted a wooden trapdoor as if it were mechanized. Standing, he faced them. "Go."

Jess's blood ran cold. She knew exactly what that was—an oubliette. A place of forgetting. She'd read about them in a British Lit course. A veritable hole in the ground where prisoners were thrown and never retrieved, about the size of a coffin or smaller. If she looked closer, would she see bones in there? Wanting to run but dizzy with fear, she gaped, speechless. He couldn't be serious.

"You can't put her in there!" Traline's voice raised.

"In she'll go, and you as well. No time for arguing. There's a death warrant on Lady Neale. This tunnel is known only to the men what made it. A sorry lot is a guard's life under the earl's command, but this little escape sweetens 'er up. Smuggling brings in comforts we'd otherwise never know and coins to line our pockets."

Jess pulled her eyes from the hole to Faulk's severe face. "Why should I trust you? How do I know you're not lying?"

He spoke with an intensity she'd never before heard. "Because 'tis my life that'll likely be traded for yours."

Her eyes went wide. He meant it. He meant every word.

"Will you go?"

She glanced over at Traline, who nodded in agreement.

What choice did she have? Turn around and face Tarne, or possibly the king's men? Or take a risk on a man's word that freedom was a black tunnel away. Maybe a hole in the ground wouldn't be so bad. "Okay," she said, inching forward

Traline stepped to her side. "I'll go first, M'lady, if it eases your mind."

"Yes, thank you." She squeezed the girl's hand, grateful for her thoughtfulness.

"'Tis not a long drop, but take care. 'Tis dark, but a sure-footed path, downhill all the way with naught but a few twists and turns. When you reach the end, heave aside the door, for 'tis well hid in the side of a ravine."

"Aye," Traline said. "Let's get this behind us then." Faulk delivered her into blackness so complete, it blinded.

"Traline?" Jess strained her ears, desperate to prove true everything Faulk spoke.

"Aye, M'lady." Traline's voice reverberated from the hole. "There is hardened earth beneath my feet, and my hands touch solid walls."

Faulk eyed Jess with an unreadable expression, crooking his head for her to move.

"Wait!" She stopped at the edge, suddenly shamed at thinking only of herself. "Tagg. I can't leave the boy here."

Faulk's hand grabbed her arm, the pressure of his calloused fingers driving home his words. "We will all rot in here if Lord Tarne comes upon us. You must go now."

"I won't."

Faulk grimaced, his grip tightening. "Get you gone. I'll see to the boy's safety. You have my word."

She gnawed her lower lip, trying to decide. Did she trust him? "Colwyn said to go to Boar's Head Hollow. Will you bring Tagg there? Do you know where it is?"

"Aye, aye, aye. 'Tis directly west. Now go!"

She clutched Faulk's forearms as he lowered her into the abyss, and as her feet touched ground, the thud of the trapdoor sealed her in. Frightening how alive complete absence of light could be. It lived and almost breathed. The rich depth of blackness sucked the breath from her lungs.

Stretching out both arms, she willed her feet to move. "Why didn't Faulk toss that torch down?"

"Mayhap he didn't think of it, M'lady, or perhaps he held reason for which I cannot account."

A few more steps and her fingers met with Traline's shoulder. Her other hand rested against the dirt wall. The contact eased some of the tension coiled around each of her nerves, until something with many, many legs tickled across the back of her hand.

She jerked from the wall, bumping hard into Traline.

"M'lady?"

"Torch or not, we're about to set a new record for getting out of this tunnel. Let's go." As soon as they clasped hands, she yanked Traline's arm and led the way down the gradual descent. She swept her free arm back and forth, back and forth, like a crazed metronome laid on its side. Whenever she brushed fingertips against dirt, she adjusted their direction. All the while, her skin crawled with the thought of what creatures inhabited this hole. Good thing Faulk hadn't lent his torch.

Only once did she have the urge to stop and turn around when a fleeting surge of regret tingled through her. She'd left behind her waistpack. That one, small bag holding her few belongings from home was her last physical link to her son—and only tangible proof that she wasn't insane. A tenuous trust in God was all she had left.

It took forever until her hand met a wooden slab. New wrinkles would surely be evident next time she glanced in a mirror. "Okay Traline, let's push."

"Nay, M'lady. Let me peek out first."

"Why? What do you think might be on the other side?"

"I know not, M'lady, but if we chance upon the earl's men, 'tis your head that bears the death warrant, not mine."

•

Thwack. Thwack. Thwack. Tarne reached for another dagger, then sneered at the empty table top. Twenty blades wobbling from impact lined a timber across Great Hall. The diversion had been soothing while it lasted, but now he tired of waiting games.

The easiest weapon to retrieve had lodged in the door frame. He pulled, then tugged with both hands, and finally threw all his weight into yanking out the knife. Squeezing the hilt as if it would be crushed, he stepped through the threshold. Now where would that plague of a wench be? Of course—in caring for his wastrel of a brother.

He spared no time in climbing the stairs to Colwyn's chamber, then flung open the door. The antechamber offered no sign of life. He crossed the empty room, surprised to find Colwyn sitting up at the edge of his bed, his skin pale except for the yellow and purple bruises on his face.

"Well brother, I thought you'd be dead by now."

Colwyn met his glare. "You thought wrong."

He picked at his ear. Nay, he couldn't have heard right. "The girl, Lady Neale, where is she?"

"What makes you think I would know?"

"Impertinence ill becomes you. Simply answer my question before my patience ends."

Colwyn didn't cower, nor even look away, but stared back and lifted his chin. "I know not."

"Liar!" He stretched tall and looked down his nose. "Surely you've seen her. She stays at your side like a dog in heat."

"Mind your words."

Was that contempt he detected? "Mind my words? What is that? A threat from you? Tell me where she is."

Colwyn looked away.

"Tell me!"

Kneading the back of his neck, Colwyn took plenty of time before answering. "As I have said, I do not know."

He squinted, reading what he could from Colwyn's expression. What kind of sorcery had that little wench worked to influence his brother so?

With two paces and a quick jerk of the dagger in his hand, he bent and parted the bedskirt to uncover what might be hiding on the floor. Instead of a frightened girl, he found nothing but a warming pan and an old chamber pot settled on a carpet of dust. When his eyes met Colwyn's, he wanted to rip the knowing regard from his face. "If and when the wench returns, you will send her to me at once."

A gleam of rebellion flashed in Colwyn's eyes. Tightening his grip on the hilt of the blade, Tarne toyed with the temptation to end that challenge, but the girl must be dealt with first.

He stalked from Colwyn's room, resuming the search. Jess's quarters stood empty. Traline's as well. Where else? With who? Ahh, yes. She had as soft a heart concerning the boy as she did for Colwyn. He strode across the expanse of the courtyard toward the stables.

"Hyah!"

He twisted just in time, narrowly missing a collision with a warhorse at full gallop. The boy blurred by, seated in front of a brawny man as they sped through the gate.

Tarne sprinted forward. "Stop them!"

From atop the gatehouse, guards cried out, "M'lord, that's Faulk, Sir Colwyn's man."

"I know who it is. Shoot him. Now!"

Released arrows whooshed through the air like an unholy wind.

"Bring them in." Guards scrambled to carry out his bidding. It didn't take long before a tear-streaked boy and a body, pin-cushioned with feathered shafts, were deposited at his feet. He kicked at Faulk's head with no response. "String him up. I want this body displayed as a token for any man courting betrayal. And I want a contingent of guards sent to search for the woman, Jessica of Neale. As for you, boy—" he grabbed hold of the boy's ragged hair.

Dragging the lad like a wriggling, yelping puppy, he crossed both outer and inner baileys, gained the castle stairs, then pulled him down a long corridor. Dislodging a torch from the wall nearest the dungeon, he hauled the boy through the door and down the stairs.

"Where was Faulk taking you?"

"I, I, I—" Sobs stuttered his words. "I don't know, M'lord."

He yanked the lad's head up to read his face. Wide, fearful eyes met his. A quick backhand sent him to his knees.

"Stupid boy." Tarne searched for the end of a length of chain, the boy's incessant crying shattering his concentration. "Oh, shut up!"

Then he found it—the end of a chain with manacles gaping to snap shut like a monster's mouth.

It pleased him well to leave the sniffling boy locked up and crying in the dark. This bait would prove alluring, no doubt. Once the plight of the boy reached Jessica Neale's sympathetic ears, she'd return to beg for his release. Aye, he'd send the best riders to make it known in all the villages. She'd hear. She'd come.

And he'd be waiting.

Chapter 17

Jess set the last stick of brush against the camouflaged tunnel door, then followed Traline up a steep ravine. As they hiked on, a breeze rushed through the dappled leaves, carrying a peppery scent, while the afternoon sun played peek-a-boo through the trees. If she weren't running from a wacko nobleman, she might've enjoyed this.

Birds twittered a chorus, but wait. Something inharmonious, almost off-key joined in. Trill, *abba-abba-abba*, trill, *abba-abba*—pounding.

Pounding?

She raced up to Traline. "Hey, hear that? Stop. Be quiet."

Birdsong continued, but the pounding grew louder. Traline's eyes widened an instant before her mouth opened. "Run!"

Sprinting after Traline, Jess dodged left, then right, but the pounding never ceased.

"Down!"

Without question, she plowed headlong into a green sea of ferns and slid to a stop. Traline rustled on a few seconds more, then all became silent—except for the approach of galloping horses. The ground vibrated, and her heart beat in her throat.

God, help us.

A horse to rival Old Black stamped to a halt, pawing at the earth, little more than an arm's reach away. She held her breath.

"Here!" The guard nearest her shouted.

Please God, no.

Fear churned in her stomach as the big horse snorted his impatience. Survival instinct screamed. She slid her hand, ever so slowly, down to her thigh, reaching for the dagger strapped to her leg.

"What have you?"

She froze. If she so much as flinched, they'd find her.

One of them dismounted, bracken crushing beneath his feet. Had he seen her move? Her temples pounded. Dizziness closed in, squeezing out her breath. She waited, somewhere between reality and a bad nightmare as seconds turned to hours.

"What is it?"

Insects danced around her face, but she dare not shoo them away. How many more would swarm over her if she died here on the forest floor?

"Oh, fie!" The man coughed up a wad of phlegm and spit it out, inches from her elbow.

"Now what?"

The heavy boots stomped back to the horse. "It was naught but a bloated deer carcass. Let's head back. It grows dark. We'll have an early start in the morn. She'll not get far on foot, if she makes it through the night."

"Aye."

The tense muscles in her body slackened, but she remained hidden. It could be a trick. As time passed, buzzing flies and chattering birds resounded with an absurd loudness.

"M'lady?" Traline's whisper signaled it safe to sit up. "You all right? Have they gone?"

"Aye."

Jess stood, shaky but thankful. "That was closer than I would've liked. Let's get out of here."

"We must take shelter, M'lady. The shadows have already turned to dusk."

"Good. Then they'll have a harder time seeing us if they return." Jess squinted into the gathering gloom. The maze of trees appeared to be unending. "Which way?"

"But M'lady, we—"

"Which way?" A hesitant look crossed Traline's face. "Come on, Traline. What if they decide to come back and we're still here?"

Frowning, Traline averted her gaze, then sighed. "Very well. 'Tis this way."

Jess followed, glad to increase the distance between herself and the castle. She'd not miss the dark corridors or the smelly, lewd men of Great Hall, and especially not Tarne. Colwyn either. Ungrateful man. He hadn't even thanked her.

Water skipping over rocks pulled her from her thoughts, and she licked her lips. "Do you hear that?"

"Aye, but—"

She bolted ahead. Growing darkness made it hard to see the knobby tree root that caught her toe. She fell, landing on both knees and grinding her palms into the dirt. Pain shot up her arm from her wounded hand and she staggered up. But thirst overrode reason. She sprinted on.

When she reached the shallow creek, she dropped and slurped like an animal, drinking long and deep. Cold and sweet, not even an iced latte could compare. Satisfied, she raised her face, hair dripping a waterfall down her shoulders. Ahh—

Her sigh competed with a grunt-like snort in the night air.

She stiffened. The sound came from the other bank. A hairy snout, long white tusks, and a bristly back held a stance of challenge directed at her. What in the world? Whatever, its beady, black eyes bored into hers, and it pawed the ground. Standing with fluid movement so as not to startle the pig-like creature, she edged her way back.

No good. The thing snorted like an enraged bull and leapt. In that freeze-frame instant, she imagined the amount of flesh that could be ripped by one of those tusks.

Her flesh.

She flew through the woods along the creek's edge. Stumps. Rocks. Brush. Nothing would stop her. Or the thing. The animal practically gnawed her heels. She'd be overtaken in no time, knocked down and gored through the back.

Giant oaks blurred past, and then she spied an ash tree large enough to hold her weight but not too broad to climb. Could the monster climb too?

She sprang, clutching at the rough bark. The impact jarred loose her knife. On its plummeting flight to the ground, it nicked the fat side of the animal, further inciting it.

Sharp tusks slammed against the trunk, barely missing her legs. The thing tugged at the hem of her dress, tearing away bits of fabric. It rammed again and again. Each time more of the cloth shredded, and less of her grip held. If she slipped any further, it wouldn't be material that lay in pieces on the ground.

Another squealing grunt came. The tree stopped shaking. One more of the pig-monsters advanced toward her adversary. The predator became the prey. Now that she had a minute to think, she recognized the demons as wild boars. No wonder Traline had been so determined to find shelter for the night. And where was she now?

"Traline!"

No answer, although it was hard to hear over the snorting ruckus.

The two hogs circled, each pawing at the dirt and popping jaws with a frightening noise. Frothy slobber flew as the two collided. Their tusks locked, then disengaged. They drew back with an unearthly squeal, only to charge again. This time the larger black boar hit off center, gouging through the other's thick hide. A spouting stream of blood splattered everywhere.

Jess shook. Her arms and legs quivered, and her slashed hand throbbed as if she held a swarm of angry bees.

The bloodlust beneath rose to a frenzied crescendo, growing louder with each inch of bark slipping through her hands. She'd never given a thought as to how much pain a body could tolerate before the last beat of a heart, but she did as her grip gave way, and she fell into the fray of carnage below.

•

Colwyn avoided Gallimore's main entrance and slipped out a side door near the stables. The journey from his chamber thus far had taxed his limits. His breath came in short, painful bouts. Would he even be able to seat Old Black?

Holed up in his quarters for the past two days, he'd labored hard at stretching knotted muscles, working through the pain. He strengthened his legs in the adjoining corridors, and in all that time, his fortitude and his hope increased, for he'd not seen Jess, Tagg, or Traline. Not even Faulk. Surely they'd made it away.

A familiar whinny called to him, ending with a snort and a stamp. Colwyn patted Black's silky coat, noticing for the first time how big this animal really stood. Maybe Jess had been right with her label of horse-beast. He smiled, remembering the way she'd clutched his surcoat that night he'd retrieved her from the stocks. How small and out of place she'd seemed atop Old Black. How warm she'd felt in his arms—the soft, shorn curls of her head brushing against his skin.

What was he thinking? He ran his fingers through his own mane of unruly hair. Time to set his mind to the task at hand.

He heaved the saddle over the horse's back and thankfully it met its mark. His hands worked smoothly as he tied the cinch and tugged on the leather strap to tighten it. But when he reached up to mount, he gasped. Pain sliced across his back as sharp and severe as a flogging.

Catching his breath took some concentration. Hopefully he hadn't split open the wound, not that he'd let that stop him. He led Black over to a barrel, and though humbling, it was the only way to gain his seat.

Leaving the stable, he pulled hard to the right in effort to side-step the courtyard, then trailed along the inner edge of the outer wall to the gate. A ruddy-faced guard drew himself to full attention as he neared. "The men are searching off past Warnborough today, Sir."

Without stopping, he nodded, and set off that direction. Once out of range, he guided Old Black along a different course. Boars Head Hollow was as east from west in relation to Warnborough, and for that he inhaled a breath of fresh thankfulness. Thankfulness? Moments ago he'd felt a twinge that could be construed as longing. And now gratitude? These feelings should be kept at bay, not running rampant through his heart.

He kicked Black's side and a rush of wind filled his ears. Summer's verdant colors blurred by. The morning sun rose higher in the cloudless sky and sweat tickled down his back and temples. As he neared a creek, the woodsy growth became thicker, and he slowed Black. Each step of the warhorse crushed plants into oblivion, releasing an herbal fragrance. Finally halting, he slid off, stiff and sore.

Water babbled over smooth stones and a few dragonflies skimmed the surface, but with a battle instinct he long ago learned to trust, Colwyn stood immobile, senses alert. Something terrible had happened here. Cloven-hooved imprints. Battered tree bark. Bloodied shreds of fabric. Countless times before he'd witnessed the remains of a boar skirmish, but this one chilled him.

Leaving Old Black to drink his fill, he continued on foot. At the base of a tree, its trunk ripped open to expose white, fleshy pulp, a dagger lay half-buried in the dirt. Dragon-hilted, edged with blood, this knife belonged to his brother. He laid the cool blade across his palm. How had it gotten out here?

He tucked the weapon in his belt, then squatted in what must've been the eye of battle. A swatch of material lay battered in the dirt. He picked it up and turned it over. Once a rich blue with silver thread adorning the edges, now blotches of reddish-brown spread out in ugly stains. He knew this cloth. Jess wore it when he'd thought her an angel standing in his doorway.

His breath stopped and he stumbled to his feet with a wild look around. "Jessica!"

Bird chatter and the breeze rustling the leaves answered his call, but she did not. Batting at bushes, he scoured the grounds for more clues, all the while calling her name. Then he spied it. A trampled trail.

Colwyn ran.

His pounding heart blocked the sound of underbrush giving way beneath his feet. God only knew what he'd find as he tracked along flattened, blood-splattered ferns. He'd been the one to send her out here. Had he sent her to her death?

"No!" Birds took flight and the anguished cry startled even him. He'd sent many to their death with never a second thought. Why start caring now? Care for a sharp-tongued, willful woman who claimed to be from the future?

Did he?

Panic twisted his guts. That small, plucky wench had stood up to Tarne for his welfare alone, risking everything for him. He owed her his life.

"Jess!"

No answer. Nay, he would not lose her. He'd never again lose anyone he cared about. A ghost of a memory he'd long ago tried to forget pushed him forward at an insane pace.

He stopped just in time, not realizing he'd pressed on uphill. The vegetation, the bloody clues, and the ground itself ended with a sheer drop twenty-feet down to the river. Whoever came this way had fallen and been swept along with the water.

Retracing his steps, he snagged Black's reins to continue his search. Much time did he spend combing the banks downstream, and all the while his wounded back screamed in complaint.

No stranger to tracking, he used every bit of his skill. Nothing. Surely if she'd been mortally wounded he'd have found her body—unless she'd become a feast for the animals of the night. Even then, he'd likely find some bones with a bit of sinew attached, licked clean of blood and cracked open with the marrow sucked out. The thought unnerved him as nothing ever had.

Exhausted and defeated, he dug in his heels and reared Black around. The sooner he reached Boars Head Hollow, the sooner he'd know if any hope remained.

He rode until darkness claimed all visibility, and then went through the motions of settling in for the night. After tethering the horse, he threw his blanket on the ground and eased down his aching body.

But sleep evaded him. The pain of his unhealed wound would've been reason enough, but he gave it no mind. Rather, he lay awake, obsessing over an impertinent bit of a girl whom he desperately wanted to find unharmed the next day. The fate of Jessica Neale mattered to him. It mattered very much, and a desire burned within to let her know his last words to her had been false.

Chapter 18

Jess sat in the dirt, its chill permeating through layers of her dress. What else could she do? Were it not for Traline—well, no. She wouldn't think about that. Never had her mortality been so magnified as when she'd faced those boars that first night in the forest. As she'd slipped from the tree, Traline's strength had boosted her up and kept her aloft ... and Traline's leg bore the gash that should've been hers for her own ignorance. Without the servant's quick wit and knowledge, more than a punctured calf would have been suffered.

Gratitude welled in her throat, and she swallowed. She owed the woman much. Even now she depended on Traline for food, water, shelter. Being humbled to the point of basic survival wreaked havoc with her pride.

Pride? She smiled. Just look at her—sitting on the damp ground of a dirt cave carved into the side of a hill, waiting for a dinner of roots and berries. Her stomach turned at the thought. Green acorns and huckleberries, or blackberries, or what were they? Whatever, her digestive tract might never survive the funk this diet caused.

She sighed and ran her fingers through her hair. Or tried to. It felt like a bird's nest and probably looked it. If Colwyn could see her now, the smug look on his face would kill her.

Why did it always come back around to Colwyn? Forget it. She wiped her hand and tottered to her feet. Much as she hated to admit the truth, it hurt when he'd told her to leave. To make it worse, he probably hadn't given a second thought to her feelings. But unintentional pain didn't feel any less hurtful. Must a wound be agreed upon for it to bleed as much?

Love him.

She closed her eyes, trying to make the thought go away, yet it interrupted her with increasing urgency. Love was, and always would be, not a feeling but a choice—one she didn't want to make ever again.

Standing, she arched her back to work out the kinks, and hopefully straighten her thinking out as well. Stupid to quibble with herself over the moot point of love. She'd never see Colwyn again anyway, and—

Something wailed outside the cave and she jerked her neck in the sound's direction. When the screech of it repeated louder and closer, her nerves cracked, then shattered.

"Caw!"

A raven. Tarne's? Did he lurk nearby as well? She reached trembling fingers to massage the tightness in her neck. It was only a bird. If Traline could take on a boar, she ought to be able to handle a bird.

How close? Her ears strained to listen.

Small animals rustled the tall grass, sparrows chirped their happy tunes, but no more sharp bird cry. No. Something worse. Something that sucked away all her remaining breath.

Pounding hooves.

Quickly prying a loosened rock from the wall, she waited, arm raised to strike. Would she really hit someone that hard? Could she? If it was Tarne, absolutely.

A rider dismounted, and only one set of footsteps approached— twig-snapping, heavy steps. Whoever it was, he knew this place, for he marched with determination. He'd soon be at the cave where she stood sweating, her hands clammy and her stomach in knots. She clenched the rough rock, the weight of it strengthening her resolve. She could do this. A few more crunching, crashing steps. Closer, and closer, and—she swung. Hard.

And totally missed.

The man snarled like a wounded mountain lion and pinned her to the wall. Her ears rang from the impact, and she cried in pain, but not with fear.

She knew that growl.

"Colwyn?"

He gave no answer, nor did he release her. He held her, close enough to inhale his musky scent. The smell of warm flesh and horses—of one who'd traveled far.

Corded muscles of anger she'd often seen chiseled along his jaw softened. Sparks of green fury disappeared from his eyes, replaced by a look she'd never seen. No. Couldn't be. She must be wrong, but couldn't stop the thrill inside her.

"Jess." The stern edge of his voice broke as he half-whispered her name.

"You scared me half to death!"

"I thought—oh, God." His eyes squeezed shut. A swallow convulsed his throat and a tremor shook through him. "I feared I'd never see you again."

She frowned. "I thought that's what you wanted."

"Nay." His gaze held hers, searching and intimate. "I spoke only what needed to be said to turn you away from Gallimore, but the words—" His voice turned husky. "I meant them not."

"Then why—"

"Save your questions, for I must speak. I know well 'tis by your hand that I live and breathe. You risked everything to stay and care for me, and I am hard-pressed to think of why."

"Colwyn, I only—"

"Nay. Do not explain. Not now. Though I know not why you've come, or even from where or when, I owe you much. I owe you my life. But what's more is that I pledge to you my heart."

The kiss happened unexpectedly and quickly, yet was so powerful and passionate, that her own hunger betrayed her. She leaned into his embrace and his strong arms wrapped tighter, pressing her against him. The heat of his mouth warmed hers, and she shivered in response to his need. An appetite that'd slept dormant since her husband's death awoke deep inside, and she reached up, burying her hands in his damp hair, molding her body to his.

He pulled away, taking his warmth but not the fire burning inside her. Where had this longing come from? This was bad. Very bad. She shouldn't be feeling this. She'd buried that part of her with Dan, hadn't she? She tried hard to conjure up her late husband's image, but all she could see was the battle-scarred face of a knight focused on her with an emotion she didn't want to acknowledge.

So, she did what she did best—run. Out the cave's opening, across the hollow, and into the woods, her feet moved as fast as the tears slipping down her cheeks. Branches snagged her clothes and scratched her arms, but she'd run until nothing was left of her.

Cramps stabbed her sides. Her chest burned and her vision blurred. She finally stopped, falling to her knees, giving in to ragged sobs which actually felt good. For so long she'd forbidden herself to cry, to really cry, and Colwyn's embrace had somehow poked an irreparable hole into the dam she'd built.

In the midst of her weeping, she visualized her clenched fists clutching onto the grief of her husband's death. With each tear, her fingers unfolded more and more, releasing the misery she'd held onto for so long. She wept for what had been taken from her, and for what Colwyn offered her now. Mostly, she wept because she didn't know what else to do.

God, I don't understand this, any of this. When Dan died, I thought that was the end of love for me.

The embrace of her Creator wrapped around her with as much reality and promise as Colwyn's warm arms had held. As the tears subsided, she lay back on the ground, tucked beneath a blanket of peace. A cancer had been removed, and a pink skin of healing knit its way around her bleeding heart.

Looking up through a leafy mosaic, she could honestly say it was good to be alive—in spite of all she'd been through, and suddenly knew at least part of the answer to her long-standing question. It came with little more fanfare than the clarity of a single thought.

She was here because she never could've experienced this peace in her own time. She wouldn't have let it happen. Only when wrenched from her element into a world beyond her control, could she ever have been set free from her self-enforced bondage. Though she'd always miss Dan, the demon of denied grief had been cast out, exorcised by a pledge of love from a medieval knight.

Now, what to do about that declaration. What if she accepted his love? Scarier yet, what if she returned it? Weak and a little shaky, she pushed to an upright position, then rubbed her puffy eyelids, trying to scrub away some of the crazy thoughts.

Of course she was attracted to him, though it annoyed her to admit it. She herself had labeled him overbearing, ungrateful, even a bully. But those six small words changed everything—*I pledge to you my heart.* That offering drew her emotions and pulled her in the direction she'd been heading all along.

Love him.

Rising to her feet, she let out a long, slow breath. She wouldn't think about this, not now anyway. It was too much to consider all at once.

Turning to trek back to the cave, she stopped short. Colwyn stood not far from her, leaning against a mossy tree trunk, his face weighted with a look of concern. She blinked and wondered if she could remember to breathe.

"How long have you been here?" She gave her bangs a self-conscious swipe.

"Long enough."

"Long enough for what?"

"Long enough to wonder why a simple kiss from me would send a woman such as yourself to her knees sobbing."

Heat rose and spread across her cheeks at the memory. "What is that supposed to mean?"

He raised his chin with a superior tilt. "I've seen you locked in the stocks, thrown into a tower cell, and facing the torment of my brother with nary a tear. Why cry now?"

If she told him, would he understand? "I, uh ... I—" The risk of opening up to this man, even though he claimed to love her, brought a sour-tasting panic to the back of her throat. "It's not you. I mean, it's not because of you. Not really."

He frowned, but not his usual angry scowl. "M'lady, if my words have caused you such distress, I will not speak of them again."

The big man suddenly seemed much smaller, and compassion squeezed her heart. "No, Colwyn. It's not you or what you said. It's about me. I've been running a long time, hiding from something I didn't want to face. It's time for me to stop. You've helped me see that. It's painful to let go of the past. That's why I cry."

He didn't answer—no sarcasm, no arrogance ... nothing. "You speak in riddles," he said at last.

"You're a man of riddles yourself."

"Me? How so?"

"It was you who couldn't wait to get rid of me at Gallimore. You who sent me away, and now you tell me you didn't mean any of it. How do you explain that?"

He stepped from the tree and her stomach churned at his approach. If he kissed her again, here, alone, how far would she allow him to take it? But the thought that heated her most was how far she wanted him to take it.

She held her breath and watched him pull from his side a dragon-hilted dagger, the one she'd lost. Extending its sharp tip downward, he stooped to catch up the ripped hem of her skirt, raising it for inspection. Then he stood, fumbled inside the chest of his tunic with his free hand, and produced a remnant of bloodied fabric. "How do you explain this?"

Right. How to explain her own stupidity? "I, um ... I had a little run-in with a wild boar."

His brows rose to hide under a fringe of dark hair. "And you came out the victor?"

"Well, I'm standing here talking to you."

Half a smile lit his face. Not the full smile she'd once hoped for, but it pleased her nonetheless.

"Why does that not surprise me? And what of this?" He held the dagger in an open palm. His half-smile disappeared. "This is Tarne's. Dare I ask what manner of 'run-in' you had with him?"

That was Tarne's knife she'd been toting around? Fingers of dread crept up her back. That could only mean that at some unknown point, Tarne had been in her cell. "I didn't know it belonged to him. I found it and I kept it, that's all. I thought it might come in handy some time."

"Then I suppose I should be grateful 'twas not in your possession when I arrived."

"Oh, Colwyn, I'm sorry. I didn't know it was you."

"Truly? Had you known, you would not have swung at me?"

"Well," she paused, "maybe not as hard."

And then he did smile, the light of which highlighted his dark features—a handsome face she realized she'd never tire of looking at. Genuine and heartfelt, the warmth she saw there made her smile back.

"M'lady," he stepped closer, his tone low and sensual, "are you aware that you torment me like none other?"

The earnest truth in his voice tingled deep in her belly. Should she be flattered or offended? Either way, standing this near to him affected her thinking, and she retreated a step. "I, uh ... I think we should go back."

Without varying his gaze from hers, he tucked the fabric scrap into his shirt and silently offered his hand. He led her along the helter-skelter path she'd cut through the woods, the strength in his calloused grip and the warmth of his fingers wrapped around her own. Oh, how she'd missed a man's touch.

When at last they broke through to the hollow, Colwyn untwined his fingers and busied himself tethering Black. The faithful horse had remained, tail swishing and ears twitching, not far from where Colwyn had left him.

As Jess drew near the opening of their crude shelter, the hum of a lilting folk tune floated out. "Hey, Traline's back. I'm pretty sure that means we eat soon."

"Aye, that we may," he answered, retrieving a cloth-wrapped parcel and wineskin from a worn saddlebag. Like a child bearing a gift for his mother, he appeared quite pleased with himself. "I thought to bring food and drink."

She let him pass into the cave with his bundle, then followed behind. The enclosure smelled of freshly dug potatoes, and her stomach churned for real food.

"Sir!" Traline stood in greeting, listing to one side as she favored her sound leg. An assortment of roots, berries and nuts lay on an apron at her feet. "You are well?"

"Traline." Colwyn barely acknowledged her as he looked around the full area of the shelter. "Where is the boy?"

"Tagg? Why, he's with Faulk, Sir."

"Faulk?" He spun around to where Jess stood near the rough opening. "The boy is with Faulk? Why did you leave him behind?" She sensed his anger. Nothing new, really, but this time a strange sense of loss descended after having experienced his gentler side.

"There was no time. Faulk said he'd find Tagg and bring him here."

With two strides of his long legs, Colwyn came near enough to turn her cloud of trepidation into a storm. "Step aside. I'm going back."

"Are you saying I shouldn't have trusted Faulk?"

"I'm saying step aside."

He used his determined tone, inciting a sliver of fear to fester in her thoughts. If he meant to go back, he must have doubts about Tagg's safety. She should've never left without the boy.

"Then I'm going too." She turned, but he grabbed her arm and whirled her around.

"You'll not be coming."

"I will if I have to walk all the way by myself."

"Nay!" He thrust his face into hers.

She would not be intimidated, and she certainly wouldn't be told what to do—not even by him. "Do you really think telling me no will stop me?"

The fine-drawn lines at his eyes stretched tight. If he were an animal, the hair of his hackles would be raised. "This is none of your affair. You have nothing to do with the boy."

"What?" Her voice rose, matching her growing anger. "I have shown Tagg more concern in the little time I've known him than you have in all the years of his life. He's nothing but a slave to you, someone to order around. He's been my comfort in this crazy world. That boy means more to me than he ever will to you."

"Mind your words, M'lady. You know not of what you speak." A dangerous intonation accompanied his words.

"I know what I've seen. He's your servant, nothing more."

Colwyn's breath came out hard and fast. Tension pulsated like a living creature between them, but neither would back down.

"Sir, beggin' your pardon, but you've got to tell her," Traline's voice sliced through the air.

Colwyn winced as if he'd been hit, and the sight unsettled Jess with a physical force. She stepped back.

He shoved her aside, and his words left her speechless.

"He's my son."

Chapter 19

Colwyn stamped off to where Old Black stood tethered. Jessica Neale changed everything. Her very nature forced him to speak and feel that which had long been hidden. He could almost hate her for it—if he hadn't already grown to love her.

His back ached and head pounded, his eyes burning from lack of sleep. He did not feel up to a ride back to the castle, nor would Black appreciate leaving the tender green shoots he nibbled.

With a glance at the cloud-dotted sky, he calculated one hour, two at best, of remaining daylight. He'd not get far.

Bending over, he coaxed up the horse's front foreleg. The wound had healed well, though he'd noticed a time or two when his mount favored this hoof. Black could do with a good night's rest. So could he.

But what of Tagg? Where was his boy now? Why had Faulk not yet brought him?

Something had gone wrong. Terribly wrong.

•

His son? Stricken, Jess turned to Traline.

"Aye, M'lady. 'Tis true."

"But how, I mean who, or—" A bombardment of questions nailed her, and she sagged against the wall, seeking its support. What a curve ball he'd thrown this time. "Tagg told me his mother had died and that his father walked out the day he was born. He said you hadn't seen his father since. How can Colwyn possibly be that man?"

"Sir Colwyn's not the same man he used to be, M'lady. He changed the day Tagg was born. The boy wouldn't understand."

Jess shook her head. "I'm not sure I do, either. You're telling me Tagg doesn't know he lives under the same roof as his father? That's not right. You've lied to him."

"Nay, M'lady. The boy was told what he needed to hear."

"He needs to hear the truth!"

Traline's lips pursed. "If you'll pardon me, M'lady, there's a history here you know nothing of. Sit ye down, m'um, and I'll tell you the way of it."

Jess pushed away from the wall but did not sit. Instead, she paced circles around the small shelter. "That boy needs to know he hasn't been rejected, that his dad's been there all along. It's not right Traline, and you know it. If you lied about his father, then what about his mother?"

Her agitation surged to new heights, and she met Traline head-on. "Are you Tagg's mother? Are you and Colwyn—"

"Ach! Not me. Now sit ye down!"

She sank, glad for the solid ground beneath her when all she'd believed seemed to be dissolving.

Traline eased herself to the dirt floor, facing her. "I was hardly more than a girl when I first came to Gallimore with my older sister, Saris. After our father's death, we were sold to pay off debt.

"You have to understand this about Saris. She had a way of making you smile whether you felt like it or not. Her gentle spirit encouraged the most timid of souls. She shone as the brightest day—fair of face, with grace in her every movement.

"Sir Colwyn noticed her right off, and Saris returned his attentions. He was a different man when he was with her, not the Colwyn you see today. His laughter came easy then, and a scowl on his face a rare occurrence. Saris was his delight, and she loved him as none other.

"When Colwyn made his intention to marry my sister known to his family, Lady Haukswyrth would have none of it. Only noble blood was good enough for one of her sons, even a second born.

"Ahh, but she was ever a shrewd woman. She arranged to have Colwyn called on king's business, an errand he dare not refuse. While he was away, Lady Haukswyrth quietly sold Saris off to the highest bidder. Saris did not leave Gallimore willingly, for she had a secret known only by me. She was with child. Sir Colwyn's child. But she had no choice.

"Colwyn returned months later to claim his bride but found her gone. His own mother told him Saris had been taken by a fever. Of course, I knew the truth of it, but had been sworn to secrecy on pain of death by Lord Tarne. I know well of that round room you spoke of when you first came, and even now I shudder at the evil it contains. 'Twas there Tarne revealed what would become of me if I said anything to Sir Colwyn, and then he, he—" Traline stared off, as if ghosts of her past had entered the cave, and she wrapped her arms tight around her chest. "I'd never known a man before, and never would be able to again."

Jess's blood went cold, but she remained silent, giving Traline time to slay the specters that haunted her still.

"Aye, fear bound my tongue," Traline went on at last, "but not my heart. I ached for the grief Colwyn bore. Grief that need not have been his, for I knew my sister was alive somewhere. If I told him, surely he'd go looking for her. Whenever I chanced to meet him in a corridor, or serve him in Great Hall, I longed to tell him— but I didn't, and that will forever be my great shame.

"Time passed, and late one night I heard a scratching at my chamber door. There stood Saris, but not the sister I remembered. She'd been mistreated to such extent that she could hardly stand for want of strength, and she was great with child.

"I took her in immediately, knowing I could be silent no longer, no matter what the earl would do. I ran for Sir Colwyn, who thought I'd gone completely mad, until he came and saw for himself. By then, Saris' time had come.

"Oh, M'lady, if you could have but seen Sir Colwyn's face at the birth of that child, his own son, you'd not judge him so harshly. That giant of a man holding with such tender care a wee babe—but complete joy was not to be his.

"The birthing took its toll on Saris. She passed on within the hour, leaving behind a helpless lad and a man whose love had been taken from him not once, but twice.

"My fear of Lord Tarne faded when I saw the look of revenge in Colwyn's eyes upon my sister's death. Were it not for the child, there'd have been no restraining him. But for the sake of Tagg, he swallowed his rage, where it has bubbled ever since. I imagine he's biding his time until the boy's old enough to fend for himself, and then there'll be no stopping him."

Traline paused, giving Jess time to think on all she'd heard. Her stomach cramped as if it'd been punched. Hard. What a horrid life.

"I'm sorry. I'm so sorry. I didn't know—"

"No one knew, not even Tagg. Colwyn's kept an eye on the boy and cared for him in the least obvious ways. If the earl were to find out Colwyn has a son, an heir to Gallimore, he'd kill him. You know Lord Tarne well enough to know 'tis truth I speak."

Jess nodded, horror snaking through her. Poor little Tagg. Never knowing the love of his father, just like her own boy. Her heart broke and she longed to hold them both in her arms.

And Colwyn ... Perhaps she wasn't the only one who'd experienced grief to such a degree. If she'd not been so caught up in her own feelings, she would've seen the burden he bore. She'd been wrong. Very wrong.

Standing, she lightly rested her hand on Traline's head. "Thank you, Traline. Thanks for telling me, and thanks for your loyalty to Colwyn. I think you're more like your sister than you realize."

She paced to the jagged cave opening, intending to walk long and far to think on all the events this day had brought. But as soon as she stepped into the brightness of sunlight, she stopped.

Colwyn hadn't left.

She approached him, unsure of what to say though compelled to say something. He stood near his mount, arms folded—a pensive study in years of sorrow. He stared off across the hollow, and she tried to see what might hold his interest. Drooping yew trees and dead pine needles littered the landscape, not much else.

Black greeted her with a sharp, horsey snort. Colwyn refused to look at her. She cleared her throat, hoping the action would make words magically bubble out. Nothing brilliant came to mind, but she wouldn't settle for the thick silence hanging between them. "I see you haven't left yet."

He grunted.

So, small talk would get her nowhere. "Colwyn, about what I said. I was angry, and—"

"I wish to be alone." The massive, medieval warrior seemed more like a lost little boy. His voice, haunted and hollow, bore testament to the years of loneliness he'd already endured.

She choked back a sob, knowing exactly how he felt. "I didn't know. I mean, about Tagg. I said horrible things and I'm—"

"I bear you no offense. Say no more." But he still wouldn't look at her.

She batted at a fly zig-zagging near her forehead, frustrated with the insect and with Colwyn for not making this any easier. "I'm trying to say that I'm sorry, Colwyn. I've been wrong about you. I'm sorry about Saris—"

"Don't." He turned to her then, and she read the suffering in his reddened eyes.

Her mouth dried to dust, and her own chest tightened in response to his heartache. "I know how it feels to lose someone you love."

"You know nothing of what I feel." His voice raised, ragged with emotion. "I need not your pity. I do not want it."

Her compassion dissolved, and she wanted to smack him instead of the stupid fly. "If you'd let go of your pride for a split-second and listen to me, you'd find that you're not the only one who's ever been hurt. You asked me before why I cried, but you didn't ask me why I ran. I lost my husband two years ago to a stupid, needless accident. I died that day as well, and I've been running from the pain ever since. So don't go thinking you own the sole rights to grief. I've lived and breathed emptiness for so long, I don't know how else to live."

A single tear trailed down her cheek. He stepped toward her, reaching out as if to wipe it away, but she twisted from him. She'd said too much. More than she'd ever admitted to anyone. She didn't want his pity any more than he wanted hers, and if he dared show her any sympathy, she'd—

His voice came soft and low. "Perhaps if you'd let go of your pride, M'lady."

Her own mocking words slapped her hard. A brick to the head would've been a kinder conviction than the sudden clarity of her own character. Humility left a bitter aftertaste.

She shifted around to face him, and her heart missed a beat.

He stood with open arms. Silent. Inviting. Offering solace, not sympathy. The comfort of his strong body pressed against hers filled her heart. How long she clung to him, she couldn't say, but not long enough. It would never be long enough.

"Does this mean you'll take me with you when you go back to get Tagg?" She broke the rhythm of the forest's serenade, liking the muffled way her voice bounced off his chest.

He pulled back and raised her chin with the crook of his

forefinger. "Did I ever tell you what an obstinate, bull-headed wench you are?"

She smiled at his teasing tone. "Yes, and don't forget vexing, but you haven't answered my question."

His hand dropped to his side, and his voice took a serious turn. "Nay."

"Colwyn, please. It's my fault Tagg got left behind. I can't stand the thought of waiting for days before I know he's safe. Don't leave me here to wonder."

He cocked his head and regarded her before answering. "If you are from the future, then surely you know what will happen."

Her bottom lip jutted out with a will of its own. "That's not fair, and you know it."

"What I know is that my son's life may very well be in danger. I lost his mother. I will not lose him." He stepped away and rubbed at the days' growth of stubble on his chin. Lowering his hand, he shook his head. "Nor will I lose you. There is a price on your head. I am not willing to take that risk."

"But I am. Look, I'll stay out of sight. I can even show you a secret tunnel to get inside, the one Traline and I used. Let me go. I'll do whatever you say."

His brows disappeared under the fringe of dark hair sweeping his forehead. "You will do as I say?"

"I will. At least, I think I will. I'll try, anyway. Please?"

He exhaled the kind of sigh reserved for an obstinate child. "Why do you badger me so? You persist until I can't think why. Most women would be content, nay, grateful to remain far from danger. Not you. You face everything head on."

"You make it sound as if that's a crime."

"The crime is, M'lady," he paused and allowed half a smile, "you know not when to cease."

She put every effort into pleading with her eyes.

He looked away. "I'll think on it."

What could she say to persuade him? "Colwyn, I want to be with you. I know that now. It's been a long time since I've felt anything, and you ... You make me feel ... Please don't leave me behind."

He let out a long, slow breath before answering. "I leave at first light, but I make you no promise."

She kept her victory cheers to herself. He'd take her. She knew it.

And if he didn't, she'd trail along behind him.

•

Tarne loved the feel of fondling young, supple flesh. No, not loved. Coveted. And as his fingers explored the warm skin beneath the squirming servant's bodice, his covetous nature let loose. Her struggling increased the enticement. He needed more.

Shoving her up against an outside shed in a shadowed corner of the inner bailey, he ripped the fabric from her trembling body. Ahh, a young one, this. She whimpered, but did not cry out. Smart wench.

His darting tongue wetted his lips as he lowered his head. First, he'd—

A cold, wet shock washed against his back.

Enraged, he wheeled about and a guard immediately dropped to one knee, an empty water bucket with broken handle rolling away in the dirt.

"M'lord, forgive me. The bucket—"

"Stupid, half-witted man! I ought to have you flogged. Rise and face me."

The girl wrenched free and fled the length of the courtyard to the sanctuary of the servants' quarters, adding to his fury.

"My apologies, M'lord. 'Twas an accident, nothing more."

Tarne assessed the soldier standing before him. One of Colwyn's men, and one he particularly disliked. A certain innocence, nay, righteousness shone from his clean-shaven face and neatly pulled-back hair. Something about the way he held his broad shoulders decreed this man to be almost—holy.

And Tarne hated him for it. "Geoffrey, is it not?"

"Aye, M'lord."

He snaked out his hand and slapped the man full across the face, making sure the drag of his pointed nails drew blood. Geoffrey's head jerked with the force of the blow, but he spoke not a word.

Deprived of the wench, this man might serve to entertain just as well. He raised his hand to strike again, but flapping wings from far off, a sound he sensed more than heard, made him pause and lend a keen ear.

"Go. Leave me."

Tarne ran to the center of the courtyard and held out his

forearm. A dark dot in the sky loomed larger and blacker until it swooped to perch on his outstretched arm. Beady eyes locked onto his, but the raven did not caw. It couldn't. Its beak carried a gift.

"What have you brought me?"

He extended his free hand palm up, where the gift was promptly deposited.

Hair. Human hair. A shoulder-length tuft of dark locks with a bit of scalp still attached to the roots.

His lips pulled into a tight smile. He clutched the ripped strand and stroked the inky feathers of his companion with one finger.

"He is near then, eh? Well done, my friend. Well done."

Chapter 20

Colwyn reined Old Black to a halt at a break in the thick forest. He rubbed the sore spot on his head, wishing he could as easily work out the ache in his back.

"Why are we stopping here?" Jess's words came out on half a yawn.

He dismounted and helped her to the ground before answering. "I'm tired." He still couldn't believe he'd let her come along, leaving Traline behind at Dalbroke Abbey. It'd gone against all his better judgment and he'd recanted many times since. But this woman had a way with words—rather, she had a way with him.

It'd been a long day of riding. He'd pushed to make up for the time lost the day before. His injuries, though healing, had been sending warnings for the past hour. Not that he'd minded having Jess sheltered against him atop Black, but he couldn't keep it up much longer. This small clearing, encircled with beech and ash, would provide an adequate campsite once he cleared a few of the alder saplings. They'd reach Gallimore next midday, and he'd need as much strength as possible to face Tarne.

Jess stifled another yawn. "I didn't think mighty knights like yourself ever got tired."

She was as fatigued as him though she'd never admit it. He smiled. "Aahh, so by your own admission, I am a mighty knight."

Her reply was a snort while she stretched her legs, exploring the patch of forest they'd claim as their own for the evening.

An earthy, moist smell of approaching dusk hung on the air. Night insects would be whirring soon. From the pack on Black's side, he retrieved the last of the provisions the nuns had supplied. He stomped down a flattened area and sat, then unwrapped a chunk of hardened bread.

Jess returned from her prowling and sat beside him, taking the half-loaf that he offered. As she did, her hand brushed his, and her touch gave him a hunger for more than food. It would be a struggle indeed to keep his desire under control for the span of a long, dark night. Every fiber of his being wanted to show her the passion she stirred. Her cheeks deepened in color. Did she feel the same way? "Why did you come back to me?"

"Where else is there to go?"

"Nay, 'tis not what I meant." Hmm, how best to phrase his words? Barking orders was all he knew, but he couldn't command this woman to share her thoughts and feelings any more than he could order the wind to stop blowing. "I meant when I'd left you behind at Gallimore. The earl offered you freedom, yet you did not leave. You stayed and cared for me. Why?"

"It wouldn't have been right for me to leave you to die."

Right and wrong—something he knew little of—but he'd try. "Neither was it right for me to have locked you in the tower. You owed me nothing after the way I treated you."

"That was the choice put before you. I had my own choice, to do what was right, regardless of your decision."

He stopped chewing and stared, trying hard to fathom her meaning. It went against all he knew—an eye for an eye, tooth for a tooth. He'd treated her ill, yet she'd shown him compassion. It made no sense. "As I've said before, M'lady, you speak in riddles."

"No, not really." She took a big bite of the bread and swallowed before continuing. "We'll all be held accountable one day for the decisions and actions we take. And when I stand before God, I don't want to have to do a lot of explaining."

"You are beginning to sound like Geoffrey."

"I'll take that as a compliment. He's a wise man. You should listen to him."

He had been listening to Geoffrey, for years and years, but he'd never understood him. Colwyn knew little of religion, and less of the God of whom both Geoffrey and Jess spoke. The tiny chapel in the castle had long since been abandoned, and it'd been nigh on two generations since a priest had been welcomed on Gallimore lands. London street plays and a fellow soldier's convictions provided the sum total of his religious knowledge. Deep within his soul, he knew that wasn't enough.

"I'm listening now."

She stopped gnawing on the crust. "What?"

"If Geoffrey were here, what would he say?"

"Well, uh—" She brushed at loose crumbs decorating her lap. "I don't know him well enough to tell you that."

"Then what say you?"

"About what?"

"About God."

She inhaled so deeply, he feared she might explode. Her cheeks puffed out as she exhaled.

"You know, I may sound like Geoffrey, but you sure sound like my son. What can I say about God? That's a whopper of a question." She paused, and he wondered if she'd say more. He wanted her to, but at the same time almost feared what he might learn.

"Well," she searched his gaze. Did she question his sincerity? "I suppose it boils down to this … What's in your heart? Either you've pledged your soul to good or to evil."

"I've made no such pledge."

"Ahh, but you have, whether you realize it or not. By not making a choice, you have made a choice. There is no in-between. You're either for God, or you're against Him. As for me, I know the keeper of my soul, and He is good."

Good? He'd known precious little goodness in all his years. "I know naught of this 'keeper.' What I know is that 'tis how much gold you have to pay the priest that matters, and they'd not take kindly to your pledging without paying."

"Colwyn, God's not about money or priests. He's about forgiveness—and that can't be bought or earned."

With a swipe of his hand, he rubbed his tired eyes. This girl had no idea the kind of life he'd led, the lies he'd told, or women he'd defiled. Blood spilled by his own hands. He couldn't even meet her eyes.

"I've much to be forgiven," he finally admitted. "Too much."

"God is bigger than anything you've done."

Her voice carried a certainty that pierced him as sharp as any arrow. He stood, feeling naked and ashamed. "You'd not speak so if you knew me."

"You're right."

"What?" Did she toy with him, then?

But her voice did not tease. It carried compassion. "I don't know all you've done, but God knows. And even in the knowing, He chose to love you. You don't need to pay a priest for forgiveness, because the payment has already been made. It's yours for the asking. Only when you repent and accept the offer will you know peace."

When the way of peace is revealed, seek it with all your strength.

Counselor Aedmund's words roared back, or had she said them aloud? How could she possibly know what she talked about? He must've worn his perplexity on his face, for she defended her position.

"See the big rock over there? You can deny the reality of it your entire life, but it'll still cause you to stumble if you don't walk around or step over it. Or how about that low hanging branch," she pointed past Black to the forest's edge. "You can choose to believe it doesn't exist, but it'll knock you from your horse if you don't duck. The forgiveness and peace I speak of is just as real, whether you believe it or not. What I'm telling you is truth."

"And as reliable as your claim to have come from the future I suppose." His mockery disgusted him, but he couldn't stop it.

She looked up, a glimmer of hurt in her eyes. "Yes, exactly."

The rest of the Counselor's warning flashed like a beacon in Colwyn's mind.

Do not allow your pride to hinder you.

He had. The most ancient of sins stopped his ears from what she had to say. Pride made him lash out at her. Ironic. Deep down, he knew he had nothing to be proud about. Not one thing.

"I am—sorry." He'd never said those words before, not even to Saris. To his astonishment, the apology felt good. "'Twas me who asked you to speak your mind. I had no right to be so cutting."

She offered him a smile, then stood, batting away the last bits of bread dotting her skirts. "It's okay."

Shifting his weight from one foot to the other, he attempted to contain the unrest her words caused. His head throbbed with such thoughts. Turning, he busied his hands with rummaging in the pack on Black's side. He tossed out his surcoat and a blanket, then tugged off the whole bag to whump on the ground. "Take this and bed down. I'll scout the area and return."

"I meant all that I've said." She laid her hand on his arm. Her touch burned through his tunic, but he would not meet her eyes. Not now. He pulled away and grabbed the horse's lead.

"And I believe you," he answered as he lead Black away to tether him for the night. "I must agree with your earlier sentiment that I am a mighty knight."

A dirt clod sailed past his ear as he hiked off. The excuse of surveying the area was truly valid, but of more importance, he needed time alone. Time to think on all she had said.

•

Jess tromped down a patch of tall, green plants the way Colwyn had earlier. Their conversation left her uneasy, and the activity released some of her stress. Who was she to spout off such theological ideas? Her own faith had been on the verge of nonexistence until a mere few days ago. Preaching to Colwyn felt hypocritical. God really should send him a missionary or a monk or something.

I sent you.

She stilled her feet and squinted into the dusk, then up to the sky. "You talking to me?"

Nothing but a percussive cricket melody answered. She stood a moment longer, scratching the nape of her neck, then walked over to the other flattened area where they'd shared bread. She eyed the frayed blanket, then the surcoat, finally deciding to go with her first choice. Woolen and scratchy, it would cover more ground than Colwyn's leather jacket and likely not smell as sweaty.

Grabbing the blanket, she shook it out and marched back to where she'd bed down. She folded the brown wool sleeping-bag style and settled into her nest. A yawn overtook her, but her eyes wouldn't close. Where had Colwyn gone off to?

She turned over and ran her tongue across her teeth. Plaque city. A hygienist's nightmare, as if she even had a chance for dental care in this crazy world. She shrugged off the blanket and stood, then walked the short distance back to the pack. The weathered bag lay where he'd dropped it, though it was hard to distinguish in the fading light. She rubbed and scrubbed at her teeth with the sleeve of her dress, then stooped to retrieve a skin of watered wine to rinse her mouth. By no means ADA approved, it was the best she could do.

Following the path now worn between the two areas, she

returned to her blanket. She straightened it once more and lay down, deciding not to cover up this time. The damp night air would no doubt settle into the fabric of her dress, but she felt too warm otherwise.

She let out a gigantic yawn and scratched behind her ear. Lice again, probably from spending the previous evening bunking on an abbey mattress that had never seen the likes of clean linen. Linen at all, for that matter. The accommodations hadn't appeared to have bothered Traline, however.

The sky changed from charcoal to ebony, and still she couldn't sleep. Her body and mind were beyond tired, but her soul wouldn't rest. Why?

I sent you.

She squeezed her eyes shut, and then opened them. No good. This time she knew where the thought-voice came from, and it wasn't from anywhere in the field or the forest. Tempted to shake her fist at the sky, she instead pushed up to a sitting position. Sleep would not be hers until she complied.

"God, my explanation of you to Colwyn was probably, well, lacking. Salvage my lame attempt, and next time give me words that will be more meaningful to him. You sought me when I ignored you and even when I ran from you. Seek Colwyn out like that. Show him your peace."

•

When Colwyn returned to the clearing, the dark of night had arrived in full. It was a fair challenge indeed to find Jess curled up in a bed of bracken, although she was not far from where he'd left their provisions. He crouched, half hoping she'd stir, but she lay still beneath a rumpled blanket.

Though he'd intended to clear his thoughts, he could've gone to London and back and still not comprehended all she'd spoken of. The kind of forgiveness she'd described set off a chain reaction inside ranging from disbelief to desire. He ached to know, to experience for himself, the peace of that forgiveness, but it seemed too easy. Too ridiculously easy.

He reached out, brushing back the soft curls hiding her face, but her breathing remained even. Her thick lashes didn't so much as flutter. Probably a good thing. It wouldn't take much to coax his mouth into meeting hers once again—or more. A light breeze blended her scent with the night air, promising warmth and softness. She slept so peacefully, with such serenity. And why not? She claimed to know the keeper of her soul.

But who kept his?

The question wrapped around him like one of Tarne's incantations, inescapable and frightening.

He stood, looking up to the heavens. No twinkling stars nor wash of a silver moon. Infernal blackness hid any hint of light—exactly how he felt inside. Was there truly a God out there who could see through that darkness? See him, and not turn away in disgust?

Jess seemed to think so, as did Geoffrey. But neither of them knew the secret sins. The evil ones. The hate from which he'd fed for years.

I know.

He jerked his gaze downward. Jess hadn't moved, but he could've sworn he heard a whisper. He scrubbed his face with the palm of his hand, fatigue weighing like a millstone. But something more than fatigue pressed in.

A gust of wind shook the branches of the trees at the edge of the clearing and swooped across the underbrush as if a mighty dragon flew over. The tall grasses rustled, but without the usual shushing sound.

More like a giant breath.

Seek.

His hair rose from the draft of sweeping air. With one last look to Jess's safety, he waded through the saplings he'd meant to clear earlier, out to the center of the small field. The wind blew stronger, increasing in pitch, all the while speaking as if it had a voice—and it called to him.

Seek. Seek. Seek.

Then it stopped. Acute silence filled the void.

He was not alone in the middle of this clearing. His heart pumped hard and fast, the rushing blood making him dizzy, and he dropped to his knees. But his pulse did not race from fear, rather—awe.

"Who are you?" he whispered.

No answer.

"What do you want?"

Again, no answer, but something listened. Or someone. He swallowed with a dry throat and tried again. "Show yourself."

The stillness stopped up his ears until all he heard was his own increased breathing. Nothing appeared in the dark field, but he desperately wanted to see whoever or whatever had called him to this place.

"Show yourself, please. I wish—I wish to see you."

Warmth radiated into every bit of his being, but not uncomfortable heat. More like acceptance. Nay. Much more than that. Something bigger enveloped him that he didn't understand, but yearned to know more fully.

Could this be love? Could this be God?

Could a good and loving God care for a cruel and evil man such as himself?

Ask me.

He sprawled forward onto the ground. "My—my Lord?"

He whispered in the dark, his focus shifting from trying to say the right words to the astounding majesty and mercy of the One to whom he spoke.

With open eyes, he saw the filthiness of his own soul in light of the holiness of God. Every black sin he'd ever committed covered him like open, festering sores. Awful and inescapable. He wanted to hide, to run away from the terrible light that exposed all the ugliness inside of him.

But even more, he wanted to be clean.

Sobs tore up from his gut and spewed out like a storm, until he lay spent and broken, face down in the dirt. With the last of his energy, he croaked, "I am sorry. Could you—would you forgive the likes of me? I am not worthy, but I beg for your mercy. Indeed, I cannot live without it."

Deep into the night, he lay prostrate. Emptied, but owning the peace of which Counselor Aedmund had prophesied.

He'd never be the same.

Chapter 21

Jess eased up from the rock-hard ground, swiping at a transparent cloud of insects. Her neck kinked, and she jerked her hand up to rub it. Definitely time to put her sleeping-on-the-ground days in her past. Daybreak arrived with a sluggish gray mist, much the way she felt, and the air smelled like a basement.

Colwyn tended Old Black not far from where he'd slept—if he'd slept. She'd waited up, intending to talk with him, but she'd drifted off late in the evening. He didn't appear any worse for lack of sleep. With little more than a careless run of his fingers through his hair, he gained a roguish, tousled look.

She patted her own curly locks, a throbbing heat in the palm of her hand reminding her she should've removed the filthy bandage long ago. She unwrapped the layers and found the gash from Tarne's blade swollen and flaming. This had to get cleaned before the infection became worse. Didn't people die from silly things like this in the Middle Ages?

She padded along the short trail to where Colwyn hefted the pack onto the horse's back. "Do we have any water left?"

He turned from his chore. "Good morn to you as well, M'lady."

"Oh, uh, yeah." Sheepishness was not a feeling she'd hoped to embrace this morning, but here it was, hugging her tight around the middle. "Sorry. I should've said good morning first. So, do we have any? Water, or watered wine, or whatever?"

"Nay, nor food. Let us be off and see to both."

She stared at the nasty wound. What to do? She couldn't put that strip of cloth back on, but the fabric of her dress wasn't much cleaner. She'd have to leave it uncovered for now. Maybe air would do it some good, anyway.

"Why do you look as if the weight of the world is your burden to carry?" He raised one of his brows—a killer look that almost made her forget the burning pain.

"Oh, it's nothing. Just trying to decide what to do about my hand."

"May I see?"

She laid her hand on his open palm. Warmth traveled upward to her cheeks.

He didn't say anything for a long while, time enough to make her wonder what he thought. Finally, he spoke. "This does not bode well."

"Thanks. I could've told you that." She pulled away, but he held on.

"I do not mean to provoke you. This must be cleansed, and—"

His head jerked up, and he looked past her into the unending vegetation.

"Wha—"

His finger pressed against her lips, and she tensed.

Squirrels jabbered and birds chattered, teasing the jittery feeling Colwyn created, but her pounding heart eventually subsided. He released his hold and inspected the area with a sweep of his eyes.

"What was that all about? It's a little scary when you get all psycho-knight like that."

He stopped his surveillance to smirk. "You? I thought naught frightened you."

"Really?" She cocked her head and his grin pleased her.

"Come. 'Tis time we left this place."

"Fine. Give me a minute." She turned to hike away.

He stopped her before she'd gone a yard. "Where are you going?"

"I have to, ah, well, something to do before we leave."

"I will attend you."

"No." She whirled back. "I need to be alone, if you know what I mean."

"Nay, I'll not leave you alone."

How to say what she needed to do without embarrassing herself or him? "Colwyn, it's kind of a girl thing." Annoyed at having to explain, she shoved her fist into her hip and waved toward the woods. "It's not like I can go over to a tree and—"

"Oh." Understanding dawned in his eyes. "Do not go far, and be quick about it."

She nodded, but determined to be out of his sight before lifting up her skirt.

•

Colwyn watched her retreat, hoping she'd not go far. Long before daybreak he'd lain awake, alert to the tiniest sound. As of yet, he'd seen nor heard anything to prove his forebodings, but something lay in wait among the trees, and not the same sweet presence he'd encountered during the night.

After shaking crushed leaves and dirt from his surcoat, he folded it to pack away, then thought better of it. His cloak would serve to keep the dampness from settling into Jess's garments.

What an odd thought. How peculiar to consider the comfort of someone other than himself. Had his mind been transformed to that of a doting old woman? Was that the way of it then?

He cast his eyes to the blanketed sky. Either fatigue skewed his thinking, or his prayer of the night before really had brought about quite a change.

A deep yearning to know more of this God to whom he'd spoken deep in the night took root in the pit of his soul. He'd discuss this with Jess. She'd have much to say. Looking toward the path she'd taken, he wished to see her coming back. She'd been gone long enough.

•

Even without the sun, the beauty of the lush surroundings impressed Jess. Colors so true—deep greens, rich browns, brilliant bits of red—the tones blended with shapes into a kaleidoscope of untamed nature.

Fronds of lacy ferns bowed before a cathedral of stalwart oaks and feisty scrub trees. Near a rise, not far from where she stood straightening her dress, small violet flowers dotted the emerald growth. So deeply intense a purple, almost indigo, they climbed up to—

The artist in her froze.

Two eyes, the kind that could bore a hole through any one of those trees, stared back at her. It seemed a dare as to who would move first. Time stopped, and her heart along with it.

This time it might be her own back that would feel an arrow.

•

A persistent sense of danger haunted Colwyn as he re-checked the cinch strap on Black's saddle. They should've straddled the big horse hours ago, but his heart softened when he'd gone to wake Jess. In the dawning light she'd slept, sweet and innocent, like a child worn thin by a day's worth of play, her dark lashes resting against her smooth—

"Colwyn!"

With a warrior's reflex, he drew his dagger. If he had to, he'd kill or be killed for her sake.

She ran headlong toward him as if stalked by an angel of death. Even with years of experience at dodging enemies, he saw nothing that should make her flee. He caught and held her to him, continuing to scan the trees.

"There's a, a man. He's chasing—me." Frantic breaths chopped her words.

The gray morning showed an unmoving canvas of trees and shrubbery, the same backdrop he'd eyed countless times already. Nothing out of the ordinary. "You are certain?"

"What?" Twisting from him, she gave a hard look at the empty forest. "I swear, he was right behind me."

She looked back at him with such pleading regard, it seemed to be important that he believe her, and a jolt went through him. Somewhere along the way, his opinion had come to be of value to her.

"Then we ride." He sheathed his blade and laced his hands for a foothold. She mounted and he settled in behind, giving the horse full rein.

Leagues beyond, he slowed the horse and bent toward her ear. "What did you see?"

She turned her head, her cheek brushing against his lips, and his blood raced.

"I was straightening my skirts, when I saw a man. At first, neither of us moved. I'm not sure who was more startled. But then he ran, and I thought that'd be a good time to get back to you."

Who could think with her mouth so near his? Fie, no time for this now. Oh, but later … He tilted his head back. "This man, did he wear a tabard?"

"Like I'd know a tabard if I saw one?"

"Lady Neale, the longer I know you, the more I believe you are from the future. A tabard is a sleeveless garment worn to show allegiance. Did he bear the colors blue and silver? Did a rampant lion fall center on a black crest?"

"I did not stick around long enough to admire the man's taste in clothing." She frowned, and it took everything in him to keep from kissing it away.

He straightened and pressed his knees into the warhorse's side, urging Black on, but she would not be put off. "Who do you think he was?"

"A King's man, scout perhaps. Hang on!"

Tightening his grip, he kicked Black and leaned forward, this time not allowing the woman's charms to muddle his thinking. If she'd seen a king's man, Black would get them to Gallimore ahead of the royal troops, but with no excess of lead time. He'd have to find Tagg with great haste, and beat an even faster retreat. Hopefully he wouldn't cross paths with Tarne.

But if challenged, he would not back down.

•

By the time they sighted Gallimore's grounds, Jess's head ached from the teeth-chattering ride. They stopped short of the fortress, but near the tunnel's ravine.

Colwyn dismounted and reached to guide her down, his solid arms bearing her weight. Her legs wobbled and her inner thighs burned. "Are we walking the rest of the way?"

"I am."

A red flag went up at that statement. "What do you mean?"

"No price is on my head." His arms held her fast, and his soft voice caught her off-guard. "Beloved, hear me. I will not lose another I hold dear. Stay here."

Beloved. He'd called her beloved. All fight drained away as the word pierced her heart. She swallowed back the tightness in her throat and tears obscured her vision.

He took a deep breath and let it out slowly. "I know not what will happen. My brother is a formidable foe. Should I have to face him, well … I'll do anything to get my son out of Gallimore before the king's men arrive. Anything."

His voice carried such intensity that she stiffened. Would she ever see him again? Even in the heat of the sultry morning, she trembled at the chilling thought. No. She couldn't handle this. It wasn't fair.

A small smile tugged the corners of his mouth. "You know," he smoothed back her stray curls, "'twas not so long ago that you hoped for a chance to be rid of me. Your wish may be granted, M'lady."

She bit her lip, hoping the pain would distract her from bursting into tears. "But that's not how I feel now. Colwyn, I—" Her voice cracked. As much as she wanted to tell him how she felt, the words would not form, but her heart shouted with an emotion she'd never expected to experience again.

"Shh." He touched her pouting lips softly with his own. "Do not fret."

Who could fret when their breathing mingled as one? She couldn't even think.

"I am not that easily beaten, and I do not go alone. Because of you, and no doubt the countless prayers of Geoffrey, I go with God's grace."

She clutched him, grasping the material of his tunic, and dropped her head against his broad chest. Closing her eyes, she marveled at the change she'd witnessed in this man. He wasn't the same anymore.

Neither was she.

He raised her chin to gaze into her eyes. "I would like nothing better than to return to your side. Someone must keep you from all the trouble you manage, and I aim to be that man."

In a caress gentler than she imagined his strong hand capable of, he stroked the length of her face with the back of his fingers. "Do not wait for me should I tarry. Go back to the abbey. Traline knows of my ally at court, a counselor who'll plead mercy for the lot of you before the Queen—therein is our hope. Do not fight me on this."

His hopeful eyes searched hers, the depth of which shone with love. She'd be a fool to refuse. "All right."

His head lowered, and she tipped up hers. This time when their lips met, it came slowly, as if he sought her permission. Soft at first, and as she wrapped her arms around him, deepening to a level that aroused a longing for this man—a man she'd once seen as her enemy. She soaked in all the safety his arms had to offer and submitted to the ownership of his kiss. Her body trembled, and self-control faded the closer she pressed.

By the time he walked away, she was left wanting more.

She watched him go, memorizing how the length of his dark hair gave way to the broad width of his shoulders, the sure gait of his long legs, and the power and strength he wore like a well-fitted mantle. When the mist of the gray day consumed him, sadness settled deep and low in her stomach. Her eyes burned with the pressure of unshed tears. She wouldn't fit in this upside-down world without him.

No. She wouldn't cry. She would not have him return to find her a blubbering mess. He'd come back. He would. He had to. *God, please.*

Black snorted his worry as well. Shoot, if the king's men came before Colwyn returned, Black would give her away. What to do with a monster horse?

She grabbed the reins then waited to see what would happen, hoping the beast would not get angry. One snort, but no big whinnies of complaint. She tugged, and the warhorse followed.

The humidity of the damp day grew intense as she coaxed and lured the big horse into a rocky crag she found. Sweat soaked her undergarments by the time she made it back to the ravine. She scooted to the gully's bottom, hoping for a low-lying patch of cool air.

A low rumble rolled in from the west, resounding in her chest. Great. As if she weren't wet enough, it had to rain? She climbed up and looked in the direction Colwyn disappeared. Not a sign.

Footsteps approached from behind. Behind? She jerked her neck around.

Three men stalked through the brush, their feet snapping twigs and rustling foliage. They were far enough away that they likely hadn't noticed her, yet close enough to distinguish tabard colors— blue and silver.

King's men.

And here she sat like a fox in an open field. Where to run? Where to hide?

Where was Colwyn?

Chapter 22

Leaving Jess alone and unprotected in the wilds of Gallimore made Colwyn's feet move faster with each step. He almost turned back, but 'twould be folly indeed to let his emotions rule. Still, he could not find Tagg and return soon enough, especially with the feel of her yet in his arms.

Earthy moisture hung suspended and one look at the low clouds told him what he didn't want to admit. A storm brewed. All the more reason to hurry. He didn't stop until within bow range of Gallimore's walls.

"Halt!"

He recognized the gatehouse sentry. He'd trained with him many a hot, dusty day. Colwyn made eye contact. "Open the gates. I wish to enter."

The sentry turned aside and shouted an order, but the gates remained closed.

"Drop your weapons!" The voice from the gatehouse roof grated as a minstrel with a sour voice. Rollo. The tension between them chafed like a blister rubbed raw.

Colwyn scowled, sliding his dagger from the sheath, then threw it down.

"All your weapons!"

He set his head in defiance but slowly reached behind his back, fumbling beneath his tunic. Seconds later, another blade met the trampled soil.

Rollo only grumbled at the action. "I said all of them."

Colwyn hesitated. All he had left was a small dirk inside his boot. Could he free Tagg unarmed?

"Now."

Bending, he removed the knife and dropped it onto the

stockpile.

"Hands behind your head."

With slow, exaggerated movement, he raised his arms, letting his muscles bulge in contempt. If Rollo looked for a fight, he was in the mood to deliver. The big man only sneered, descending from sight.

The familiar grind of the portcullis lifted its spiked jaws. Weathered oak doors parted, and Rollo stood like a bull threatening to gore.

Colwyn glowered at the smug tilt of his chin. "How is it I merit a criminal's welcome?"

"Save your questions for the earl."

Rollo snapped his thick fingers and two guards flanked Colwyn. He could force the issue now, being they were his own men. He knew their strengths and where their skills would falter. Taking them on would be his victory. The unknown factor, however, was Rollo. He'd be a match to reckon with, especially unarmed. No, better to follow and perhaps catch a glimpse of Tagg.

Crossing the outer bailey, he scanned for the boy. It looked deserted—no wonder, with so many soldiers at their posts. Did Tarne already know about the King's men?

They passed through the second gate into the inner bailey, and he scouted the nearby perimeter. Tagg could often be found pestering the blacksmith, but that shed stood empty. Or sometimes the boy would watch the men wager at games of chance in front of the barracks, but not one loitered near them. Even the servants' quarters showed no signs of life. A far-off roll of thunder added to the eerie atmosphere of the empty yard. Something was not right.

A keen odor, one that should never assault the nose of the living, made him forget about Tagg. He stopped near the base of the keep's stairs. His hands curled into fists, until his knuckles threatened to split.

Rollo glanced back before climbing the steps. He raised a hairy arm to point at the source of the sickening smell. "Look long and well, for no doubt you'll soon be joining him."

At the top of the stairs, secured from a broad beam by a stout rope, hung the remains of Faulk, bloated and gray. The disgrace punched Colwyn hard in the gut. Bracing his hands on his thighs, he could not contain the bile that rose in his throat, and retched.

Rollo laughed.

"Behold the mighty Captain of the Guard now, eh boys? He don't deserve what this man got. Too much glory in it for him. Better he go back to the womb what bore him. Out back. In the dirt. Unknown and unmarked. A fitting end for Lady Haukswyrth and her bastard son."

Rollo closed the short distance between them, his stinking breath giving evidence of his rank character. "But I don't think Lord Tarne will let you die as quickly as he allowed your mother. Now, move."

Colwyn clenched his teeth until he feared the pressure might crack his jaw. He mounted the steps, waiting, waiting … then lunged for the guard, shoving him off the stairway. Wheeling around, he planted his fist into the other guard's stomach, doubling him over. Rollo turned, and Colwyn landed a solid blow, knocking the big man flat.

He raced to the wrought-iron hooks securing the coiled rope and unwound the binding. His friend's body thudded aground, putting an end to the humiliating spectacle. He'd freed Faulk. Now to free Tagg.

Wham. His face mashed against the closed door of Gallimore, teeth puncturing into the soft flesh of his lip. A salty taste filled his mouth. His arms wrenched behind him so forcefully, he expected to hear something pop.

Rollo grabbed a fistful of hair, wrested back his head, then smashed his face into the door once again. Cartilage gave way and bone crunched against wood. Warm blood ran over his lips and down his chin.

"I ought to kill you here and now." The voice roared in his ears.

Colwyn worked his mouth despite the pain. "Try it."

"I'll save that pleasure for Lord Tarne." Rollo cuffed the side of his head, and his vision swam.

"Noble of you." The blood streaming from his nose made it hard to talk, and he turned to spit before they entered Gallimore's gloom. As he passed through familiar corridors, memories of the years he'd served under his brother's oppressive rule tried to snuff out the fledgling peace he'd been given.

God, help me.

Tarne waited in his mock throne-room, perched atop the dais

like a hook-nosed vulture ready to pick his flesh. A shove forced Colwyn to kneel, cracking his kneecaps onto the stone floor.

"Leave us." Tarne waved away the guards and turned to him. "So, brother." He tugged at the sparse whiskers comprising his beard. "I see you've come crawling home. Where have you been, and where is the girl?"

Wiping the blood from his chin, Colwyn stood on shaky legs. The image of Faulk's body burned in his mind. "Why hang Faulk in shame? And what have you done to Mother?"

"Ahh, Mother. You know as well as I that she'd outlived her usefulness. As for Faulk, he was disobedient. A trait I'll not tolerate. He attempted to flee with your wastrel of a page instead of bringing M'lady Neale to me. You will deliver the woman or share the same fate. Now, where is she?"

His heart skipped a beat at the mention of Tagg. If Faulk, and even his own mother, had exacted such a price for defiance, what had happened to his son? He fought to remain in control. "Where is the boy?"

"Locked up, where you'll be if you'll not answer." Tarne's voice increased its pitch. "Tell me where the wench is!"

"I'd sooner rot than hand her over to you."

"That can be arranged." Tarne curled his lip. "Better to put an end to you and the girl now, before you rut like a buck with her and sire a whelp as worthless as yourself."

Years of anger and bitterness rose to the surface, almost choking Colwyn. He let a mixture of saliva and blood pool in his mouth, then spit it out, every bit, onto his brother's face.

He tensed, waiting for retribution, but Tarne merely raised his fingers to wipe the mess.

"Do you see what she's done?" He asked in an octave so low, Colwyn wondered if the voice even belonged to him. "She's turned you against family. She will be the downfall of the Haukswyrth name. I've foreseen it. Bend your knee to me now, and I'll forgive this little incident."

Colwyn's jaw dropped. "Forgiveness? From you? All my days, I've not seen it from you once. In the short time that girl has been here, she's shown real forgiveness when I didn't deserve it. She's shown me the true meaning of the word and its source. I cast my lot with Jessica Neale and her God. Never again will I bend my knee to you."

Funny how Tarne appeared haunted and cornered now that fear and hatred no longer skewed Colwyn's vision. All the years he'd spent plotting revenge receded, leaving him nothing but pity as he beheld the miserable little man before him. "I've been told, brother, that God is bigger than anything you've ever done. If you will but repent of your wickedness, you can know the same forgiveness of which I speak."

Tarne's face mottled into a strange shade of purple. Trembling overtook his body, and his eyes turned blood red. This was not a good sign. Colwyn had witnessed this rage directed at other people before.

None lived to tell about it.

•

Jess eased back to the bottom of the ravine. It couldn't be too far to that smuggler's door. If she waited there until Colwyn returned, no one would be the wiser, provided she could find it.

She crept on hands and knees, difficult in a long skirt. Where was that door?

The step of a boot came way too close, right above the ridge where she lay. She froze and held her breath. Loosened dirt fell on her head.

As the footsteps moved along the rise, she let out a slow breath and continued her search. The door had to be nearby, but nothing looked familiar. Green and rocky and—no, that pile of sticks looked a little too symmetrical.

Dirt jammed under her fingernails as she laid hold of the camouflaged door. She struggled as loud as she dare, and it gave way enough for her to squeeze through. Pulsating blackness closed in. This time she wouldn't hear Traline's comforting voice.

Surely Colwyn and Tagg would be past Gallimore's walls soon. Maybe if she counted, she could gauge the time. Twenty minutes. She'd wait twenty minutes, then leave her hideout. A good plan that would give her something to think about besides what else hid in this creepy hole.

Near as she could tell, the time came to heave against the door. She opened it a crack. A waft of fresh air and shaft of thin light crawled in. It also let in the bass vibration of approaching thunder and men's voices passing along orders. She couldn't make out what they said, but heard enough to know that leaving now would not be in her best interest.

Darkness taunted her when she eased the door shut, the moist dirt smelling of a grave. Bugs or not, what she wouldn't give for a little light. She knew where a torch was right outside the dungeon door, but had the dungeon remained empty the past few days? Worth a try.

Thick, stale air left her breathing hard by the time she bumped against a wall. End of the trail. She reached up and brushed against wooden planks of the trap door. How would she ever force it upward? She had nothing to pry it open. Still, Faulk had lifted it so easily.

She crouched and braced herself for the inevitable pain to her wounded hand, then sprang up. It opened, all right. It opened with such ease, the sound of it would give her away if anyone were nearby.

And someone was.

A rattle of chains and a familiar whimper traveled through the darkness. Without pause, she climbed out of the tunnel to the straw-covered floor of the dungeon.

"Tagg, that you?"

"M'lady?" His voice carried a mix of fear and surprise. "Are you really here, or are you but a ghost?"

She groped around and found the boy with little trouble, then held his thin body close. "Oh, sweetie." The mother instinct in her flared. "What have they done? Why are you in this awful place?"

His chest shook as he fought back tears. "M'lady, there is great danger. You mustn't let Lord Tarne catch you. After what got done to Faulk, I fear for you."

No, better not to ask. "Shh, it's okay now. We'll both get out of here, together. Colwyn will find us a new place to live. Somewhere far from Tarne. Would you like that?"

He leaned against her, and his breathing evened. "More than anything, m'um."

"Me, too, Tagg. Me, too." Maybe this crazy nightmare could have a happy ending.

"Let's get you out of these chains. Please don't tell me the guard keeps the key on him."

"No, m'um. It hangs on a hook up near the door."

"Okay. Be right back." Finding the stairs and then the key turned out to be one challenge. Padding cautiously back down in the infernal darkness proved another. Fortunately, she made it without tumbling headfirst. Colwyn would be proud of her. He'd been impressed by her wild boar escape, but this would be—

Groaning hinges and a glow of torchlight interrupted her. Her heart skyrocketed to her throat.

"Run, M'lady, run!"

She did. Reaching the boy, she fumbled with his fetters. Her hands trembled more violently with each stair the man's pounding boots gained. The key clicked, but she had to force open the iron jaws biting the boy's ankles. By the time she released the lad, she knew without a backward glance that she'd not been fast enough.

"Go, Tagg! Down the tunnel, to Dalbroke Abbey." She didn't have to tell him twice before he scampered away.

Jess turned to the man, stalling for time. If she followed Tagg, he'd catch them both. If she ran the other way, at least the boy might have a chance.

"What have we here?" Torchlight illuminated a frightening face. This man had seen battle before. A scar crawled like an earthworm from brow to jaw. She stepped back from the unearthly appearance, banging her foot against a bucket. The jostle sloshed the contents, sending out a waft of human waste.

"I wager you're the lady the earl's been looking for. My, but you are a pretty one at that." A wicked smile parted to show what had once been teeth. His eyes lusted up and down the length of her body as if she didn't wear a stitch of clothing.

She grabbed the pail and flung it, smacking it against his chest. The impact and splash startled him, and the torch fell. Hellish flames leapt to life in the straw, a wall of fire erupting.

The tunnel was no longer an option.

"Why you—"

His curses followed close behind as she fled up the stairs.

Chapter 23

"God!" Tarne screeched the name. His maggot of a brother dared address him on spiritual matters? "You go too far. If the woman and her God is where your allegiance lies, then die the fool's death you deserve."

He flung his arms wide and chanted in monotone. Every last bit of air expelled from his lungs, and then he waited. An eerie silence filled the room. Even the beating of his heart stilled.

From nowhere in particular, a rushing whoosh smacked his chest, knocking him back a step. With a gasp, he sucked in an energy so malevolent, it rattled his bones. Sweat rained from every pore. He brought his palms together as if in prayer, then pointed his fingertips at Colwyn. His eyes rolled up into his head, and all went black. He panted, breathless.

But something was wrong.

His eyeballs descended to their rightful place. The light of the room stung his pupils, and he blinked.

Colwyn stood unharmed.

Nay. Impossible. He howled his outrage. Calling upon every black bit of magic that he knew, he tried again. Focus. Focus. He would not be thwarted. Not now. This power was his. He owned it. He would direct it.

Without warning, his concentration shattered by the interruption of a guard's shout. "M'lord! The King's messenger stands outside the gates. He'll speak to none but you. Shall we let him in?"

All the fury he'd intended for his brother shifted to the soldier. The man fell to the floor, convulsing. Every muscle rippled and wriggled as if larvae crawled beneath his skin, and then he lay still as the cold stone beneath his corpse.

Tarne glared at Colwyn. He'd have to answer the King's messenger first. "This is not finished. I will find you."

Talons of questions clawed at his mind as he erupted out into the corridor. Why had Colwyn not fallen? How did he stand against such power?

Something had blocked his attempts much the same as the night he'd tried to sink his dagger into the woman's neck. It was her. She'd caused this. She'd duped his stupid brother into—

He stopped all thought, all reason, all movement. There in the foyer of Gallimore Castle, the age-old tapestry bearing the unsolved riddle glowed. He stared, mesmerized by the brilliance.

> *When night bends to kneel*
> *At the throne of the sun,*
> *A new realm dawns westward,*
> *Bringing all wanderers home.*

And then he knew. The revelation grabbed him by the throat, and he issued a primordial cry, wolfish and resounding.

> *When knight bends to Neale*
> *At the throne of the Son,*
> *A new realm dawns westward*
> *Bringing all wanderers home.*

A powerful force slammed him backward. He hit the wall so hard that his legs gave way, and he slid to the floor. Dazed and shaken, he mumbled an incantation, and … nothing.

Supporting himself against the rough stone behind, he pushed up to stand. Louder, he evoked every spirit he could name.

Nothing.

Nothing happened. Nothing answered. Nothing opened its big, black jaws and swallowed him whole. All power, all authority, all that had been his was gone.

The tapestry's glow faded, and he was left standing in an empty foyer. Abandoned. Deserted. The darkest arts he'd given his life to, inexplicably gone, leaving him with a dried snakeskin of a soul and an ash heap where his heart once had been.

Alone. Forlorn.

Godforsaken.

His eyes traveled heavenward for a whisper of time. What was it Colwyn had said?

But his fingers curled into fisted balls, his back stiffened, and his jaw set, then he bolted down the corridor.

Colwyn and his God be damned, and the King's men along with them. If a new realm indeed dawned westward, with or without supernatural power, that realm would be his.

•

Colwyn gazed at his shaking hands and then at his whole body. Unharmed. But how? Luck? Nay. Someone watched over him to be sure, and as he stepped over the lifeless body of the guard at the door, he was sure. That should've been him lying there, cold and motionless.

Thank you, God.

In spite of his brother's warning, he sprinted down the hallway. The commodity of time held more value than a noble's ransom, but even so, he took the serpentine route to the dungeon. It would not do to follow so closely behind Tarne, for that was the direction he'd taken. If he swept around the back corridors, then cut through Great Hall, he'd have the added consolation of acquiring a greatsword from the arms cache on the walls.

If Great Hall was empty.

Corridors blurred by. No one tried to stop him. The halls of Gallimore echoed barren and deserted.

Approaching from a servant's entrance, he sped past the table where he'd dined since childhood. No more. He'd not eat another meal in this hall.

Behind the raised table where only those handpicked by the earl were favored to sup, weapons adorned the wall in a show of strength. The exhibition served to impress guests and visitors with their embellishments of jewels and silver, but the trimmings didn't make them any less lethal.

He reached for a greatsword, choosing one with a blackened steel hilt. As he stretched, something sailed past his ear, and pain stabbed through him. Cold metal pinned his hand to the wall, a boot knife protruding at the base of his middle finger. Blood snaked past his wrist and down his arm. Whomever did this toyed with him. He suspected who even before he jerked out the blade with a grunt, then grabbed the greatsword from the wall with his other hand.

Turning, he dodged, scarcely avoiding an arcing overhand swing. Just as he supposed—Rollo. He swallowed. Did he have enough stamina to bring him down?

God, help me.

Rollo's blade struck the table with a mighty crack. Splinters of wood shot from the chasm gouged in the surface. Colwyn sought the center of the room as Rollo pulled the blade from the oak.

"I should've killed you when I had the chance." Rollo circled, sword at the ready.

"Your misfortune."

"Not to worry. 'Tis a task I'll entertain now."

"I would not be so certain."

The big man stopped his incessant circling and crouched, poised to spring. "I know the wounds you bear. You've not the strength."

"Try me."

Rollo swiped a vicious swing, the beginning of a wild melee of blows. Parrying, Colwyn's whole arm jarred from the big sword vibrating in his hands. He held his ground, but they both knew the offense belonged to Rollo.

It took all the effort he possessed to ward off each strike. Sweat stung his eyes and his muscles burned. His footwork turned sluggish as Rollo drove him back. The buffeting exacted a toll higher than he could afford. If Rollo killed him here and now, what would become of Tagg? What of Jess? He couldn't protect them any more than he had Saris. The realization struck him harder than any of Rollo's swings.

His lungs heaved and judgment slowed, and he took a deep gash on the arm in payment. He couldn't keep this up.

The next thrust ripped the sword from his hand with such force, his arm almost followed it. Drained and beaten, he dropped to his knees.

God, I don't deserve your help, but I call upon it.

"Behold the fearsome Sir Colwyn on his knees. I've waited many a long year for this."

Breathing hard, he watched Rollo's gleaming blade in slow motion. Sound receded, lending every movement, every color, a surreal effect. *Rushing air in, rushing air out—is this what it's like to die?*

He slipped from reality as Rollo's face contorted like a candle left too near a hearth. The rage Rollo wore wavered, then melted. His puffy lips formed into a big oh, and his eyes blinked in rapid succession. Colwyn braced himself to bear the brunt of the swing that would take his life.

Instead, a hot, hairy body knocked him backward, not the severing blow he expected. Rollo lay on top of him, unmoving.

Shoving the dead weight aside with the last of his strength, Colwyn stood, supporting himself against a table. A dagger stuck in Rollo's back, embedded to the hilt.

Across the room, a guard advanced.

Geoffrey.

Breathing too hard to speak, Colwyn nodded once.

"You are well, Sir?"

"I am—"

"Nay, hold your words." Geoffrey ripped off an edge of his tunic and wrapped it tight around Colwyn's bleeding arm.

Weary beyond his years, Colwyn fought to catch his breath. "I owe you my life."

"Say no more, Sir. You've saved my hide countless times."

"Nay, you do not understand. I owe you, and Counselor Aedmund, even M'lady Neale much. You never gave up. You always spoke truth. God's truth. I know that now."

A slow smile spread across Geoffrey's face, and he offered his hand to lock forearms.

"I would know more, Sir, but there is not time. Most of the men have fled. Those remaining are loyal to Tarne and will think it an honor to bring him your head. Worse, the King's men threaten at the gates even as we speak. There's nothing left for you here, Sir. Let us leave while we may."

"Nay. I am not free to go. Not yet. I release you of service to me and the Haukswyrth family, but I pray we will meet again. Godspeed."

He hesitated, then dipped his head. "God go with you, Sir."

"And with you."

As Geoffrey strode from the room, Colwyn retrieved the sword he'd dropped, then jogged to the main door of Great Hall. The scent of an uncontrolled hearth blaze filled the air and a transparent haze lingered overhead. The worry of fire could not trouble him now—there was no time. He scanned the foyer before sprinting across, for he could ill afford another skirmish.

The last one had almost killed him.

•

Jess worried her knees might buckle as she bolted down the corridor. Her heart pounded in double-time with every step as the guard behind her gained ground. She could see the hallway soon ended in a tee. Left or right? Didn't matter. She hadn't a clue which way to go.

Veering right, the sound of her name slowed her feet, and her fear. She teetered off balance, scraping her shoulder against the wall.

"Jessica?"

She turned, and there stood Colwyn. Had she chosen to go left, she'd be in his arms by now. Instead, the flat of her back hit the floor hard, knocking the wind from her. The weight of the foul-smelling guard on top of her pushed out the last of her breath. His grotesque face pressed against hers. Prickly stubble on his chin scraped against her cheek as his lips sought hers, then fastened on with bruising strength.

Colwyn roared, and a moment later the heavy burden lifted. Instinct urged her to roll to the side and get to her feet. By the time she stood, the guard lay at Colwyn's boots, a pool of blood oozing into an ever larger stain on the floor.

She stared, sickened. That could've been Colwyn's blood. She spun away, covering her mouth with her hand.

Colwyn turned her back. "What are you doing here?"

Smoke thickened overhead, and her chest started to burn. "We've got to get out."

"Nay. Not without the boy—"

"No, listen, Tagg is safe. He's already out of the castle."

"You are certain?"

"I just told you—"

"Then come." He offered his hand—his rough, blood-stained hand that yet trembled from exertion. She clasped it, and his strong fingers wrapped around hers.

Parts of Gallimore she'd never seen before whipped past in fast-forward. When she didn't think there could be anymore stairs to ascend, he'd find another twisted column. Her thighs cramped and her lungs ballooned against her ribcage, but she pressed on, trusting him.

As they drew near yet another door, she suspected she'd

better brace herself. Downpouring rain and deafening boomings warned her they'd soon face the elements, but even expecting it was not preparation enough. She shivered the instant they stepped outside.

Above the thunder cracks, Colwyn spoke, but she couldn't decipher his words. "What?"

He leaned close, and the warmth of his breath stopped the rage of the wind. "Wait here. I'll return shortly."

Wait here? He couldn't have let her wait inside? She didn't like how he disappeared, though admittedly she couldn't see much past her own nose.

Leaning against the outer wall of Gallimore offered no protection other than the psychological benefit of its solidity. Buffeted by nature at its worst, she stood helpless, watching streaks of lightning herringbone across the sky. This was no ordinary storm, and she shook even more.

Colwyn returned with a long coil of rope wrapped around him, nodding for her to follow. She slipped and slid across the battlement in a dress tangling against her legs.

He stopped and bent, wrestling one end of the long cord to loop around the crenellated parapet, then secured it with a tight knot. He stood and drew her close, enough to speak into her ear. "I'm going to wrap this rope around you and lower you down."

Alarm buzzers went off in her head.

"I'm not going down there alone. Did you know the King's men are out there? Can't we go together?" She yelled to be heard, and the effort released some of the panic fluttering in her chest.

"As much as I'd like to carry you down, this rope won't hold the weight of us both. I'll follow once you're aground."

"Shouldn't we wait until the rain slows?" She grasped for a reason not to go. Any reason.

"Nay. Surely the king's men have taken cover and won't be at the base of the wall. This western battlement is the least likely to afford an escape because of its sheer drop and rocky bottom. They'll not have it guarded now."

"This is not sounding very safe, Colwyn."

"I never said 'twas safe, but I'll pledge my life to see you soundly put to ground. As long as I live and breathe, I'll not let harm come to you. Will you trust me in this?"

His gaze locked onto hers, intense and pleading. As scary as the thought of going over that edge would be, she believed him. He would do everything in his power to keep her from getting hurt. The acrid smell of smoke urged her on. "All right."

The white of his smile shone even brighter with a close flash of lightning. "You see, 'tis not so hard to obey. I'll have you calling me Sir Colwyn in no time."

She lifted her chin. "I can still change my mind."

"Nay." With that he began to twist, twirl and knot the end of the rope into two loops. "Step into this."

As soon as she had one foot in each circle, he raised and tightened the rope so that it became like a rock climber's harness. "Now with your good hand, hold here. I'll lower you."

She neared the edge but couldn't keep from peering below. It descended like an abyss into hell. She whirled around. "I can't do this. I can't."

"Shh." He leaned his forehead to rest against hers. "Look only up at me. You once told me how big your God is. Between Him and me, I wager you've a good chance. Remember, keep looking up no matter what. I'm here for you. Do you hear me? I'm here for you."

She let him ease her over the edge. They both knew she'd not do it of her own accord. She tried to package her fear and tuck it away, but the Pandora's box would not be closed. Her breathing turned erratic as her feet left the footing of Gallimore, and she dangled into the slamming winds of the tempest.

I'm here for you. I'm here for you. She let Colwyn's soothing words replay like a broken record, a strange accompaniment to the howling storm.

Inch by inch she dropped, but she kept looking up, watching Colwyn's muscles strain against his wet tunic. He let the rope slide smooth, but even at that, she swung like an insane yo-yo. His wounded arm would not be useful much longer.

Strobed lightning blinked off and on, but the sky above Colwyn's head brightened. An orange, incandescent glow penetrated the dark of the storm, and fire erupted high into the air above the battlements. An unbelievable scene freeze-framed in the hellish light.

And her heart stopped.

A thin figure stood behind Colwyn, the glint of a blade lifted high to strike. Tarne.

"Colwyn—no!"

Her cry reverberated with a clap of thunder as the rope gave way. Her freefall broke only once by a rough scrape against the curtain wall. Wild, unpredictable snatches of her life came to mind as she hurtled toward the bowels of the earth.

Chapter 24

"Jessica? Jess?"

The voice sounded far away, like the time she'd fallen off the dock at her grandpa's cabin and been trapped underwater. She should answer, but the effort was overwhelming. A moan was the best she could offer.

"Jess, I'm here for you. I'm going to get you some help. Hang on."

She floated, lifted up by strong arms. Who would hold her and why? Her head pounded too hard to think.

Other sounds seeped in one by one, a beating heart, the patter of rain, someone's feet tramping through wild terrain. Her ears worked, but the rest of her would not cooperate.

At least the incessant thunder had stopped, making it easier to try to collect her—whoa. Hold on. Thunder and a storm? Lightning and—

"Colwyn!"

She forced her eyes open. Shades of gray and black receded, and she focused on a pair of emerald greens staring back at her. What a gift. What an incredible gift. Leaning her head against the warm chest of the man who carried her, tears of fear and worry slipped down her cheeks.

"I was so scared. I saw Tarne behind you with a knife, and I thought he'd killed you. I thought you were dead." Her tears turned into sobs. "I—I didn't get to tell you that, that I love you—"

"Shh. You'll be all right. A little distraught and out of sorts maybe, but I think you'll be all right. That gash on your head worries me, but hush now, and catch your breath. We'll stop here for a minute. I'm afraid shock might be setting in."

He lowered her to a rock, then sat next to her, one arm slung around her shoulders. Night air shivered through her, and he scooted her closer. She relaxed, resting her head against his shoulder, and allowed his body heat to radiate through her dress. Her breathing slowed to the rhythm of the light rain.

"Feeling better?"

"Mmm. Much." Wow. She did feel better. Oh, her head still hurt, and her bumps and bruises throbbed, but the topsy-turvy world she'd been living in didn't seem so frightening now that she had someone who cared about her to share it with.

"Pardon my asking, and perhaps this is not the appropriate time, but I must inquire. How did you know my given name?"

His tone soothed, but the question disturbed her—as unsettling as his shirt fabric against her cheek. Definitely not rough homespun. And was that aftershave she smelled? "What?"

"You've been spouting some pretty random things, but I'm curious as to how you knew my name is Colwyn. I've always, only, gone by the name of Cole. No one but my sister and my mother would know that."

"Sister? I didn't know you had—" She pulled away to look at him. A thick shock of dark hair threatened to hide the piercing green eyes that scrutinized her. Without a doubt Colwyn's face, but taking in the larger picture, his tunic had been replaced by a button-down shirt, his leggings and boots changed to stone-washed denim and running shoes.

"But you—uh. I don't get it." She squinted. He sure looked like Colwyn, but— "Where'd you get those clothes?"

"I might ask the same of you. When I invited you to Gallimore, I didn't expect you to dress the part. And how did you crash your car into that tree?"

"What? What are you talking about?" A swirling sensation stirred in her stomach, but she stumbled to her feet anyway. "We don't have time for this! The King's men could find us. We've got to catch up to Tagg. He's out here alone."

She glared at him but that made her see double of Colwyn, or Cole, or whatever he wanted to be called. The ground rose up to meet her as she lost balance, but once more his embrace steadied her.

"Please sit down. If you pass out with that wound on your head, I'm afraid you'll never wake up."

Cold, clammy sweat tickled her from head to toe, and her body shook. She let him settle her next to him on the rock because it took everything to regulate the rapid, irregular breaths suffocating her.

"What's happening to me? I'm thirsty, and dizzy, and I'm not sure about anything anymore." Tears choked her. Where was Colwyn? "Make it stop. Make it better. Tell me Tagg's okay. Tell me you're okay. Tell me—"

"Hush now. It'll be all right. I'll tell you anything, but you've got to calm down. Can you do that for me?"

He peered into her face, worry etching wrinkles on his brow.

"Oh. Okay. I'll … I'll try."

He smiled, then began to talk in a low, tranquil tone. "On my way to meet you earlier this afternoon, I got hung up in traffic. I'm not sure if the heat, the fumes, or the triple-scoop chocolate marshmallow ice cream affected my niece, Margie, but she lost it all over the back seat. Of course, that made everyone grumbly, so I thought it best to reschedule Gallimore for another day.

"When I returned to my sister's flat, she'd gone out, expecting to have the whole of the day to herself. I tried ringing you, but the innkeeper said you'd left hours ago."

His story started clicking rusted gears in her mind, but a vein in her head throbbed out of control when she thought too hard. She squeezed her eyes shut, but he kept talking.

"Well, it wasn't long before Margie started up again. I didn't know what to do with a vomiting child, so I packed them all off to the pediatrician's. Oh my, what an absolute zoo that turned out to be.

"It was well after dinner by the time we made it back to my sister's. I rang your innkeeper once more, quite a nice chap actually, and he said you'd not yet returned. That's when I thought you'd very likely gotten lost, and it'd be me to blame."

Lost for a day? No, no. She'd been lost for weeks. Maybe even months. Let's see—in the stocks for a night, locked in a castle chamber for a day, or had it been two? No, one. Then she'd been restricted to grounds before the whole tower cell thing and that had gone on, and on. Just like this man who wouldn't quit talking.

"I came to find you, but such an amazing storm slowed me down half-way. I turned off in Tetbury, and as chance would have it, the drive I pulled into for shelter belonged to the shopkeeper you'd spoken to earlier. Americans don't often stop off in Tetbury, you know. So, I knew you were out here, but I had to wait till the rain let up before slogging through the countryside.

"I must admit to being relieved and frightened when I saw your car crinkled up bonnet-first against that tree. Thankfully, your head had stopped bleeding by the time I reached you, or you might not have made it."

She trembled all the more. His words carried shards of truth that sliced into her confusion, leaving shreds of reality amidst a shattered pile of emotions. Some of what he said rang true, but where was Colwyn—her Colwyn? Had she lost him forever? Her heart constricted and then sank like a weighted corpse to the bottom of the sea.

She lifted her eyes to the man next to her, wanting to believe Colwyn would magically appear. "I—"

Her breathing escalated. "I think I'm going to be sick."

She turned her head and spewed onto the rain-soaked ground. Cole fumbled in his pocket to produce a handkerchief, but she wiped her mouth with the back of her shaky hand.

"There now, we can't put this off any longer." He scrunched the cloth back into his jeans and stood, offering her his hand. "We've got to get you to a doctor. Can you walk?"

"No. No, I can't leave here. Tagg is somewhere and Colwyn is hurt. Don't you understand we've got to find them?"

"I would love to help your friends, and we will, but I really think we should get you some medical attention first."

A jumble of sentiment danced through her heart at this man's genuine regard. He did look so much like Colwyn. And he had come out of his way in the midst of a stormy night to look for her.

"Are you able to walk, or shall I carry you the rest of the way to my car?"

Cole and a car. No Colwyn and no horse. Disappointment gagged her and she thought she might throw up again. What was happening? "I can probably walk." She stood on rubbery legs, and he reached for her hand. But when they entwined together, she cried out in pain.

He released his hold at once. "What's the matter?"

She held up her hand. Even in the moonless night, she saw the angry slice across her palm, inflamed and infected. Not a recent injury caused by some car accident—more like an ulcerated slash inflicted by an unclean blade.

Before she passed out, she swore she heard nasally-pitched laughter cackle across the centuries.

•

Cole caught the woman before she hit the ground, sweeping her into his arms. The awful smell of her assaulted his nose, but he held on. Maybe she forgot to shower this morning, or more like every morning since he'd sat next to her on the airplane. Oh bother, he shouldn't be worrying about her state of hygiene at the moment. What if she slumped into a coma and died?

He set off through the untamed brush of Gallimore grounds. This girl needed medical attention and fast. He never should've agreed to let her drive alone. What had he been thinking? He'd been so preoccupied with visiting the ruins that he'd not given a care to this American's safety. This was all his fault.

God, forgive me.

Slipping on a patch of wet ferns, his feet flew out from beneath. He cradled her against him, landing hard on his tailbone. The impact rattled his teeth, but he kept her from tumbling out of his arms. He clutched her tighter, glad to feel her regular breathing, amazed at the surge of protectiveness he felt for this limp, young woman.

With much effort, he got them both upright, but his biceps shook and his backside complained. He couldn't hold her like a babe in arms anymore. He heaved her over his shoulder in potato-sack fashion, doubting if knights of the past would resort to such weak-limbed measures. Trudging through the slick vegetation once more, he took great care to avoid ferns.

At last he spied his pathetic Volvo, rusted and dented in the fender. Even the lingering odor of Margie's ice cream incident didn't lessen his gratitude as he buckled Jess into the front seat. The neglected motor griped when he turned the key, but the temper tantrum didn't last. They soon reached the M11 and sped toward the nearest medical facility. All the while, he silently prayed.

No flashing red lights or screaming sirens announced their arrival as they pulled up to the hospital's emergency entrance. At this sleepy time of night, it looked as if everyone must be tucked away in bed.

He retrieved Jess from the front seat and held her close. When he approached the glass doors, they swooshed open. Crossing the threshold, he was greeted by the smell of disinfectant, thinly disguised by a veil of flowery air freshener. A swirl of multi-colored lab coats sprang into action, peppering him with questions. Someone relieved him of his burden, laid Jess on a gurney, and began wheeling her away.

He followed.

"Sir, I'm sorry but you must remain here—"

He ignored the voice, a trait he'd perfected from many years of study. Shut out the world's noises and focus, but this time not in favor of the written word. This time to follow the flurry of personnel rushing a woman into a triage room—a woman he hadn't been able to get out of his mind since he'd first met her.

Jess disappeared behind two grey doors that flapped shut, and a strong arm on his shoulder stopped him.

"Sorry. Authorized personnel only."

Defeated, he turned to face a uniformed guard and an impatient administrator tapping a pen against her thigh.

"Terribly sorry." He spread his hands. "I'm just, you know, a bit worried is all."

Thigh-tapper stilled her pen. "Quite understandable. I assure you, the doctor will be out as soon as possible. Please come with me."

He couldn't answer half the questions the administrator asked. Besides the fact that he didn't know much about Jessica Neale, he got distracted whenever he thought he heard the flapping doors open.

Tap, tap, tap. The administrator's pen drummed a cadence on the laminate desktop. "I think we're just about finished. Why don't you have a seat in the waiting room. There's a phone, and plenty of tea or coffee."

"But—"

Tap, tap, tap. "I'm sure it won't be long before you get a report. I'll direct the doctor your way."

"Very well. Thank you." He walked the short distance down the tiled hallway, relieved to escape the administrator's endless questions and tap dancing pen.

Dim lighting and a Mozart sonata lent a peaceful atmosphere to the small room. Cushioned chairs and a few loveseats invited his sore backside, but he would not sit. It'd been nearly a half hour. Had Jess not come around yet?

Or worse?

He paced over to a shiny, beige phone on the wall and punched in his sister's number. Four rings later, her sleepy-edged voice answered. "Hello?"

"Sorry to wake you. This is Cole."

"Of course it is. I've been expecting you to ring all night. Do you realize it's three in the morning? Where are you?"

"Yes. Yes, I know the time. I'm near Harlow at a hospital—" His sister's barrage of questions flew out the receiver and he removed it several centimeters from his ear. Uh-oh. That'd been the wrong thing to say to a worried relative.

"No, no. I'm perfectly fine. It's Jess. I'm afraid she's been in a car accident. And well, I guess I'm just—afraid, actually."

"Oh. Oh, dear. I'm sorry, Cole. Is she going to be all right?"

"I don't—" A lump clogged his throat and his chest squeezed. After a cough and a breath, he continued. "I don't really know. Not yet anyway."

"Do you want me to come?"

"No, no sense in that. I'll let you know as soon as I hear anything."

Please God, let it be soon.

"Cole?"

"Yes."

"I'll be praying."

"Please. Please do. I'll ring you later." He returned the handset to its home on the wall, then sank into one of the soft chairs. Running his fingers through his untamed hair, he attempted to sort through the jumble of unexpected feelings and thoughts that would not be quieted even in the subdued room.

Though he'd known Jessica Neale for precious few days, and only superficially at that, he'd never before experienced such an inner draw to a woman. His years had been spent in pursuit of dusty books and archaic facts, but an unexplainable urge to pursue this woman usurped those yearnings. Why now? Why her?

He rubbed his tired eyes and rose to make a strong cup of tea.

"Mr. Hawksworth?"

The administrator called to him from the doorway, but this time she didn't come with pen in hand.

She came with a doctor.

Epilogue

Four Years Later

Bubbling laughter from a curly-headed toddler carried across the goat pasture to where Jess lounged on a plaid-woolen picnic blanket. She couldn't help but smile at the antics of an adolescent boy playing ride-the-wild-donkey with the shrieking tot. She'd been unsure of Jack's reaction that day she'd first told him he'd have a new little brother, but he'd loved him from the start. Two boys from two different continents, two different fathers, two different—

"What are you thinking?" Cole's voice cut into her musings.

She turned her smile to him, letting her eyes linger on the familiar cut of his jaw and the new shades of silver showing at his temples. "I was only thinking how distinguished you look."

"Oh really? That's a fine way to tell me I'm looking old and decrepit."

"I never said anything of the sort, but now that you mention it..." She paused for dramatic effect.

"Right. Well then, I don't think you deserve this birthday gift, so I'll just be taking it back." He reached for the wicker basket nearest him, but she snatched it away first.

"My birthday's not for another week. I wondered what this impromptu picnic was all about."

By the time she removed layers of sandwiches, chips, and cookies, a burgundy foil package lay at the bottom. She stopped only long enough to say, "For me?" before her fingers tore the pretty paper.

Cole's deep laughter warmed her through, even though she knew he laughed at her. "You're incorrigible. You know that, don't you?"

"That's a mighty big word to be flinging at me, Mr. Professor. After all, it's my birthday and ... Oh Cole, it's beautiful!"

She ran her hand over the textured cover of a leather-bound book. Its rich, musky scent rose to meet her nose. Gilded edges on the pages added to its classic appeal, and stamped neatly in gold, the title glinted in the sun—*Gallimore Through the Ages by Cole and Jessica Hawksworth*. She hugged it close and couldn't contain the grin tugging her lips.

"They're not all as fancy as that one, mind you. I had it specially bound for your gift. Do you like it?"

She lowered it to her lap and gave him a mock frown. "As a matter of fact, no. I don't."

"What?" His eyebrows raised to such an odd angle, she almost lost control of her straight face.

"My name doesn't belong on here, Cole, and you know it. This is your life's work, not mine."

"Oh love, come here." He opened his arms, and she couldn't stop herself from snuggling against him. The past three years as Cole's wife still seemed like a dream, and she took every chance she could to be near him. She understood too well how quickly dreams could disappear and how short life could be.

The image of Tarne, blade raised over Colwyn, would always be with her. The sorrow it brought used to choke her with tears, but she'd come to accept it as bittersweet. She often wondered that if time could be so easily twisted, maybe she would see him again on the other side of death.

"You know I couldn't have written this book without you." Cole's deep voice rumbled in his chest against her ear.

She pulled away, a provocative arch to her brow. "Of course you could have. You already knew everything back to Taggerwyn the Noble. It was you who told me Tagg ended up a favorite of the Queen, and how she reinstated to him the lands and title of Gallimore after King Edward's assassination."

"But I never understood why he was favored for that title. Were it not for you to clear up his kinship to Colwyn—"

"Hey, wasn't me. I'm sure Traline cleared that up when she got Tagg safely to court."

"Listen here," he rested his forehead against hers, forcing her to see the seriousness in his eyes. "Accept my gratitude, Mrs.

Hawksworth. Without you, without all that you went through, I never would've known what really happened to my namesake. Everything was destroyed in that fire."

"Yeah," she smirked, "too bad it was my fault."

Cole threw his head back and laughed.

She smiled, but her good humor faded. "We don't know any of this for sure. I mean, I still struggle with my own sanity on that issue. It seemed so real, like a part of my life. I've learned so much, changed so much, because of that experience. But do you really think I was there?"

"I don't know, love," he reached for her hand, tracing a fingertip along the scar running the length of her palm, "but I'm awfully glad you're here. For lack of a better explanation, let's just call it a miracle, and leave it at that."

His action and his words tingled through her. Miracle? Perhaps, though the realm of the mind could be powerful enough without the aid of supernatural forces. She knew in her heart that it was time to let go of the continual wondering and accept the fact that she'd likely never have answers for all her hows and whys.

Yes, she could label it a miracle. However it had been accomplished, she'd learned that visiting the past can be a good thing, but leaving the hurts behind and moving on in life is even better. And she knew in the pit of her gut, that's what Dan, and Colwyn, would want her to do.

"Now, M'lady, I am hungry."

"Shouldn't we call the kids over first? Jack and Tagg have been playing awfully hard. I'm sure they're starving."

"So am I." A seductive fire lit his eyes, and he leaned close, his warm whisper heating more than just her ear. "Let the peasants fend for themselves."

She laughed out loud as he pressed against her, lowering her to the blanket. "As you wish, M'lord. As you wish."

•••

Michelle Griep

Minnesota author, Michelle Griep, has been writing since she first discovered Crayolas and blank wall space. She has homeschooled four children over the past twenty years, and teaches both Civics and Creative Writing for area co-ops. She is a member of the American Christian Fiction Writers.

www.mmgriep.com